POETIC LICENCE

Kevin Price

CrotchetQuaver
noteworthy publications

Other fiction by Kevin Price

Kumakana: A Gronups Tale

POETIC

LICENCE

First published in Australia in 2022 by Crotchet Quaver, an imprint of Logorythm.

ISBN: 978-0-9942115-5-2

Inquires should be addressed to the publishers
Crotchet Quaver
119 Ridgewood Loop Bullsbrook Western Australia 6084
www.crotchetquaver.com

Cover illustration by Judith Vun Price

A catalogue record for this book is available from the National Library of Australia

For Judith

Chapter One
Superstition

If you've been around as long as me, you'll have a pretty good sense of what happens when policemen frequent bars long after closing, or politicians schedule late-nighters with interns, or property developers finagle favours at the Hilton Grill: you don't really know what's going on, but you do know what's coming off, if you get my drift.

Sleaze doesn't have a monopoly on bad behaviour, but it does slip into the workings of what is good in the world the way a dollar slides into a slot machine and messes with the gears without drawing attention to itself. If that isn't enough to send the business of life onto the rails, we are gullible about what comes next, so we don't lie in wait for the next good thing. Instead, we find our watering holes and drink ourselves into a stupor, fling ourselves at members of the opposite sex in ways that would embarrass rabbits, and take our lives — and those of others — into our hands by getting behind the wheel of a car when a sober version of ourselves would be throwing up behind the nearest hedge. And we marvel the following morning at our miraculous survival, not of the journey home, but of the copious amounts of firewater and chemical enhancements ingested. We breakfast on a box of Disprin and a wash of orange juice topped up with a dash of vodka so the day doesn't completely lose its shine or purpose. I've watched mates slip in and out of this lifestyle often enough to know it's how we wash away our suffering by inducing more suffering.

I've watched years pass by where we've put incompetents and outright crooks into seats of power with the same slippery ease that youth disappears. It happens without us noticing, and by the time we do notice, it's too late. And when the time comes around again — here, Jackson Browne sounds in my mind — there's no question that you'll get up and do it again. So you, along with the pretender, spend countless hours longing for the better times those early years held in stock. And you expect, unreasonably, for better times to be lying in wait for you tomorrow.

See, I don't believe we get to pick our fate. If we did, I'm inclined to ask why ours is a world of so much suffering, where the one-percenters get to choose the lot of the remaining ninety-nine. And if we did, I certainly wouldn't choose as my companion moments where life turns to death in the ugliest possible way. And yet, in some bizarre offence to all manner of probabilities, those moments find me. All I can say is it's a bit of a worry.

That kind of moment found me one evening when I was sitting in a cosy restaurant above the still pools of Henley Brook in the Swan Valley staring through the stipple of a stand of wandoo trees thrashing wildly in a stormy wind at a mansion fairly recently built on the riverbank across West Swan Road. My thoughts drifted to wondering who owned it and where anyone gets the audacious wherewithal to whack something like that together, dominating the skyline not just for miles around, but for years to come. The oysters on my plate turned rancid, the best Cabernet in the valley tasted corked, and I pitched and plummeted to depths I thought had long gone the way of my teenage years.

I didn't know whose audacious wealth I was wondering about.

But as it turned out he was connected to two men who later that same night — a few minutes on the morning side of midnight in fact — pulled up in a black Range Rover at the gates of a panel-beating shop located in a dead-end street of an industrial suburb south of the city, a suburb visited only by those intent on doing business. These men had all the intention in the world. Once inside, they emerged from the vehicle and set about dispatching the life of a third, much younger man, whom they dragged, gagged and hogtied, from the boot. It was an elaborate execution designed to ensure that neither the men in the car, nor the man's business interests they were protecting would attract attention. They disposed of the body in a wheelie bin and dumped it, kerbside, a couple of kilometres away where the weekly collection was scheduled that morning. They photographed their work as evidence — one assumes — for their claim of payment.

I had no idea any of this was happening, but there is a strange energy in the atmosphere that beats on me like the opening riff of *Sweet Home Alabama* when evil manifests itself in my nearabouts. It's unexplained in the normal sense of everyday happenings, so, not being a religious person, I put it down to forces of conscription that move facts around to suit a strange disposition.

I believe evil has an origin. It may be that some are born with it and others born into it, but there's another avenue trafficked by peddlers of influence who insist the high moral ground is theirs to be bought when in real life they have all the morality of a death adder. I've met these people, drunk with them, eaten beside them, attended their parties, succumbed to their charisma, given my all in the hope that a crumb or two of their good fortune will be in the sweepings when it's all over. The next time I see them, they don't even remember my name.

Perhaps that's what I was feeling that night when I reached my car. The car park sits up the slope from the restaurant and from behind the wheel, I had a direct sight to the front of the mansion across the way. The temperature had dropped to four degrees and a fog thick enough to be held in the hand swallowed the building. No lights burned. No-one appeared to be in residence. It was a block of shadow pushing against a diffusing moonlight, the golden halo spreading out into the vineyards from its sides draining into the night like blood on a carpet. I turned the key and my car purred into life, the sound system, after a short pause, surrounded me with *Superstition*. The edgy clavinet cut into my silence like battle pikes as the riff took hold and Stevie's voice worked its way in. I sat there, stared into the dark, and caught myself in the chorus, unnerved that I might believe in something. The scream closing the bridge touched a raw nerve like a dentist's drill.

Here I am, frozen in my driving seat, in the dead of winter, heading for the coldest night of the year, snakes oozing up the hill towards me. The gates of hell may not be fully open, but nor are they locked and barred.

The chills that come into my life don't only come from an August freeze. For years they've picked moments that become harbingers of somewhere, someone doing bad. For the life of me I can't explain why it comes to me. After all, this city's history of murder includes all manner of weird and unexplained happenings, the truth of many of the most notorious hidden behind doors of power and secrecy, and likely to stay that way.

But this is a feeling of a different evil. It breeds like the flies on a sheep's arse, maggots burrowing beneath the shit into the flesh while the fly, with its fifty eyes and streak of glycol green down its back, drones on to another sucker. And, like the maggot it is, this evil burrows its way into the courts of the highest power, drinking the sweet milk of the political teat as it gobbles up influence and buries the voices of truth and freedom at the bottom of iron ore pits. And somehow, even though my hidden friend Hunter might tell me it's all acalistic, I attract it and it sticks. Like chewing gum on the soles of your thongs.

Chapter Two

Shakey Ground

Monday 5 August — 33 days before the election

The funk of that evening was with me when I woke the following Monday morning, three days later. The Prime Minister's announcement on Sunday that we were heading for the polls only added to it. The politics of our country have succumbed to gravitational waves beyond anyone's ken, and sunk to unplumbed depths, which led me to musing on a way of thinking about our political chiefs so as to avoid getting too invested. Branding them TAPM, the Australian Prime Minister, and LOTO, the Leader of the Opposition, gave me release and a satisfying sense of objectification. It suited my mood to look beyond crisp media labels to the grubbiness of the dusty cellar relics they are.

It took less than twenty-four hours from TAPM's announcement for me to see truth scurrying for refuge among the carnage of three-second attention spans and a twenty-four-hour news cycle. The proprietor of the country's dominant newspaper group tweets that LOTO is some kind of rare breed for a politician. The front page of one of his papers blares advice to voters to DROP THIS MOB —

the mob being TAPM and incumbents. In the morning news TAPM reiterates his offshore arrangements for refugees, dashing their slim hopes of freedom against the rocks of our shores by shunting them off to foreign camps before they get here. In his next breath, he insists that negativity has no place in his vision for Australia. LOTO vows he will stop the boats.

The choices are stark, and the casualty of truth is a foregone tragedy. I'm thinking on this line, intending to write something profound and poetic, when the phone breaks the spell.

It's my new boss, Donna Gardner. I wrinkle my brow, the screen of my buzzing device dancing before my eyes. It's the first time she's made an early morning out-of-hours call to me. Her style is clear lines of communication, clarity all the way.

A sentence or two into the conversation, she utters the words, 'can't be avoided, I'm afraid.' It brings the hairs on the back of my neck to attention. Demurrals push truth aside — *not my fault*, or *it's just the way it is*. Outside of death and taxes, what is there, really, that can't be avoided? It's the poet in me that's picking this argument ... like, why should a particular darling be murdered and not another? When someone's bidding is being done at the expense of truth, it makes me uncomfortable.

I teach creative writing, a subject with about as much gravitas as a wilted lettuce leaf, at a small university in Perth's southern suburbs. Donna Gardner is the recently appointed Dean of the school where my discipline is lumped in with English and Comparative Literature. Unlike many of my colleagues, I have not arrived from a career forged in academia, but of lived experience that began as a journalist and descended into life as a hack, sometime stringer, occasional performing poet, subscribing, perhaps fancifully, to the notion that making meaning is a worthwhile pursuit. At work, impostor syndrome follows me around like a cloud of bush flies.

When I set out in journalism, serendipity put me among the darker of the shady people credited with moving and shaking our state's political and economic fortunes. There came a point early in that career, and in circumstances that don't need elaboration, when I was trapped and tapped — it wouldn't be fair to say coerced, perhaps, strongly encouraged — to assist certain members of our government of the day to keep an eye on certain movers and shakers exhibiting certain less than desirable connections. The contractual arrangements, although apparently for life, were inconsistent and heavily biased in favour of the buyer, leaving me in a position of not only risking terminal discredit to my profession, but of frequently having to pursue more creative avenues in efforts to tip economic fortunes my way.

In leaner times, I could occasionally be found conducting group sessions for would-be novelists and poets searching for the creative elixir guaranteed to uncover their genius and set them on a path to fame and fortune. It was on this platform that I was, one day, overheard by an elderly, bespectacled, eternally haunted, fellow poet. He sat through my discussion, listening, taking the occasional note, brow furrowing to some hidden neurotic rhythm as he regarded me with bright, olive eyes. At the end, he took me aside with a suggestion that we walk down by the lake, whereupon we sat on a bench gazing over the water at a pair of ducks as they negotiated the islands of reeds for a nesting place hidden from the predatory ravages of their world. There, he encouraged me to take up a university residence in creative writing because, he said, 'we think you might complement our faculty rather well.'

Before I'd an opportunity to question his use of 'we' and 'our', he went on the sell.

'We have a few common connections around the traps, you and I,' he said, his voice distant and reminiscent, 'and your name has been in our books for some time. The salary's better than you're making now. Plenty of leave, and excellent superannuation. There are risks of course, but I think your skills lend themselves admirably to keeping an eye on one or two people.'

The university's newly appointed vice chancellor was a member of that one or two club.

As it turns out, Gardner's call this morning is to summons me to a meeting with none other than that VC, as if he were a man bearing a chest of medals. His name is Wallace Lipschitz, *Lippers* to those of us who prefer the sentiment held in the last syllable of his name.

I say, 'It always bothers me, Donna, to hear a phrase like *can't be avoided*. Maybe best to just spit it out.'

'I mean it's my calling so early that couldn't be avoided. It didn't come up until late in the day. I was in a meeting until after six.'

'Okay. And it can't wait until I'm on campus this morning?'

'I need you at nine.'

'I have a class this morning.'

'I've checked your timetable. You are free at nine. It won't take long.' A pinch of treble is added here to enhance clarity and punctuate the imperative.

'I get the sense that I'm not going to like this, Donna.'

'I can't speak to your likes and dislikes, Art. The VC has scheduled a meeting with you and me.'

'Why on earth would Lipschitz, of all people, feel the need to meet with me?'

'I have no idea, Art. He can meet with who he bloody well likes. All I know is he's called this meeting. Senate boardroom, nine o'clock.'

With *whom* he bloody well likes I mentally correct as she disconnects.

I pour a coffee into a travel mug and dash through a sudden cloudburst to my car, turn the key and drive off with The Temptations' *Shakey Ground* funking up the interior.

Chapter Three

Mystery Woman

Fremantle harbours more than its fair share of people who have fallen through the cracks of life into its dank doorways, huddled beneath threadbare blankets and holding hastily inscribed cardboard placards that lay bare the dire needs and bleak circumstances of their lot. Perhaps it's in the city's genes. As most of the population roar full-throttle night and day from boutique to barber, from café to bar, they see only a blight, a monochrome fog of rust that smears their world which, given a little political will and gumption and a large enough microfibre cloth, could be wiped away in the next spring clean. The one glaring fact of which the majority seem to be in complete ignorance is that homelessness is not usually a choice.

Except, perhaps, for Hunter.

Out of the fifteen hundred or so souls in Fremantle who are homeless on any given August night, Hunter may be the one who chooses to be. It wasn't always this way. Before, he'd had a different life. And name. One that was on electoral rolls and rate notices and press club memberships. In the early nineties, he collected a Walkley for helping bring the bastards of WA Inc. to account. But nine years ago, things went arse upwards. He was deep in a story digging into criminal activities and political connections on the wharf when he was given a choice by the Gordionis, a powerful family with powerful connections: disappear or his wife and daughter would die. Disappearance was a no-brainer — lost at sea was how the news reported it. He returned a couple of years later, leaner, bearded, bearing a limp, a new name and the demeanour of the down-and-out. Ever since he has taken advantage of the rusty blight to remain hidden in plain sight, confident that any Gordioni would sooner cross the street than look a homeless person in the eye. It was a conscious choice of survival and revenge.

This Monday morning, like every other, he set himself against the wall of the church opposite the city's post office in Market Street and read aloud the poetry of CJ Dennis to any who cared to stop and listen and perhaps drop a coin or two into the briefcase gawping next to him like a koi at the surface of a pond.

Strains of Joe Cocker gravelling *Can't Find My Way Home* wafted from a nearby shop doorway through the morning's grey drizzle as a straggle of pedestrians drifted up from the train station, umbrellas hoisted and heads bent towards their daily toil in the offices and shops that lined the commercial and tourist precincts, many nursing paper cups of steaming lattes or long blacks.

A lanky, grey-haired form in sneakers and jeans, checked shirt and brown corduroy sports coat with elbow patches stooped briefly to drop what looked like a banknote into his briefcase. A sly nod and he was on his way. Hunter's gaze followed him as he crossed to the post office, smiling at his failure to dodge the spray from the wheel of a passing motorist as it splashed through a kerbside puddle. Not quick enough, my friend. The *Mandolin Rain* — it falls gently, takes you by surprise. A small smile lifted the corners of his mouth and wrinkled the edges of his eyes, but just as the brown coat faded into the building's gloom, the smile faded. Something else caught his eye.

It was a girl he'd noticed the previous evening, a ghostly form huddled in the shadows of the arcade that housed post boxes — a statue unnoticed by those entering and leaving the enclave. What took Hunter's eye, even from across the street, was the blank expression. He met her gaze and immediately wished he hadn't, the effort to turn away shadowing a momentary flush of embarrassed impotence he hadn't felt in years.

He hadn't seen the face before. It offered nothing out of the ordinary as its image played across his mind; eyes heavy with a burden of fear burrowed so deep nothing reflected; a pasty mouth, its thin line punctuated at each end by cheeks sunken with despair; strokes of stark contrast in the pallor about the gills and the grey beneath her eyes. Nothing familiar, yet everything the streets had shown him before.

It was late morning when Hunter managed to retreat under the cover of a mob of Chinese tourists. He struck a forbidding image with his injury-laden stride that, for all its apparent handicap, enabled a deft navigation of the footpath. His tall rakish figure, gaunt, unkempt, rough and dour, with yellowing teeth and a chisel-pointed beard, more salted than peppered, kept the gaze of onlookers averted as he headed north towards Beach Street. He turned up past the deserted woolstores to a narrow-fronted, dilapidated building wedged between two giant warehouses and waited, studying the street from the confined space of a gangway between the buildings. The sky above the harbour was thick with cloud the colour of bitumen and spitting needles of icy rain. It was like looking through a welding glass.

When he was sure he hadn't been followed, he forced a rear door and found a space in what was once a kitchen. It stank of rat shit and stale drug use and was littered with food remnants that a horde of ants had industriously reduced to crumbs. With his boot, he scraped away the rancid mess beneath a window where a splash of daylight promised meagre warmth. Here he read the mail he retrieved from the envelope disguised to look like a ten-dollar note. Here he could sit and think and let the afternoon pass away. He thought on the meaning that might be attached to the haunting appearance of the girl. And about the day he would reclaim his life.

That night, after ten, the city centre seemed deserted except for a gang of listless youths Hunter followed along the cappuccino strip. They were looking for action, verballing a load of hoons jockeying past in a souped-up Subaru, its hot-dog exhaust *blatting* under acceleration, windscreen fogged from excess testosterone. The cafés were quiet. Several had closed early, the bitter cold assaulting the few footpath diners who had ventured out, sending them home early to the warmth of wood-fired heaters and heavy doonas.

You don't get pity from the streets. Down is a permanent state once you've got there and, for Hunter, survival at the most basic was a day-to-day engagement with the enemy, leaving the peak of Maslow's pyramid of needs far off. Shelter was as personal as his coat, the lining of which had gone, and a tear under the sleeve gaped like an open window sash. Still, he wrapped it tightly around his scrawny frame, covering a grubby, white rayon shirt he wore buttoned to the collar. The weave of the tee shirt beneath was held together by the faded logo of a long defunct rock band. His army surplus trousers were held up by a rough leather belt threaded through the three remaining loops, their one redeeming quality being the numerous pockets where he stashed various knick-knacks of his secret self in separate places in the event that he were mugged by younger, more desperate men.

He turned a corner into an unlit alley that took him towards the Esplanade. He was known to some of the chefs and sometimes, particularly on slow nights, picked up a decent supply of victuals that, under council regulation, had to be thrown out. Several days earlier, he'd made a mental note to check out Calderos, a new tapas joint along Packenham Street. A short lane took him towards the rear of the restaurant. He returned with half a loaf of sourdough bread, a container of marinated olives and half a dozen lamb empanadas stowed in his briefcase. A sealed Styrofoam cup of hot spicy broth warmed his hand. At the point where the lane turned back toward the street, a muffled scream reached his ears. It came from the car park of the end building.

He froze, cracked the top of his briefcase, reached in, and withdrew a taser he'd scored six months earlier when a cop dropped it during a street brawl. It was kicked into a gutter and Hunter picked it up and continued walking while the brawl raged. It no longer had cartridges, but it still delivered an effective stun and had saved him on more than one occasion. He placed his briefcase and soup on the ground and entered the car park under the shadow of the near wall. On the opposite side of the lot he saw the shape of a large man dragging a struggling smaller figure towards the road. Even in the dark, and from this distance, he recognised the garment she wore.

'Hey!' Hunter shouted, moving towards them with uncommon swiftness.

Before the assailant had time to turn, the full jolt of the taser burned into his left kidney. He doubled over with a pain-filled grunt. Hunter jabbed a second time, this time onto the back of the neck and held fast. The pain sent the attacker to the ground. Hunter trod heavily on a hand. Loose stones on the rough bitumen surface bit hard into skin. The assailant's free hand reached down his leg for a sheathed knife, but Hunter twisted his boot on the hand underfoot and kicked viciously, catching the other forearm just below the elbow. The knife clattered to the ground from a hand that could no longer form a grip. As the thug's breath wheezed from him in a trained attempt to gain control of his breathing, Hunter directed the taser at his genitals, producing a moan that echoed off the building walls. It died as Hunter swung the butt of the weapon down into the contorted face. The assailant's head cracked against the tarmac, producing a sickening thud. He was still.

———

They were sat on the kerb of a vacant parking bay at the rear of the Collie Street multistorey car park, close to the stairs, well enough lit and sheltered from the wind. The floor was devoid of cars except for two at the far end. Hunter had used the car park as a late-night respite often enough to know where the limits of surveillance cameras ended. Even though it closed at midnight on weeknights, the rear emergency exit stairs were never locked. The girl drank the spicy broth and he watched some colour return to her face. The left side was swollen and colouring up like the clouds of a bad storm. Blood oozed from a split in her lip.

He could feel a nightmare looming, the snare of involvement tightening, trapping him like the whirling blades of an advancing helicopter. *Who the hell are you?* his head demanded. *Why are you following me? What have you got to do with me?* Then he asked softly, 'Who was he?'

Her English was lightly accented. 'He wanted to take me back to them.'

'Who is "them"?'

A sudden rush of blood exploded from her lip as she bit down on it. The gash was deeper than he'd first thought. It needed dressing. Hunter handed her a napkin and coaxed a promise to stay put while he went in search of something for the wound.

'Five minutes,' he said, and left by the fire door, jamming a nail into the door bolt to ensure it didn't latch.

He went to a pharmacy a few doors up, purchased his supplies and was stopped just outside by a man towering over him and built in all dimensions like a brick shithouse.

'Excuse me,' the man said, and held a photograph in front of him. 'Have you seen this girl?'

It wasn't unusual for people to search Fremantle streets for lost and missing persons, God knows there are enough of them, but two things struck Hunter. The girl in the photograph was the girl he'd left in the car park. And the character asking politely after her appeared to have been cloned from the man he'd left unconscious in a car park. Only this one was bigger.

'No,' he said. 'Who is she?'

'She's been missing since Saturday,' the man said. 'She's not well and her family are worried.'

Hunter studied the man's eyes. Cold, hard eyes. Deep brown and hooded and observant. He stood with a bearing that comes from years of military training. He was clean-shaven, head and all, and his fingers holding the photograph were precise and steady. Hunter saw them curled around a trigger. He turned away to look down the street, as though following the direction of someone, and as he did so, pulled a key ring from his pocket. A couple of keys dangled from it and at the end of a short chain what looked like a small light but, instead, was a miniature digital camera capable of crystal-clear night-vision shots.

He turned back to the man and said, 'There was a guy up there, I think, asking the same question a while ago.'

The man's eyes followed Hunter's gaze, searching among the bodies walking the streets. Hunter hid his camera hand behind his pharmacy bag, bent over in a coughing fit and snapped off a series of shots, hoping to capture the man's face.

'Yeah, there's a couple of us,' the man said.

'I haven't seen her, but I can ask around. Where's she from?'

'From?'

'She a local?'

'I don't know the details.'

'Well, I haven't seen her,' he repeated, 'but if you've got a card or something...'

'A card?' The man fixed a cold stare on Hunter.

'In case I see her, and you want me to let you know...'

'Never mind I'll keep looking.'

'Suit yourself,' Hunter said, and moved past him.

She was where he'd left her, the soup cup cleaned out and half the empanadas gone. He dressed the wound on her mouth and sat in silence while he removed the data card from the miniature camera and inserted it into a tiny portable viewer. He clicked through the images and brought up the face of the man in the street.

'Who's this?'

She didn't answer, just bowed her head. He asked again.

'A bad man.' She said it to her feet.

Hunter persisted. 'Why is he looking for you?'

She continued to study her feet. 'You're a good man,' she said. 'He's a bad man.'

'And the other guy? The one from earlier?'

'He is also a bad man.'

'So, two bad men. And you. Why have you been following me?'

'You're a good man.'

'You don't know that.'

'I can tell. You help people. I think you can help me.'

'I can take you to a women's shelter.'

Her head came up suddenly. Her eyes flared. 'No. They will find me. I stay with you.'

'You can't stay with me.' Although he said this with some force, he sensed that her roads had come to a complete dead end.

'I have to. If they find me...' — her eyes caught Hunter's gaze directly — 'they will kill me.'

Hunter's words, even to his ears, had the hollow ring of a drainpipe. 'The women's shelter is safe—'

'No. Not from them. They have connections everywhere. They can find people. I must stay with you.'

Hunter's frustration mounted. What to do with her? Can't just leave her here. Aloud, he said, 'You said they want to kill you ... why?'

'They murdered my brother.'

Hunter pointed at the photograph. 'He said your family was worried.'

'My brother was all I had left.' She stifled a sob with a sudden intake of breath. 'They killed him. And now they want to kill me.'

Hunter was silent for several moments as though contemplating a different tack. Eventually he said, 'I have a daughter about your age.' He thought about what he would expect of a decent man were his daughter in a similar situation.

'Is she gone?'

'Gone? Yes, she's gone — they've all gone.'

'She is dead?'

'No, she isn't dead. I'm dead.'

She smiled at that. 'How long have you been dead?'

'Nearly ten years. The only reason I'm still here is because I don't exist. And I can't risk that — you understand?' She nodded. Once again, he held up the picture of the man in the street. 'You need to tell me why you think this guy wants to kill you? Who is he?'

'He works for people who want to kill me and, if I tell you, they may want to kill you too.'

'Too late. I told you, I'm already dead.'

Chapter Four

Free Ride

I have a standing appointment on the first Monday of the month with Dr Eli Mendopulos, a psychiatrist. The appointment is always in the early evening because it suits both our schedules, and Eli is treating me on instruction from some hidden handler. I'm undecided whether it's treatment or conduit.

Eli has a mass of tangled grey hair and he wears black, thickly rimmed glasses that extend his eyebrows out both sides of his face like rosemary branches. He rarely smiles, nor does he frown. A long time ago he held the chair of clinical practice at the University of Western Australia. His office these days is a far cry from there. He works from a decrepit old house on Victoria Street in Midland, the front yard overrun with weeds and litter, and a solitary wandoo that drops leaves on the roof. Passing drunks find the yard a useful repository for empties. A crawl through the weeds would end with stick injuries and a lifetime of hepatitis. The front boundary is shielded by a half-height compressed cement fence which has been kicked into a sieve with holes big enough for escaped circus elephants to crawl through, a scene I have no doubt many locals have witnessed. A sign out front advises there are no drugs kept on the premises. Good advice, if the locals were in a fit state to read.

I dare not park nearby, so I come by train and run the gauntlet from the station past massage parlours with neon signs, and bottle shops guarded by uniformed brawlers. I shun cries for a dollar or a smoke from loiterers begging in the doorways, and wear the abuse of being a white cunt like a shawl for keeping out the light. The weather is blowing in from the coast in heavy sheets that drop from sooty skies in cold, black misery. I muster through the shadows of the driveway and enter via the back door. In his office, I wait and watch as he sifts through a sheaf of pages, getting up to speed on where we are on my pathway to recovery. Eli doesn't own a computer — or at least there are none here. I wonder if he is Freudian or Jungian.

'When we last met,' he says, without lifting his eyes from the page before him, 'we spent some time in hypnosis.'

'I remember,' I say, thinking that it was me who spent the time in hypnosis. There is no *we*.

'But there are some holes in your past. You were reluctant to revisit—'

'Yes, well... Eli, there are some things I can't talk about. I doubt even sodium pentothal would get you there.'

'I know you *think* you can't talk about them, Art, but if I am to help you, we have to. These conditions don't just arrive by themselves. Our test results suggest that something happened and we need to talk about it.'

I spot the opening. 'Would they be Freudian or Jungian — these tests?'

He's not biting. 'You are protected here, Art. Doctor–client privilege.' It's not the first time he's said this, although it's not that kind of protection I worry about. He continues. 'Why did you stop working as a journalist?'

'Freud would probably say it has something to do with unmasking unconsciousness. But Jung might put it down to individuation and my self-regulation of mental processes. What's your opinion?'

'I think you're dodging the issue.'

'I can't explain it further.'

'Can't? Won't? Don't want to?'

'Wouldn't do any good. A paranoid journalist is no good to anyone. Can't be objective and looking over your shoulder all the time. It's like having a personal unconscious and the collective unconscious arguing over who's in control of your diary. Is anyone in control of your diary, Eli?'

'It's not about me, Art. An analysis based on Jung or Freud isn't going to help if you don't.' Almost as an afterthought, he says, 'Although, I would have thought a healthy dose of cynicism was a basic job requirement in your profession.'

I think *Yeah, now who's being a cynic?* And say, 'What do you mean, my profession? My real one or my pretend one?' I don't wait for an answer. 'And I don't agree. I think it helps to know the basis of your magic. In my understanding, there's about as much difference between Freud and Jung as there is between being a cynic and being crushed by gravitational waves. You want to treat the cynic? Fine. But perhaps the crushed soul needs the treatment more.'

His eyes light up behind the black rims of his glasses. 'Good, Art. Good! What do you think were these gravitational waves, as you put it?'

'See, there you go, *individuation*, right? Am I being the Trickster, Eli, and you the Change Maker?'

'Archetypes are unhelpful, Art. I think we can peel back the layers, little by little, and get at the underlying cause.'

'Oh, so Freudian! Yeah, again, Eli, you're not getting it. Unmasking only reveals the next mask. How many times do I have to say it?'

'Was it Kalgoorlie?'

'Was what Kalgoorlie?'

'The gravitational waves?'

'Can we talk about something else?'

Dr Mendopulos has remarkably rapid mental reflexes. 'Sure,' he said. 'How about your new boss?'

'Donna Gardner?' So smooth is his segue, I react without thinking. Perhaps that's his intention.

'Yes. Still getting unwanted intrusive thoughts about her?'

I laugh. 'Freudian again?'

'It's quite natural to have sexual thoughts about people we work with, Art.'

'You know what, Eli? I'm hearing strains of *All Along the Watchtower*. I just can't quite figure out if one of us is a joker.'

'You're looking for a way out?'

'I think Lipschitz might be on to me. He called me to a meeting yesterday with her — actually, *through* her. They're in cahoots.'

'On to you about what?'

I want to answer, but I if I do, I feel sure I will make matters worse. Instead, I deflect. 'They made me feel a fraud.'

'They don't have access to the triggers for your feelings, Art. What unsettles you about him?'

'He's so clean-shaven his skin glistens. He enters a room like he's riding a Segway. He fiddles the corporate credit card. Probably fiddling Gardner for all I know. His mates land lucrative consulting jobs paid for by the university. He's got a plan to spend millions on a film studio and it's crawling with contacts of his — actually told me that's where he wants me. "You can be the doyen of the creative industries," is what he said. But you know what? He wouldn't remember my name if we bumped into each other in the toilet at an awards ceremony, which, by the way, is where we did meet. He's a shadow, a bit like...' I peter out.

Eli looks up from scribbling notes on the page in front of him. His eyebrows tilt like apostrophes above his glasses. 'Go on...' he circles his fingers, urging me to keep rolling, 'a bit like...'

I recount the events of the previous Thursday evening, as if they were miraculously connected. Perhaps Eli thinks they are.

When I finish, the silence hangs like a cloud around a mountain peak. And then, in a slow, deliberate voice, Eli points out the obvious.

'There are different ways we can divide events in our lives, Art, but one way I like to consider is splitting them between events we can control, and those outside our control. You can't take responsibility for those in the second group, and you can't always take full responsibility for those in the former. You can, of course, choose not to go along with it. Any of it.'

I'm shaking my head now, commiserating with the impossibility of such action. What's worse, I can't provide an adequate explanation.

'Sometimes,' I say, my voice draining with my mood, 'I'm just like a fisherman. I throw a baited line in the water and wait. The thing is, when the bite comes, I don't even recognise the fish on the hook. Other times, I feel as though it's me and I'm just waiting to be hauled in.' I look at him. 'Is that Freud or Jung?'

Chapter Five

Black and White

Tuesday 7 August — 32 days before the election

It was almost three in the morning when Hunter led the girl to a hideaway he'd managed to keep secret for nearly five years. The weather had turned as foul as a waking drunkard's breath as he guided her through a maze of city blocks. They stopped before a gate hidden beneath a grove of broad-leaf banksias, wandoo and flooded gums, their crowns whipping like sails busted loose from their riggings. The wind swept horizontal pellets of rain into their eyes as it howled in from the harbour, dragging the smell of salt and diesel and dead seaweed with it. A sheet of water sluiced from the limestone as Hunter ducked into the safety of the tunnel, its trickles crawling beneath his collar, down his back, inside his shirt. He led her through the dark, treading by memory, until they reached a point where the limestone walls and ceiling had collapsed. He knew the precise location of the narrow crawl-through without light, and coaxed her carefully through. A sharp turn lay on the other side which left them in a main tunnel where they could stand. They walked the remaining fifty or sixty metres by torchlight, ending in a

23

good-sized room.

He had found it in 2009, and concluded that the room was originally a World War II bunker. Although the tunnel could have been part of a network between the harbour and the prison built at the end of the nineteenth century, a quick inspection gave him a clear impression that the room hadn't been visited for nigh-on fifty years. He couldn't believe his luck. Two old steel-framed wire-mesh cots sat side by side against one wall, their kapok mattresses frosted in calcified dust, cockroach husks and rat droppings. There was a square green Laminex table and four chairs in the middle of the room, and a plywood kitchen safe stocked with canned goods from the early nineteen-forties lined a wall beneath a single lightbulb and a Bakelite power point. He was pleased to discover they were still connected to an electricity supply. A shallow alcove held a solitary water tap servicing an enamel basin that drained into a sluice and ran out through the rock. Hunter claimed it that day, changed the lock on the gate, and had used it as his hideaway ever since.

The room the girl entered was clean and homey in the manner of a sparsely furnished single man's quarters. It had the impermanent permanence of a golden orb's weaving. Any night here could be his last.

Her name was Falullah Salim. He quickly established she had fled Iraq with her older brother Ishmail in May 2004 when she was eleven years old. Getting to the here and now came in dribs and drabs. For Hunter, there was no going back after he learnt about her escape from community detention, where she had been held since her release from Christmas Island in July 2010.

The escape was spontaneous and daring. She was in a bus with no windows, the bus in which she had been transported to and from a factory for hard, unpaid labour six days of every week for the past three years.

On Saturday evening, the bus had pulled up at a set of traffic lights and, without giving it a second thought, Falullah wrenched the handle of the vehicle's side door, flung it open, leapt out into traffic and ran. She ran with nothing in her mind except putting as much distance between herself and the vehicle as Allah would provide. By good fortune she ran towards Fremantle and hid in the shadows of the streets, where she happened to see Hunter assist an elderly woman who had fallen. She decided it was an act of a good man and followed him feeling, somehow, he would protect her.

The man who stopped him outside the pharmacy, she said, had been hired to take her back to the compound, where she was certain she would be killed — like her brother. Her eyes were heavy and red-rimmed, and when her head fell towards her chest, she straightened up in sudden jerks. She was exhausted, but Hunter pressed on.

'Who runs this compound?' he asked.

'Yusuf.'

'Does Yusuf have another name?'

'Many names, I'm sure — none of them the one he was given at birth. But I know him only as Yusuf. He's a bad man.'

'Just Yusuf? On his own?'

'No, Yusuf has many men who work for him.'

'Like those two tonight?'

'They don't work for Yusuf. I have only seen one of them before. He visited Yusuf with another man, a small man with shifty eyes. Yusuf's people are Asian.'

'All men?'

'Yes, all men. They have dogs that patrol the grounds. Two men drive us from the compound to the factory every day. The bus has no windows so we cannot see out. The compound has high walls. Men guard its doors — we are not permitted to leave. At the factory, we are kept separate from other workers. We prepare and pack food, but not talk, we are not allowed.'

Piece by piece, her story unfolded.

Her family had lived in Baqubah, a small town forty kilometres north of Baghdad. Her father was a driver who worked for the French Embassy. One day early in 2004, armed, masked men came to town and started rounding up and executing people who spoke languages other than Arabic. Originally, they targeted Kurdish speakers, but once they had the taste of blood, any language would do. The Salims spoke several: French, German and English among them. They were separated. Falullah and her brother fled to Baghdad where an uncle helped them. News reached them that their father had been executed in the town square, but her mother and two younger brothers were hidden by friends and later escaped to the north. The uncle arranged for Falullah and her brother to travel to Pakistan, where they met an agent who promised to get them to Australia — the safest place in the world, he'd said. Similar arrangements would be made for their mother and brothers to follow.

'Your brother was with you?'

'After we left Christmas Island, we were separated ... we were not allowed to see each other. Then they killed him.'

'Who killed him? How do you know?'

'One of Yusuf's men showed me a picture. He was hanging by his feet from a chain and his throat was cut.'

For a long time she didn't say any more. Hunter scratched in a tattered notebook, his writing more like hieroglyphics than letters shaping words. It was a codified form of shorthand he'd used for years.

She slept for the better part of Tuesday.

While she slept, Hunter wrote on a miniature laptop he extracted from beneath the kitchen safe. He worked at a feverish pace, words hitting the screen at the speed of thought. He felt as if he were witnessing society sinking. The values of media institutions he once treasured sacrificed to politics that demonised asylum seekers while the privileged sat safe behind walls of wealth. These people were blind, resentful and mean to the level of an art form. Their money protected them from the criminals their own greed created, from the underbelly they didn't want to see. An underbelly that produced asylum seekers.

At the time of his exile, Hunter's daughter was eleven. Last birthday she turned twenty. Every year, on May the fifth, he buys a gift. Nine gifts sit unopened in safe storage waiting for the day he can deliver them.

The girl sleeping in the cot had been eleven when she fled Iraq with her brother. Seventeen when she was taken from Christmas Island into community detention. Although she seemed skinny and undernourished, she was pretty, with fine bone structure and a golden hue to her skin. She moved with an elegance that belied her years of suffering and captivity. He looked on her as she slept, the way a father looks over a daughter, the old, grey, woollen army blanket tucked around her, rising and falling on her breath. Her breathing was laboured, catching in an asthmatic rattle that wasn't helped by the cold and damp. He made a mental note to pick up a Ventolin when he went out.

Hunter drummed away at the keyboard, working on a weekly column he wrote for the *Herald* under the by-line, *Balsa Mick*. It was a regular job he performed for one of the two people he trusted with his identity. Some of the income came to him, but most went into a secret bank account for his wife and daughter, neither of whom knew of his survival. The editor and proprietor of the paper was Ree Porter, long-time friend and bureau chief during Hunter's years at *The Kalgoorlie Miner* in the seventies.

Soon after his return to Fremantle, he pitched an idea to Porter to give a view of life from and for ordinary people — humanity's flyweight in a morally corrupt society is how he described Balsa Mick. A cartoon character who sucks irony out of bombast, irreverent and self-deprecating, speaking the language of the street, putting it in black and white. The scheme they concocted keeps a safe distance between them, and channels the fruit of his labour back to his wife and daughter under the disguise of a journalists' benevolent fund. Porter is the intermediary who ensures they never know of Hunter's survival or the source of the income they receive.

Every Monday the lanky streak passes by his corner near the Wesley Church and drops an envelope into his briefcase — what Hunter calls his mail. The envelope's contents vary, but usually there are five crisp twenty-dollar bills and a micro SD card. Sometimes there was a hastily scrawled note in Porter's own unique shorthand — practically indecipherable to anyone but himself and Hunter — containing news of his wife and daughter, a comment on his column or a response to a request for information.

Porter was well liked in Fremantle. His paper held a reputation for support of worthy causes, providing a timely and comprehensive coverage of political, social and corporate happenings in the city. He sits on the boards of the Fremantle Arts Centre, OneTree Aged Care and St Pat's Day Centre, which is where, every Tuesday evening, a plain envelope finds its way to him. The package Hunter delivered that evening contained the memory card with the week's column — 'Balsa Mick's Theatre Experience: A Canberran Tragedy'. He also included images of the man he encountered in the street searching for Falullah and a request that Porter discreetly try to identify him.

When Hunter returned that night, she was sitting up. He fed her and gave her the inhaler, checking that she knew how to use it. He heated water over the Primus stove, and she took a duck bath at the enamel basin behind a hastily erected blanket curtain. Later, they sat at the small table and Hunter asked about her mother and brothers.

'They died,' she said.

'Yes. You said. But how do you know that?'

'They told me.'

For a moment Hunter was confused. 'They?'

'Yusuf and another man.'

'Do you know this other man?'

'He got us from Christmas Island. I think he is a lawyer. His name is Mister Singh. He was a bit arrogant. He said we would do well with Yusuf because we could speak English. He said we would have a good life.'

'We — your brother and you?'

'Yes. There were others, too.'

'And you were taken to the compound under the care of Yusuf?'

'Not my brother. He was taken somewhere else. I wasn't allowed to see him, but a man called Mahmoud was sometimes on the bus to the factory. My brother worked for Yusuf cleaning offices. Mahmoud would tell me news of him.'

'How did they know your mother died?'

For a long time, she didn't answer. She stared into the depths of her teacup, as though somehow the secrets of her past might be hidden in the soaked-out tea bag.

Hunter prodded. 'Listen, Falullah, if I'm to help you, you have to tell me what you can.'

She shook her head. 'I can't,' she said. 'They will kill me. It is why they killed Ishmail.'

'They can only kill you if they can find you. What I propose is that we make it very difficult for them to do that while your brother's killers are brought to justice.'

'How can you do that?'

'I know a man we can trust to do both,' Hunter said, almost as though convincing himself.

Chapter Six

Pick up the Pieces

Wednesday 7 August — 31 days before the election

In the movies, some characters let go their big secrets moments before they front the gates of paradise and feast on the sugar cakes of eternity. This makes for good entertainment, but there's a lot people don't tell you when they weigh you down with their secrets. Don't tell anyone, they say. What they mean is, *you're mine now, and forever.* They lay levels of exhaustion on you that sap your strength and, before long, you realise the more important a secret is to your life, the more time you will spend thinking on it. It will consume you and produce levels of shame you never imagined possible. To borrow from Shelley for a moment, there's little quite as shameful as the heavy weight of hours that have a man chained and bowed to a past he cannot redeem. The west wind blows, and your face changes forever. It's best not to poke your tongue out.

My journey into the dark has led into the playground with characters of nefarious histories: associations that must remain under lock and key. It has included gang members with plantations buried under domes the size of aircraft hangers, racketeer arms dealers running nightclubs on the side for pocket money, police officers who think racism is a competition. And worse.

One of them is now a maturing code cracker called Will Feynman — WiFi for short — whose dubious career began when he was about thirteen and somehow, notwithstanding charges related to breaking into the security system of the Perth Mint and his part in the biggest heist in history, he went on to land government contracts he can't talk about. His criminal records were expunged and, even more curiously, he landed a job on campus at about the same time as me, where he installed a hidden email server on the university's IT system with the apparent purpose of giving me a secure encrypted address and a back door to Lipschitz's communications. We call it Days of Vanity.

Hunter's message reaches me through Days of Vanity just after three. The message is in the form of a wordplay we cooked up together when I started at *The Kalgoorlie Miner*. Newsrooms everywhere are hotbeds of wordplay: it's part of the culture and, apart from scoring top points for the next day's page one headline, it breeds codecraft for keeping sources safe and communicating important information in ways not easily compromised. Ours started with pieces of paper left on desks and notice boards, communicating our reporting on the shenanigans of men with mineral wealth of unimaginable sums and their commerce in political backhanders, drugs, robbery, vice and wild west policing. It was silly rewriting of famous Australian poetry.

A poem by CJ Dennis, who Hunter argued had more wordplay skills than Webster's International, indicated a meeting, its place and time buried in the words. And I'm looking at one right now; deeply intrigued.

Hist Hark, until it's fell'ed dark ...

Six Glugs of Gosh partake their nosh

Across the dossing park.

Frith Froth, it's paddy dons the cloth ...

Two bugs to squash a mackintosh

And sup the brother broth.

Brother broth — a poetic coincidence — an indication of more afoot than either of us would consider normal.

Just before five thirty, I park in a Fremantle side street behind a historic building, once the lunatic asylum, but now, fittingly perhaps, the Fremantle Arts Centre. I retrieve a threadbare sport jacket, old lumber shirt and canvas trousers from a bag I keep in the boot of my car. My transformation takes a couple of minutes and is completed with a pair of broken sneakers, a filthy Fremantle Dockers beanie on my head, and an old carry bag stuffed with rags. A bottle of cheap wine I've grabbed from a drive-through along the way is wasted over my hands and face, and I smear dirt and grime to complete the image. I affect a slouch and shuffle my way down the hill across Fremantle Park and along Queen Victoria Street to arrive at St Pat's on the dot of six. The wind is bitter, low clouds the colour of powdered asphalt hover over the harbour.

Hunter sits at a table partly obscured by a niche wall remaining from the abutment of what were once two separate buildings, his nose buried in a notebook, pen screaming across the pages, a steaming cup of tea in front of him. The rich aroma of pea and ham soup and steamed vegetables storms from the kitchen and I realise, at that moment, I am famished. I drop my rag bag on the floor at the table and saunter to the servery, order soup, lamb stew and vegies, a cup of black tea and return to the table to sit opposite the man I'd come to see.

He glances at me and looks back down. 'You smell terrible, Lazaar.'

'You did say, "don the cloth".'

'I didn't say drown it. What the fuck did you use?'

'McWilliams Muscat. Wouldn't want to waste something I'd

rather drink.'

'You're a cheap bastard.' He looks up at me and a smile lights his eyes for the briefest of moments. 'Although you do look as though you could do with a decent feed. A shave and bath probably wouldn't go astray either.'

I wait and, eventually, Hunter puts his pen down. He surveys the nearby tables, probably to decide the level of voice to use. My stomach growls. I tear up a slice of bread and float the pieces in my soup. Hunter watches me shovel generous spoonfuls into my mouth, my slurps signalling both my hunger and my appreciation.

'You got Middle Eastern girls at your university?' he asks.

I'm a little taken aback. 'Some. Why?'

'We need to hide one — best if she can be one of a crowd.' I must have kept my stunned look. 'Like me — hidden where people won't see,' he adds.

'Jesus, Hunter. How can I do that?'

'There's murder involved.' He's dropped his voice to a whisper, but that's a word I hear loud and clear. Like a fix to a junkie. 'And if we don't protect her' — a pause to let the we sink in — 'there'll be another one.'

He launches into sketchy details of Falullah Salim's story and explains what he has in mind. My soup grows cold as I sit spellbound, attempting to come to terms with what — on the face of it, at least — seems preposterous.

'Slave labour? Here, in Perth?'

'Looks that way.'

'A serious worry if it's real.'

'Trust me, the blokes looking for her are very real. And they mean to find her.'

By this stage, my brain is clocking time-and-a-half. 'Are we supposing they are the murderers?'

'That's what you need to find out, Lazaar. Before they — whoever they may be — find her.'

'Better to leave it to the cops, surely.'

He ignores me and ploughs on. 'Doubt they'll make much progress. Porter did some digging and tells me there's a murder investigation, but they haven't released any details. Apparently they haven't identified the victim. I don't know if it's her brother, but it seems a reasonable assumption.' His grey eyes, clear and steady, drill into me. 'This is a young girl's life, Lazaar. She's in deep shit and the feeling in my bones tells me it's way beyond the league of local cops.'

'Twenty thousand leagues beyond?' I say, reminding him of the first time he uttered that sentiment to me thirty-nine years ago. 'You know, Eli Mendopulos keeps wanting me to talk about that shit in Kalgoorlie.'

'Well you can't. Whoever that is.'

'He's my shrink. They should never have got away with it, Hunter.'

'Well, they did. Get over it.'

'Get over it? People died, people got rich, people got powerful — people who shouldn't have, all because some fucker wanted to—'

'Hey!' He shook his head, slight movements. 'You think I don't live with it?'

'It wasn't your ethics that were compromised. You kept your job and your career.'

'Look where that got me. Anyway, you've got a better job — better than mine at least.' He smiles.

'Until some pink-faced spook comes along and suggests I take up another calling. Maybe I'll be a lawyer next. I might need to be. As it is, the subject assassins put my job on notice yesterday.'

Hunter looks at me, his face hardened to the realities of what we've become. 'Look, Lazaar, what happened, happened. You can't change it, I can't change it. The people you do these jobs for — you're never going to know who they are. Even if they did organise this shrink for you, if you talk about this shit, it's not only you who's fucked, is it? A whole government went down because of what you saw and just because forty years has gone by, it doesn't mean it's forgotten. These pricks remember things across generations. So, can we get on and solve *this* fucking murder?'

We sit in silence while I assembled the facts and my own version of events. It went a little bit like this.

Ishmail Salim's murder came about because of a complicated deal with a network of people smugglers that unravelled on 15 September 2010. That morning, an asylum-seeker boat crashed into rocks at Christmas Island, broke up and sank, leaving ninety people struggling in wild and treacherous seas. Forty-eight died, among them the mother and two younger brothers of Ishmail and Falullah Salim. The travel arrangements for the mother and siblings were made when the man called Yusuf secured their release from Christmas Island into community detention. The journey would be paid for by their indenture: Ishmail and Falullah would work for him for five years to pay off the debt. After that, Yusuf told them, they would be free in Australia and together as a family. It was too good a deal to refuse.

Mahmoud told her of her brother's death. He said Ishmail had an argument with Yusuf because he'd failed to deliver their mother and brothers safely to Australia. He insisted there was no debt to be paid, which meant he and his sister should be free. Yusuf refused and Ishmail threatened to go to the authorities. He was caught escaping. His murder was the logical solution. Except now Falullah had escaped. And that compounded the risks to whoever was behind it all. We needed to find that person.

'How does she know?' I ask.

'Know what?'

'The murder. How did she know they murdered him?'

'They took a picture and showed it to her.'

I sit back, watching the fleeting light of my escape fading in the distance. 'So, she knows who did it? Seems simple enough. If the cops have a murder, she knows who did it because they showed her a picture, all she has to do is tell them. They'll connect the dots. There's no point me getting involved.'

Hunter stares at me. 'She doesn't know who did it. The picture doesn't show who did it. The guy who showed it to her didn't do it. At least she doesn't think he did.'

'But he had the camera. Did he take the picture?' That stops him.

'That's unclear,' he says, finally. 'Anyway, she's not safe, so she can't speak to police.'

'These two thugs don't fit the other facts of the story,' I say.

'Now that's a brilliant idea. Figure that out and you've got it solved.'

My stomach churns. It's one thing to be fighting for my academic future with Lipschitz on the prowl, but to do what Hunter is asking is at an altogether different level. He demands that I find a way into the secret places of the souls of dangerous forces about which I know bugger-all. And if I don't, at least one young woman will likely die.

It's 1974 all over again.

In 1974, in Kalgoorlie, Hunter (then called Calvin Bishop) was my editor and Ree Porter our bureau chief. As the junior, they had me reporting the courts, where I met the young detective Nick Fairgough. I walked into the wrong room and the wrong meeting with a gathering of the wrong people surrounding the naked body of a young girl. Under threat of being fed through an ore crusher and my remains dropped down an abandoned dig by a cop the size of a mountain, I could choose the crusher or leave with no choice, a buried truth, and a poetic licence. I opted for the latter and have lived with the roaring tinnitus of a ten-tonne jaw crusher pounding in my skull ever since.

'Look, Hunter—'

'No Lazaar. You look. I didn't ask for this to land in my lap, but it has. That means it's also in yours. You have no choice.'

It's funny how songs just invade your mind at unexpected

moments. I felt as though I'd killed a lawman. 'Did Porter happen to find out who got the case?'

Hunter smiles, tilts his head back and looks at me through narrowed eyes. 'It's all acalistic, Lazaar. You'll see.'

I gesture with open hands.

'Kelly Boulter.'

Chapter Seven

The Next Phone Call

Acting Detective Sergeant Kelly Boulter has an office about the size of a broom closet located next to the male toilet on the first floor of the Fremantle detective's building. The building, narrow, two storeys, painted white with no signage was a relic of the sixties with its most recent interior fit-out at best twenty years earlier. From her desk she heard the squeak of toilet cubicle doors when they opened, a bang when they closed, and every flush, grunt and fart as the other eight detectives in the unit relieved themselves of their bodily waste. If she swivelled her chair, she could look through a narrow window that hasn't seen a cleaning rag since last century. The view terminated at a solid red brick wall across a small car park, a space with insufficient bays to include her vehicle, forcing her instead to park at the nearby multistorey car park at visitor's rates.

Boulter's posting to Fremantle was in line with a long-standing tradition in West Australian policing, where the South Metropolitan District Office, Fremantle, is a punishment posting, a stigma that respective commanders and commissioners have worked, over many years, to remove. Their failures remain a mystery to anyone above the rank of superintendent.

It's a tough town. Much of the population, particularly when confronted by police, choose not to speak English, and then dissolve into a cultural quagmire. Many of Boulter's investigations stalled because those involved hail from families who preferred to stay silent, to exact their justice privately and physically, where nobody saw or heard anything. Witnesses disappeared, victims lost their memories, suspects were never heard from again.

Yet the superintendent expected case closures, convictions, and reduced crime numbers — statistics that make his branch look good in the annual report, statistics that produce promotions. And all too often he got them from detectives eager for re-posting; detectives who became involved with petty crooks and their victims; detectives who subverted police resources to cook up charges and false evidence in the pursuit of a better life.

Boulter's posting to the South Metro followed a long investigation in which she found cause to pursue allegations of corruption against a senior sergeant who was, at the time, under cover and seconded to the Australian Federal Police. She had been part of a team investigating one crime while an AFP investigation targeted the same group of criminals for a different crime. Hers was drugs; theirs, immigration fraud. But they failed to share intelligence. The allegations against the officer went away and Boulter ended up in this foetid old-boys' club, waiting on a long-overdue promotion. To add insult to injury, the senior sergeant she'd had in her sights had since been promoted to superintendent in the Australian Federal Police.

But there was one man who she blamed. Although he did connect the dots that led her to the drugs evidence, that was small profit at great expense. He blew her cover, and her actions were seen to undermine the feds. That meant Buckley's chance of securing evidence against a crooked copper. And, of course, she had to kiss her drugs bust goodbye. He miraculously escaped charges. If she ever lays eyes on him again, it will be too soon.

Boulter preferred working in the situation room, a space more conducive to thinking than the dogbox they gave her. Here she could look at the active crime boards — a cork-lined wall, pinned with notes, photographs, diagrams and connecting threads of evidence that provided the narratives of active open investigations. Her ideal time for thinking was late in the day, when she could avoid the sexist slanging of juvenile male officers ten years her senior who puffed their chests and mounted their crime scene evidence the way she imagined they mounted the women in their sad lives.

It had just gone six thirty, and a freshly printed forensics report from the crime scene she'd dubbed the wheelie bin murder lay before her. She'd been assigned lead investigator by Superintendent Ewen McPherson. Officially, it was because she was trained as a major crimes investigator, but because the victim was of Middle Eastern appearance, it was thought it would be of little interest to the media. Many would assume — on racial and religious grounds — that the victim deserved it anyway.

On most afternoons, the arseholes in the squad disappear quicker than a rainbow in the desert, so the floor was deserted except for her and, as it turned out, Superintendent McPherson. She watched him enter the room carrying a bottle of scotch and two glasses, which he placed before him. He chose the head of the table on Boulter's right, his gaze crawling her breasts as he fell into his chair. She shrank back into hers and folded her arms — an involuntary reaction, not to authority but a response to men who assume a right to view her body.

'SOC report?' McPherson asked as he uncapped the bottle and began splashing the golden liquor into a glass.

'Not for me, thanks,' Boulter said, holding her hand in a stop gesture. 'Yes. The wheelie bin report.'

McPherson nodded. A Scene of Crime report was the factual

record of work the crime scene investigators did immediately they took control of a place of interest. He tempted again with the bottle. 'Sure?' She shook her head. 'Clear this one, lass, and you can go back to Midland.' And then, as an afterthought. 'Permanent promotion.'

Obviously, he didn't believe it could be done. 'It's early days, Superintendent. But if you have some insights, I'd be pleased to hear them.'

'Perhaps you think it's early days, but it's coming up on a week and nothing's advanced. That's not early days, that's poor progress. You've had Robinson and Baxter all week. I'll put young Parker with you on Monday, help you along, but we need to see some results pretty smartly.' Parker was the latest transferee. He'd been reposted from the country. Narrogin or was it Merredin? She didn't know what prompted his reassignment, but her first impression suggested he had a whole book of tickets on himself. He'd fit in perfectly with Robinson and Baxter.

'If you think that's a good idea sir,' she said, and turned a page, even though she hadn't read it.

He sipped at his drink and regarded her coolly beneath his heavy brow.

'Maybe you're the one to ground him a bit,' he said, leaning forward and tapping the document. 'There's not much up on the board, so perhaps you can bring me up to speed?'

He was right. The board was practically bare. The only photos were of the wheelie bin and the victim, along with a map reference of where it was found. There were no names, no threads connecting events or people.

Boulter turned the page back on the report. 'We checked the serial number on the bin. It was in pre-delivery at David Gray's O'Connor depot.' She read down the page. 'Assigned to an address in Armadale but stolen sometime between last Tuesday morning and Thursday. It was scheduled for delivery on Tuesday and the deliveries were made on Thursday. The murder was committed between ten o'clock Thursday night and two the next morning. The only trace evidence on the bin other than the victim's is from the guy who called it in. Robinson and Baxter canvassed the neighbourhood. One odd occurrence — a broken-down four-wheel drive near a park around the corner was towed by a towing service around midnight. We haven't identified either vehicle yet — Robbo's following it up. Baxter's on David Gray's, trying to pin down the bin theft.

'There are a couple of other odd things. Before it was used, the bin had been cleaned with a chemical agent containing ammonia and sodium hydroxide, and probably with an industrial pressure cleaner. They found some grease in one of the tyre treads and red paint mixed with the victim's blood. The grease may have come from the vehicle that transported it. The paint ... I don't know. The analysis suggests it's automotive — we should get a manufacturer and batch number early in the week.'

'So, professional job?'

'An execution, sir.'

'What do we know about the victim?'

Boulter shook her head and ignored the sound of her phone ringing in her office. 'No idea, sir.'

'Well you'd better get an idea. And soon. It's not the sort of business we want ending up with SCS, is it?' The Special Crime Squad handle cold cases and, should they solve the crime, the original investigation is usually tainted with failure, levelled at the lead investigating officer or, worse, the branch. He poured another two fingers into his glass and voiced his thoughts. 'Surely if he's a foreigner there'd be a record — fingerprints, passport. Shouldn't be too difficult to get Immigration to track it down.'

'Yes, you'd think so, sir. But there's nothing in either the national fingerprint or DNA databases. It's weird. I'd put him mid-twenties, Arab features. His clothes were local. Everyday items — jeans, polo shirt, light vinyl jacket, sneakers — things you get from K-Mart or Target. No wallet, no money. Nothing.' Again, she ignored her phone ringing in her office. Instead, she read quickly through a page, turned it, then turned it back. She looked up at her superior.

'What is it?' he asked.

'*They*, or *he*, strung him up.'

'They what?'

'Hung him by the ankles and butchered him.' She read aloud: 'Contusions and abrasions around the ankles and feet, most likely caused by a chain with links two to two-and-a-half centimetres long looped around both ankles. The body was suspended from the ankles. The throat was cut with a fine, very sharp blade. A single cut severed both carotid arteries and the windpipe just above the larynx. The hands were secured through a belt loop behind the back with a cable tie. The victim bled out completely into the wheelie bin, placed in headfirst, his legs folded down and the lid closed. A plastic sheet was used as a liner, like a shower curtain, and folded down on top of the body. The abrasions show some signs of struggle, as does the blood spatter in sections of the plastic liner. Red paint spatter also found on the inside surface of the plastic liner.' Boulter looked up from the page. 'Paint? Why paint?'

McPherson drained his glass and stood. 'I guess that's what you need to find out.' He picked up his scotch and made to leave, abandoning the glasses to the cleaners. He'd covered half the length of the table when he turned around. 'Maybe some kind of ritual thing. Revenge?'

Boulter's phone rang for the third time. She slumped back in her chair and loosened the band of her ponytail. Combing her hair back from the top of her head with her fingers, she watched McPherson's back as he left the room.

When Boulter finally reached her phone, there were three messages on her voicemail, all from the same caller. A number she would much rather have erased from the earth. She was almost tempted to erase the messages without giving them a hearing, but something stopped her. She hit play.

Ah ... Kelly ... Art Lazaar here. I need to talk to you about something important. Call me back.

She deleted it and played the next.

Yeah, Kelly, Lazaar again. Call me, please. It's important.

Another delete.

The next: *Lazaar again. Look I've got something important to talk to you about. Maybe we can catch up for a cup of coffee.*

Cup of coffee? That's rich, the last time I saw you, Lazaar, I poured coffee down your trousers. She hit delete with a little more force than necessary. Then the phone rang. She stared at it while the ring tone warbled at her until the call diverted to voicemail.

Boulter, I know you're in your office. I need to talk to you about the murder you're working on. Tonight. Call me.

She didn't delete the message but shut the phone off and scanned her surroundings. The only sound was the low hum of air conditioning and a fluorescent light flickering in a distant office. How could he know? Was he watching? She looked down into the car park. Three detectives' vehicles were parked under the glare of halogen lights. The detectives would be at Rosie O'Grady's, the cars would remain late. She couldn't see anyone lurking. Perhaps he knew her too well. He would assume her working habits hadn't changed. He was like that: clever, intuitive, deductive. But he was also arrogant and not a little psychopathic, a complex man who read people like they were books, whose spheres of influence were both unknown and unfathomable.

Was McPherson his connection? But McPherson had gone to great lengths to warn her off Lazaar. Several times in fact, starting the day she arrived. He couldn't have been clearer.

'He's put you in a bit of a spot,' he said. 'Compromised your inquiry and landed you in the cack with the brass. I'd suggest you keep your distance from him. He's an opportunist, an amateur sleuth, and I won't have his kind around my nick. If it wasn't for him, your sergeant's posting would be permanent.'

She agreed. She'd asked McPherson why he hadn't been charged with obstruction or interference with an official inquiry.

'Difficult to prove,' McPherson said. 'He's a slippery devil. Aye, he knows his way around an inquiry, and he's proved useful once or twice — can get into places we can't, do things where we are limited. But he's an outsider, he plays close to the edge, and when you play with him, you risk falling into the abyss. Best you stay clear of him.'

Could McPherson have been playing her? Driving a wedge so she would rise to the challenge? She felt foolish. The kind of foolish that comes from discovering a lover with another woman and his pants down. As the fog cleared it dawned that she had been trapped.

She was the lover with the pants down.

Chapter Eight

Into the Mystic

There's something about Fremantle that gets under my skin. When the mist and the fog blows in on a miserable August night, and soaks your face and clothes and chills you through like snap frozen peas, I find myself in sympathy with that long ago ship's master who placed a buoy on a rock out in the sound and ran his ship aground by steering straight for it. The rock became known as Challenger Rock, named after the vessel, and our fair city known as Fremantle after the ship's captain. He demanded the master be hanged immediately, and most likely would have had his way were all hands not needed to free the stricken vessel.

I'm standing in a non-functioning doorway of the heritage-listed Orient Hotel in High Street, having been told by the rugged-up occupant of the one further up to piss off and find my own crib. My inner voice is riffing on Van Morrison's prophetic lines from *Into the Mystic* as I shake off the shivers and turn my gaze across the street towards Angelo's Kitchen — a greasy spoon lit in mustard yellow. I watch every face as it moves along the footpaths, reflecting for a moment on the building next door to Angelo's, now a backpackers' hostel, but a classic haunt I frequented in the early seventies when it was called Cleo's. I was among many who would line up on a Sunday afternoon for a two-hour drinking session with Fatty Lumpkin hammering out Spencer Davis Group, Grand Funk Railroad and Jethro Tull covers along with one or two of their own songs. They were good musicians, loud, with a fine repertoire. The building was constructed around 1850 and has been a hostelry of one kind or another all its life, owned by a string of notable ratbags and dealers in vices often beyond what their licences allowed. Part of the Fremantle colour palette which lives on to this day, blind eyes turning in all directions. That part of Fremantle isn't heritage listed.

I am suffering this freezing indignity because Kelly Boulter's call nominating Angelo's Kitchen doesn't come until after seven-thirty.

I arrive early and hide in the shadows to watch. My beanie is pulled down on my head and my coat wrapped tight with the collar lifted. Ghosts of my past float across my mind like the vehicles that buzz up and down the street, and every second face on the footpath as it passes in front of me has the false strain of familiarity. Angelo's sports a smattering of diners out front beneath gas heaters that glow like red mushrooms, spitting and hissing as the radiators catch the drizzle. Boulter approaches from the west, the wind and rain behind her, and I watch as she enters the café and threads her way through full tables in the front towards the rear. I let five minutes pass before I'm convinced she has no tail. I cross the street and slide into the seat opposite her, in the last booth.

'Reliable as ever, Lazaar,' she says, her face passive, giving nothing away. 'Maybe you should get a watch.'

I head to the counter and order a flat white for her and an espresso for me.

'Place is a bit of a worry,' I say, squeaking my way back into the booth and taking in the decor. The booths are cream coloured vinyl, sticky and grimy, the tables white grainy Laminex, chipped and stained, perched on chrome legs bolted to a black and white tiled floor as though a thief might find them tempting. Distorted middle-of-the-road pop music squawks through speakers in the corner of the ceiling. The atmosphere is stale coffee and frying grease. I'm glad I've already eaten.

'It's safe,' she says.

'Would that include the food?'

'Safe from anyone I know seeing me with you.'

'Ouch.' I wait while the coffees are set before us. The waitress enquires if we are waiting on anything else. We dismiss her with simultaneous shakes of our heads. At least we agree on something.

I try my best smile on Boulter, but it draws no response, so I take a bold step. 'You look good.'

'Thank you,' she says, her words devoid of warmth. 'What do you want to tell me, Lazaar?'

'Well, that, for one thing.'

She frowns. 'Give me a break Lazaar.' She pauses to ensure I get the point. 'How did you know where I was? Did McPherson tell you?'

'I don't know a McPherson.'

'Don't bullshit me, Lazaar. My superintendent, Ewen McPherson?' She studies my face and, seeing nothing, continues, 'He spends the last six months telling me how lucky I was to escape your trap, insisting you're dangerous, unstable, untrustworthy, a deviant I should have nothing to do with. Then he tells you where I am?'

'I'm sorry, Kelly, I don't know him. He didn't tell me anything. Sounds like he's full of shit, though. Either that or his ear's in the mouth of someone further up the food chain who wants to spoil my reputation.'

'Yeah, well you do have a reputation. I can't imagine who might want to spoil it. You're a meddler, Lazaar. You stick your beak into business that has nothing to do with you, you interfere, you put lives at risk, blow investigations.'

I wait a moment, assume what I hope is a humble attitude and wind my hand as though spinning a wheel. 'Yeah, yeah, I know I'm not a cop.' My gaze bores into her eyes, but the blinds are drawn, her sense of justice deeply buried. 'But I know poetry, and something here is not rhyming.'

She emits a brittle little chuckle, involuntary, soulless, unkind. 'Poetry? What the fuck has poetry got to do with it, you wanker?'

'Poetry has everything to do with it.'

'That's why we're here? Together? Talking about poetry?'

'Absolutely.'

'Bullshit.'

'We share a naturally veering path,' I say, bringing my hands together. 'You can't deny the strange attraction between us.'

'I'm not in the least bit attracted to you, you dick!'

I hold my hands up in mock surrender. 'Whoa. Whoa! Not attracted to me? Come on Kelly, you know you are. Why would you pick a shithole like this for us to meet in if you weren't attracted to me? I mean, with a B&B right next door...'

She laughs. 'Jesus, Lazaar, your memory must be as short as your penis — you do remember what happened to you when we tried that?'

I join in the laughter. The ice is broken. 'Of course, we're like Humpty Dumpty and Alice, we're connected — *pensée pensant.*'

'Sounds like a lot of cock, Lazaar. *Penises and panties?*'

On cue, Joni Mitchell's *Free Man in Paris* squawks through the ceiling speakers. 'It's French. It means thought-thinking while thinking-thought ... that moment when we connect, when things are synchronous, I feel you, you feel me.' I take a breath. 'You've been there, deep in a case, the thought bubble emerges from the froth, the thought itself takes liberties — suddenly there's a connection. It's the same machinery behind poetry as great detective work. But you know that.'

This last bit comes out as mere flattery, but I actually mean it. She's an excellent detective: thorough, clever, resourceful.

And extraordinarily beautiful.

One night, a couple of years earlier, she had sauntered into the front bar at the Railway Hotel in North Fremantle dressed in jeans and a black top that didn't just fit perfectly, it moulded the entire world around her. A long-time regular haunt of stevedores, truckers and miscellaneous wharf workers, the Railway Hotel was seedy and loud, and for many years the only hotel in the Perth metropolitan area to be licenced until 6 am. It was owned by Enzo Gordioni, a Fremantle notable. Enzo, the patriarch of the Gordioni family, the man who decided who could work the docks and who could employ them. Enzo, who would chase Hunter to the end of days.

He chaired committees and held audiences with the Minister for Shipping and Transport, and the heads of Customs and Excise, with the Premier if needs be — of either political stripe. He was an honorary member of the Maritime Union of Australia and he extended generous discounts to union members in the hotel's bars. He was eighty-three years old and lived as though he were fifty. If there was a dispute, anything from a bar fight to a waterfront lockout, Enzo could settle it. If it touched the wharf, it touched Enzo. He could prevent goods or people entering or leaving, and that leverage tended to resolve most disputes. Among the many properties he owned in Fremantle, the Railway Hotel was the one he'd owned longest. It was dingy, rundown and worth a fortune. When Kelly Boulter walked through the door, it was as though the lights came on for the first time in its hundred and ten year history.

I was there because Hunter had roped me in to chase a theory. Off the books of course. His theory was that the Gordioni family who had, eight years earlier, ordered a hit on him was also behind a surge of meth on the streets, distributed through networks of homeless people sucked in to a secret organisation called The Brotherhood. It seemed pretty far-fetched, but theories often need leaps across narrative boundaries. At first glance, his narrative — and that of the usual drug distribution — lacked enjambment. But there were people here who didn't fit.

An overweight, bearded crane driver, still wearing his hi-vis jacket and quaffing Jack Daniels and Coke like it was cordial, was murdering me at pool. Instead of sighting my shots, my eye had been fixed on a large, athletic man at the far end of the bar, his curly hair ginger enough for him to have likely been nicknamed Meggs in his youth. He wore an open-necked off-white polo shirt, brown corduroy jacket, blue denim jeans and expensive sneakers. He was sat at a small, round Laminex table in conversation with a skinny young bloke whose deeply olive complexion, long manky hair and high-bridged nose placed his ethnic origins somewhere in the eastern Mediterranean. He wore tattered jeans and sweats and looked less than comfortable with his surroundings. Although they were out of earshot, the neural lye between them created a rhythm that sat against the natural metre of the bar. At six-thirty on a Friday, they seemed as out of place as she did, perched on a bar stool directly in my line of sight.

My next shot miscued, giving away two shots, even though Crane Driver only needed the first to take my last fifty bucks.

I declined a rematch on financial grounds and took a stool next to her, scooping my now warm middy of beer into my hands, sipping, scouring the room from beneath a lowered brow. A Bloody Mary was placed in front of her and she too scanned the room, resting her eyes momentarily on mine. I tore my eyes away and looked back at the corner table. Meggs had vanished, leaving Skinny sitting alone sipping from a bottle of water and flipping his pack of smokes like they were playing cards. His eyes shifted, as though seeking a figure in the crowd, but not resting on anyone long enough to draw a return gaze.

Meggs was nowhere. I watched the toilet door, but he never emerged. Maybe he'd left.

I looked at the girl on the bar stool. It never dawned on me then that she was an undercover cop. She looked to be out for the night, slumming her way around the sleazy end of Fremantle, looking for action. Most of my money had gone on the pool tables and the one bloke who interested me had gone too. Although his skinny partner was still on the premises, he was the small cheese in the fridge. Certainly less deserving of my attention than the woman on the stool next to me.

She told me her name was Kylie, 'Like Minogue,' she added in a hyphenated sort of way.

Yeah, I thought, but live, right here, in the flesh. She was shaped and moved with a presence. Her lips had a certain natural and inviting pout to them that I liked. We bantered, volleying back and forth for some time. Before I knew it, half an hour had gone, the score was deuce and I was vying for a match point advantage. The crowd had grown larger and more boisterous, and I noticed out of the corner of my eye that Skinny's eyes had stopped roving, latching on to something behind me, deeper down the bar. I turned but there was nothing obvious in the crowd. When I turned back, Skinny was on a beeline for the door. I excused myself and threaded through the pack of punters, bursting out the door just in time to see him climb into a black Mercedes 380 coupe with an Asian man, perhaps Indonesian or Malaysian, at the wheel. I watched the car drive down Tydeman Road. When I turned, Kylie was standing behind me. She suggested we go into the lounge bar where the Dave Hole Band had just started their set. Our match was in recess, it seemed.

A little after two in the morning, we were in a late-night yuppie bar on South Terrace where, a week earlier, four off-duty cops had beaten the shit out of a mob of exchange students from the USA celebrating the end of their semester at Notre Dame University. The music was loud and awful, and I couldn't wait to get out of there. My intention was to take her to the sanctity of my bed. Although the match was far from decided, I was quietly confident.

But fortunes have a way of changing unexpectedly. Within

five minutes I'd recognised Meggs, the ginger-haired guy from the Railway, at the far end of the bar. He was deep in conversation with Vincent Gordioni. Vincent was a nephew of Enzo and, according to the licence plate above the front door, the owner and licensee of this bar. I grabbed Kylie by the elbow and went to move along the bar, hoping to get a closer look and maybe eavesdrop on their conversation. But there was a sudden change in her demeanour.

Her jaw had set, and her eyes narrowed, and she had stiffened a little. I caught the briefest of glimpses in the same direction as Meggs and Vincent, so I asked her straight out, having to be in her ear to be heard, if she knew them.

'I'm much more interested if you know them,' she said.

That threw me a little. She was suddenly standoffish. It dawned on me that some of her questions earlier in the evening could have had alternative implications. She was playing a much better game than I realised.

'I know who the young one is,' I said. 'But I don't know Curly there — the bloodnut — Meggs.'

'Who's the young one?'

'You tell me yours and I'll tell you mine.' My lips were on her ear lobe as I said this. She turned and flashed me a smile.

'I bet mine's much more interesting than yours,' she said. Then she reached up closer and her breath fell lightly on the back of my ear and down my neck like a gossamer curtain. 'I think we need to get out of here.' She took me by the hand and led me out of the bar.

The slap of the cold air doubled me over and I took refuge in the warmth of the body next to me. I would learn more that night than I'd bargained for.

I'd been living out of a small suite at the Tradewinds Hotel for fifteen months, since my home in Roleystone was burnt to the ground on a day that reached 44 degrees and a howling easterly had been ripping up through the Araluen valley since before dawn. A spark became an inferno, and by the time the fire was extinguished over seventy homes had been razed to the ground. Mine was gone within an hour. Along with it, works in progress, recordings, historical memorabilia ... stuff I could never replace.

I ushered the woman whom I no longer believed was named Kylie-like-Minogue into my room and fixed us a coffee. I needed some clarity, so I called her on the name thing. I twigged she was a cop working undercover. Her cover blown, she either had to trust me, arrest me, or call off the operation.

A few weeks earlier, a mother had lost her daughter to the Fremantle streets and tipped off Major Crime about a drug operation being funnelled through the wharf. The mother had blundered into a nest of vipers in an attempt to recover her daughter. She was too late but before her daughter died, she had given her mother information that might identify a key player. A car accident claimed the mother's life the day after she took the matter to Major Crime. It was not considered a coincidence. Without saying as much, Boulter indicated that the guy in the jeans and corduroy jacket — the one I'd nicknamed Meggs — was central to her investigation. We had common cause: a Gordioni and the enigmatic Meggs.

She wanted to identify the figure the girl implicated; a figure she also assumed to be involved in the mother's death. I pressed her on the real identity of Meggs, but she remained as tight-lipped about it as I was about Hunter. Some secrets can't become others' secrets. That's the way it is.

The sun came up that morning and we'd never got near a bed.

A month later Boulter's investigation became more dangerous than she knew. I could see no way out other than to blow her cover. To sabotage a mission is about as unethical as you can get, but she was fatally exposed, and either her superiors weren't aware, or they didn't care. She accused me of betrayal and vowed that if she ever saw me again, she'd kill me. By then I'd learnt that Meggs was Max

Glendinning, a serving police officer, but I couldn't explain to her how I had come about that information.

So here we were: one year on.

As I watch her face across the table for signs of anything other than hostility, I reflect on how she affects me. At first glance you could be pardoned for thinking there's something of a *Lucretia Mac Evil* about Kelly Boulter, but the truth is more complex. People underestimate her. An attractive, diminutive figure sends one kind of signal to a certain kind of man, but making that kind of assumption would be a mistake a man wouldn't have a second chance to make about Boulter. She's about 155 centimetres tall, probably weighs around 60 kilos, and has the appearance that butter wouldn't melt in her mouth. But she has three times been the state's weight-lifting champion for her class, has the Mhuy Thai skills to put a man twice her size on the mat in fifteen seconds and scores consistently above 4.7 on the firing range. Her nerves are as steady as a shearing shed's roof purlins, her eyesight as sharp as fleecing shears. But getting close to Kelly Boulter is much the same as getting close to molten steel. There's a good chance of getting burnt. She has hair as white as Scarborough Beach sand, softly punctuated by a pair of gold sleepers in her ears. A little mole the colour of café au lait on her right cheek rises and falls with every smile, and darkens with every frown. Tonight, she's wearing denim jeans and a checked lumber shirt under a weatherproof microfibre jacket that sounds like fallen leaves being swept by a brisk wind along a concrete footpath every time she moves. Her anvil grey eyes regard me with resentment and suspicion across the table.

'How's the murder inquiry going?' I ask in a conspiratorial whisper.

'Murder inquiry?'

'Yeah, the Arab kid?'

'Who the hell told you about that? Baxter? Robinson? Any of

those dirty fucks.'

I laugh, no more than a mild chuckle. 'Robinson's fat and bent and doesn't give a shit about who he stitches up. Remember that young bloke in Rockingham with the pharmacy job last year? You do know he was fucking the kid's wife so he could nail the poor bastard. He's a thug. If they've partnered him with you, it won't be for mentorship. Watch your arse. I don't know Baxter, but the fact that he's stationed in Fremantle tells us something.'

She sits forward and locks eyes with me. And then comes the scorpion. 'Really? What does being stationed here say about me, Lazaar?'

Message received loud and clear. 'Whatever you think, Kelly, I had to do it. If you'd persisted with that investigation, you'd be dead now.'

She forces a thin smile. 'You sold me down the river, you prick. Not forgiven.'

'Not how I see it, Kelly. You got too hot.'

'That's bullshit. I know Max Glendinning was playing both sides.'

'I don't doubt you're right, but if you had pointed the finger at him, you would have gone the same way as that poor mother.'

'What do you know about the Arab kid?' Her change of subject is smooth, but her tone remains on ice.

'I know who he is.'

'Well that's really funny, Lazaar, because we can't seem to find one scrap of information that can identify him. So, unless you're somehow up to your neck in this, how could you possibly know?'

'You couldn't find anything to identify him because there is nothing.'

'If there's nothing to identify him, how could you know? Did you kill him?'

'Don't be ridiculous. He has a sister; she knows who he is.'

'So, she can be identified?'

'No. She can't. That would be a death sentence. She needs

protection.'

'Then you don't really know if she is actually a sister?'

I stare at her. Her skills are finely honed. 'There are ways. Blood test, DNA.'

'Bring her in.'

Obviously, that couldn't happen. But I don't want to put Boulter too far offside, so I say, 'Tell me about the murder scene.'

'Can't do that. Against the rules.'

'Since when have you needed rules? This is one of those show me yours and I'll show you mine deals. I can help you get a positive identification, which could very possibly help you take the perpetrators out of the game. But the girl is vulnerable. She needs certain guarantees, and if you can't provide them, I walk.'

'I'll arrest you.'

'On what grounds?'

'Obstruction.'

'You'd never make a case.'

'Make you pretty uncomfortable.' She's right of course, but I'm not about to give her that.

'Not nearly as uncomfortable as you will be with a wrongful arrest charge over your head. I'd have thought you'd want to solve this one, reinstate your good standing and all that.'

'A good standing you fucked up, Lazaar. You and your bullshit theories.' We sit, glaring at each other in silence. Eventually her eyes soften and her lips almost make it to a smile. The little mole lifts enough to grant me hope.

'If McPherson hears of this,' she says, leaning across the table, her face in mine, 'It'll be the end of me.'

'Yeah, well that cuts both ways. No-one in your team, and I mean no-one, can know anything about what I tell you. After the Glendinning business last year, we don't know who can be trusted.'

'You know he's a superintendent in the AFP now.'

'Who?'

'Glendinning. McPherson reckons that if the Coalition win this election, he's set for a top job in their new border force.'

'Jesus! Well that seals it then. This is between us. Agreed?'

She agrees and gives me a summary of the crime scene. Her grisly rendition confirms the essence of the version I got from Hunter and fills in some gaps that neither he nor the girl could.

I sit deep in thought for a moment or two, hopefully looking as though I am working it over in my mind when, really, I am trying to figure out what she is withholding.

'A wheelie bin?' I ask at length. She nods. 'And there's nothing on it?'

'Other than the victim and his blood and fluids in a plastic liner, nothing. A smear of grease in one of the tyre treads. Apart from that, sparkling clean. Too clean.'

'Weapon?'

'Very sharp, thin, one-fifty to two hundred mil blade. Maybe a butcher's boning knife.'

I give a low whistle. 'Not your run-of-the-mill murder. Calculated, clean. No passion.'

'Okay, your turn,' she says, laying her arms flat on the table before her. I give her a rundown of the brother-sister story — how they came to be in community detention and under contract for the passage of their mother and siblings out of Indonesia to Australia. I don't name Falullah or Yusuf, nor do I elaborate on the thugs searching for her.

'It doesn't make sense,' I say as I wrap up. 'Why is there no record of this young man? His details should be on file in Immigration.' She nods. 'They were given community detention visas, but the person who kept them in detention took their papers to stop them absconding. Still, the details should be on file.' I take a deep breath, wondering who has the kind of clout to wipe out those sorts of records. Then I say, 'Anyway, I need a legend for her so I can get her into a safe environment. I need you to make that happen.'

'Fuck, Lazaar. I can't do that. I'd be putting everything at risk.'

'Everything? You're not putting your life at risk — she is.'

'Yeah, but...'

'No buts Kelly. Get her an identity so I can get her to safety. And there's another thing...'

'What?'

'These fuckers bring asylum seekers in and enslave them, and for my money, they have real clout — how else can they disappear the records? They're fucking ghosts, so getting anywhere near them will be nigh-on impossible. We have no idea of who's involved or how high it goes. So you can't let anyone know you're looking further than the murder ... can't raise any red flags. The last person we need sniffing around this is—'

'Glendinning.'

'Exactly.'

Chapter Nine

Smooth Operator

Thursday 8 August — 30 days before the election

Roger Lamord stood before the plate-glass window of his third-floor office overlooking North Cottesloe Beach and stared into a pea souper, imagining he was at the helm of a massive ship cutting a path into a bleak sea. The beachfront mansion has three above-ground storeys, an undercroft and a secure lower-level parking garage accessed directly off Marine Terrace. The top floor houses his personal suite, a boardroom, kitchen and bathroom. From here he directs SANCO, a conglomerate of companies providing food, cleaning, logistics, security and construction services to governments, airlines, hospitals and all manner of remote operations. He'd grown this corporate empire quickly and silently beneath the radar of public scrutiny, generating revenues in excess of half a billion dollars in the last quarter alone. An empire built by hand, built with cunning and hard work.

It was here that Lamord felt the thrill of making and destroying men. While his business empire had made him immensely wealthy, he had long since found money to be a small cog in the greater wheel of earthly fortunes. The real currency was influence. After serving several years as President of the Western Australian branch of the Liberal Party, he had graduated to the more noble role of serving his country. Now, he decided who could stand for a seat and make laws for the state and this side of this great nation. Others, of course, thought they had a say. The local branches. The Premier. One of the secrets of power Lamord had learnt along the way was to foster those beliefs. Eventually, their say was always what he decreed.

At five-thirty, Lamord went through his private door to the boardroom on the southern side of the building, its large, tinted windows looking west across the roofs of Cottesloe to Rottnest Island and the Indian Ocean horizon. Streetlights, headlights and lights from windows snaked and flashed in the rain. The Norfolk pines, the famous beach's iconic landmarks, stood like spires in the grey winter dusk. A polished table hewn from a single slab of tingle sourced from the Great Southern forest dominated the room. Around it sat twenty-six chairs hand-crafted from the same tree, upholstered in a green fabric made from wild hemp. A large landscape of the Swan Valley vineyard where Lamord had spent his teenage years hung on the eastern wall. The artist's fine palette and even finer eye had captured the sunburst of a spring morning's early rays as they broke over the Darling Scarp and played through a rising mist onto dewdrops clinging to budding new fruit — a symbol of the first steps to greatness.

The room was state of the art: soundproofed by a floating floor and vacuum-insulated walls, windows, and ceiling; air-conditioning ducts isolated and inaccessible; electrical and communications cables routed through non-impact media. The security team swept it for bugs, a weekly ritual to the realities of the modern world.

Sean Dower, managing director of his security firm SECSUR, and his media analyst Samantha Codlin were seated opposite each other, waiting. Lamord greeted them and reached to a wine rack beneath a credenza of polished York gum and wandoo, selected a bottle of

Shiraz from his own vintage, and poured a glass for each of them. He took his seat at the head of the table, facing the landscape. He toasted the painting and wafted the wine's bouquet with a deep breath, its heady mix of spices, berry and black current aromas planted a salivant delight on his tongue. He savoured the nose for a long moment, drawing out the full pleasure before the first tasting exploded in his mouth. He swallowed with a satisfied smile and turned to Dower.

'Are we set?'

Dower had returned that morning from a ten-day business trip to Indonesia. He leaned back in his chair. Although he had been in Australia for almost twenty-five years, his Irish accent remained strong.

'It's looking pretty fine, Roj. Seven boats in Cilicap, five in Pacitan, a dozen in Surabaya, nine in Kupang — more in the pipeline, of course.' He paused long enough for Lamord to contemplate the numbers.

'And our exposure?'

'We've commissioned a new line of packaging out of Yogyakarta. I advanced half a million toward that. And there's some new kitchen, storage, and transport equipment on order from Surabaya. We've advanced a further half million toward that. Should cover it. The money will find its way through the chain.'

'Expensive stoves and fridges, Sean,' Lamord said, a sardonic smile crossing his lips. 'Run into any problems up there?'

'Me? When do I ever run into problems?'

'It's been known. Bali last year might be something to talk about.'

'You know I'm never going to talk about that. Spotters are wary of informants up there now. The AFP have infiltrated some networks, paying big bucks for deal makers. I hear they've been fed a few dodgy ones — seems they've got our government running in circles. Typical. Word is, there's one or two on our side. How's the polling?'

'Two or three points ahead overall,' Codlin said.

She ran a team of surveillance and media specialists from a secure bunker on the second basement level at the rear of the building. Her networks tapped ministers, party officials and industry leaders across the country and the region. If it's been uttered, said in an email, spoken over a mobile phone, discussed in a party room or posted in social media, her team has sourced and flagged it. Lamord watched her as she scanned an iPad screen. It reflected onto her glasses. New, he noted. They sit a little lower and emphasise those fine cheekbones. New woman, too?

Lamord took a pull at his glass, let the wine rest on his tongue for a long moment, swallowed. 'We've got four weeks to election day. I want twenty on the water before then, and at least one to arrive on the day. Clear?'

Dower whistled. 'Twenty.' He drained his glass. 'Doable. That could be up to two-thousand IAs.' Illegal arrivals. 'Maybe another million — is that okay, Roj?'

Lamord nodded, and allowed himself a smile. 'Perfect. The current mob's hopeless solution will overload — it'll be a disaster. Make it a flood.' He shifted his gaze to Codlin. 'Media inserts?'

He was referring to people, not fliers.

'One stringer in TV, three in press, I'm negotiating with a radio jock and we've got a series of op-eds lined up. Two stringers on the ground in Indonesia — one in Kupang and one in Surabaya.'

'Arm's length?' Lamord asked.

'Oh, absolutely,' Codlin shot back. 'As far as they're concerned, all they get is a Wikileaks feed. They have no idea it's from us. They can't trace it back.'

Lamord was satisfied. Driving a campaign was about driving his people, and both Codlin and Dower cared what happened, cared that this country was at risk of a slide into social anarchy. 'What're the hot buttons?' he asked.

Her clear blue eyes held his. She pushed a recalcitrant lock of blonde hair away from her face.

'People hate the thought of illegal immigrants coming on boats. They don't say it, but it's quite clear from the research that voters don't like potential terrorists coming here aided and abetted by Indonesians. This is where the votes are, Roger. All our man has to do is keep pointing to how this government is inviting people smugglers to do business.' She flashed a smile at both men. 'And let's face it, they're raking it in.'

Lamord laughed. 'Well, we do our bit for international trade.' He took a long look at both of them. 'And let's be clear, no one in the party can ever know about any of this. No connection, right?' Although they had both signed non-disclosure agreements, it doesn't hurt to remind them of the risks. 'Leak the numbers, Sam. Then let them predict what will happen as we ramp it up.'

'We only have to get it started,' Dower said. 'The operators themselves will ramp it up — we can step back — cut the risk of exposure.'

'How will you sell it to the voters?' Lamord asked.

'Self-defence and rescue story,' Codlin replied. 'We will protect the borders, stop the boats, and save lives at sea.'

'Save lives?'

'People drown because the boats are unsafe, they're overcrowded. Safe Borders keeps them alive, Roger. That's our platform. Ask any Australian voter: what's the point of getting on a boat to come here if you're going to drown? Ask them if offshore processing or the Malaysian solution will stop the drownings. And when the time comes, we just shut them down. It'll look like it's been done with policy, and no-one will be the wiser.'

Operation Safe Borders. It was deceptively simple and a guarantee of election victory like no other in the history of this country. And he, Roger Lamord, would be the one who secretly made it possible.

Dower waited for the door to close behind Codlin as she left the room. He stood to refill the glasses. Lamord sensed the move was covering a certain discomfort. He waited. When Dower sat again, he shifted in his chair as though scratching an itch he couldn't politely reach.

'There's a problem,' he said. 'Yus-less Abacus has lost a bead.'

'Come again,' Lamord said, his wine glass poised mid-arc to his mouth. 'I take it you're referring to Yusuf? I thought you sorted that out last week.'

'Sorted one thing. The boys plugged the potential leak while I was away. But apparently' — he was careful with his words, Lamord could tell — 'there is a sister and she slipped out of the frame last Friday.'

Lamord, displeased, shook his head and waited.

Dower continued, 'She jumped the transport at Marmion Street and disappeared. Apart from a dozen IAs in the vehicle, there was only the driver and some little weasel that Yusuf keeps hanging around. They didn't stop to look for her — feckin' afraid that if they did, more would escape. Yus-less called me and I sent Swaddick and Dosek round. They've been scouring Fremantle ever since. Dosek was certain he'd found her on Monday night, but he was jumped from behind. Some tall fellah tasered him, he reckons, and then beat the shite out of him, bounced his head off the pavement. Says he didn't get a look at the guy before he passed out. Some other young homeless bloke told Swaddick he'd seen her hangin' round the post office earlier on Monday. But no-one seems to have seen her since.'

Lamord asked rapid, detailed questions about exactly what had happened, and precisely who was responsible.

'Well this is a fine thing, Sean.' Lamord's disdain was heavy on the air.

Chapter Ten
Sledgehammer

Friday 9 August — 29 days before the election

Calm descended overnight and sunshine lit the water between Cottesloe and Rottnest, bringing out people walking their dogs and early morning swimmers in body suits or paddling surf skis into the white caps that rolled in and foamed like washing suds on the sand. It felt good to Lamord to watch from on high, as if he were the only one standing.

The calm waters fired a memory of a morning forty-eight years ago, when he first saw this coastline and the silhouettes of the Norfolk pines of Cottesloe Beach through the rust-framed porthole of an ageing ship. He was six years old, an orphan, shipped as chattel from Portsmouth, England. At Fremantle wharf he was bundled onto the back of a truck with cattle sides and a loose tarpaulin to be delivered by a conspiracy of two governments into the brutal care of the Christian Brothers at Bindoon Boys Town, sixty miles north. The sea didn't break him. And nor did the Brothers — although it wasn't for the want of trying.

He was undersized and undernourished and had to fight for

everything. He fought with bigger kids over food and clothing, he fought with priests over rules and abuse, and was frequently beaten — once so badly he was hospitalised with a cracked vertebrae in his neck. The injury left him with a permanent tilt of the head. This gave a military bearing to his stature — a disability that in later years, as his hair greyed and his spectacles became rims of fine gold, afforded a certain advantage.

He learned that the only battle you win is the one you don't fight. He ran away soon after his thirteenth birthday, vowing no-one would ever dominate him again. He found refuge with an Italian family of grape growers in the Swan Valley. Every Sunday since, he made it his business to take a pew in a Catholic church and pray to be the equal of God.

Sean Dower knocked lightly on the door and entered the room, crossing the floor to stand next to Lamord at the window. Silence prevailed between the two men as they gazed upon the waking beachfront. A secretary came and went, leaving two coffees and a platter of biscuits.

'Fix this, Sean. I can't postpone important meetings with Noah Carter's campaign team because some idiot showed some girl a picture of her murdered brother.' Lamord paused to let the gravity of the situation sink in. Then he said, 'How did he get hold of a picture, Sean?'

'Swaddick took the picture on a throw-away camera to show Yusuf that the job was done. It should have been destroyed. But, either Use-less left it lying around or he kept it to show anyone what could happen to them if they stepped out of line. It was that fool Mahmoud who showed it to the girl. Maybe he's sweet on her, wanted to impress her.'

'Should never have happened. Where is it now?'

'I've got it, I'll destroy it.'

An idea formed in Lamord's mind. 'No, give it to me.'

Dower rose from his chair. 'It's in my car.'

The phone on his desk buzzed. He picked it up and listened, acknowledged the call, then replaced the receiver.

'Get it and meet me in Sam's bunker,' he ordered. 'She's got something to show us.'

As the door closed behind Dower, Roger Lamord dialled a number on his phone. He didn't identify either himself or the person who answered at the other end. He simply asked, 'Are you free for lunch?' A pause, then, 'I'll meet you at Balsamic & Olives at one. There's something I need you to look into.'

Sam Codlin's domain, a secure room similar in dimension and encasement to a pair of shipping containers face-to-face, was called the bunker because of its basement location at the back of the building, and for its sophisticated security. Codlin directed activities from a glassed-off room. She monitored technicians in half a dozen workstations spread along one wall, all at work on an array of military-grade surveillance and media equipment. The maze of screens streamed video images while live and recorded audio streams buzzed with chatter. An isolated server room that housed racks of high-end computer servers in a controlled atmosphere lay beyond. Downlights recessed into a black ceiling pinpointed areas for people whose work entailed long periods of concentration monitoring screens and audio traffic. Several chairs and small worktables sat on a raised viewing platform behind the workstations.

When Lamord entered, Codlin was at the workstation second from the far end. A young man with shoulder-length hair and mousy features sat before a pair of giant plasma screens. He was known as the Rat. At twenty-three, he was a communications technology genius — one of half a dozen such specialists on Codlin's team.

Codlin looked up and smiled as Lamord entered the room.

'Sean's on his way up,' he said, pointing with his thumb over his shoulder. He approached the workstation and looked at the image in freeze-frame on one of the giant screens. 'What have we got?'

'This is a feed from the City of Fremantle, looking at the post office in Market Street,' Codlin explained. 'The camera is on the parapet of the building opposite. The monitor on your left is footage from Monday.'

Lamord looked at the time stamp on the screen's bottom right. *20130805:08:53:00.*

A buzzer sounded and Dower's face appeared in a small monitor. Codlin clicked a button and the door opened. She continued.

'The screen on the right shows a feed, synchronised to the same time from a second camera on the corner of High Street. These are the only two cameras in that vicinity, so the picture isn't complete, but we've managed to locate your girl, and piece together some of her movements that morning.'

Lamord drew up a chair at one of the small work desks, his Mont Blanc in hand and a notebook on the table. Dower sat next to him. The Rat took over the narrative.

'You can see the time is eight fifty-three,' he said. His nasal voice carried an edge of disdain that Lamord recognised as a generational marker and not intentional disrespect for the technologically inferior. 'Working backwards, we can set the situation.' A red dot appeared on the screen at the post office. 'If you look in the shadows here, you can just make out her face.'

Lamord saw a shape cloaked in shadow, her face visible in the light.

'If we backtrack to just after eight o'clock...' Vertical streaks appeared across the screen as people walked backwards at a brisk and unnatural pace. 'Here it is two minutes past eight and right here we see her, hidden behind these two men as she hugs the wall and slips into the alcove where the post boxes are. A minute later, she goes behind this arch and stares at something across the street.

'I'll come back to that but if you watch this other screen, the one with the feed from the High Street corner' — Lamord shifted his attention to the other large screen — 'we see her at seven fifty-eight approach from the harbour end of High Street, still seeming to keep in the shadows and she waits two minutes near the scaffold on the Federation Hotel site. Watch closely.' He slowed the vision. 'She's looking at something or someone coming down from South Terrace on the opposite side. Her head turns as she watches someone walk by. And when that person is past, she waits, then ducks in behind these two men in business suits. If the person she's watching turned, she would be hidden from view. She disappears out of the frame of this camera and a few seconds later appears in the other one, here.' They all turned their attention to the first monitor.

'Curious,' Sean Dower said. 'Is there vision from the other side of the street?'

'Unfortunately, no,' Codlin said. 'Cameras are new in this part of town. They've only got these two, so we're pretty limited.'

'Okay, what else?' Lamord asked.

'She stayed in that same location until after ten,' the Rat intoned, as he shunted the footage forward to 10:52 and hit play. They all watched intently as the girl disappeared from the alcove.

'Wait!' Dower commanded. 'Where did she go?'

The Rat reversed the footage and once more took up the commentary as he replayed it. 'She's looking across the street here; her expression has changed. Then she looks across towards Cantonment Street, and then down towards the train station and again across the street. If I had to guess, I'd say she's lost her mark.'

'Yeah, but where does *she* go?' Dower asked again.

'Into the post office. See this crowd of Asian tourists? she's hiding among them, heading off in the direction of the train station.'

Lamord scribbled a note. 'Does she catch a train?'

'I don't know,' the Rat replied. 'I've scanned TransPerth footage and I can't see her, but that doesn't mean she didn't.'

Dower whistled beneath his breath. 'Girl doesn't want to be found.'

'So it seems,' Codlin said, 'but we're not done yet.'

The Rat again took up the narrative. 'If you look at these two screens' — pointing at two smaller screens beneath the two large ones — 'this is real time. The left one is the same camera looking at the post office.'

'Dosek is standing there where the girl was,' Codlin interjected, pointing at the form in the shadows.

'Got him,' Lamord said.

'And we've got a camera feeding this screen on the right, looking directly across the street from Dosek's position.' The Rat was back online. 'This is an approximation of what the girl might have been looking at.' He tapped with a stylus at the tablet on his desk and the image reappeared on the larger screen above.

Lamord studied it. He was looking at the footpath opposite, the right edge of the frame showed a covered lane at the rear of the Wesley Church, the left third a series of reflective glass shopfronts. A steady stream of pedestrians passed through the frame.

Codlin hit a contact's number on her mobile phone, still talking to Lamord. 'I think the lane opposite was what she was looking at. When you compare images of where her eyes appear to be looking and what Dosek sees when we have him look in the same direction, we think something was happening in that lane.' She spoke to the console. 'Swaddick? What have you found out?'

Swaddick's gravelly voice sounded from the audio monitors. 'There's a bloke busks here several mornings a week. Reads poetry, apparently. A guy in the internet cafe just down the street reckons he's been doing it for yonks. Says they call him Hunter. Tall lumbering bloke, long beard, grey, scruffy looking, about sixty, limps and carries a briefcase. I saw a bloke on Monday night outside a chemist's. Could be him.'

'Was he the one who clobbered Dosek?' Dower asked.

'Maybe,' Swaddick replied.

'Think you can track him down?' Lamord asked.

Swaddick's reply sent a cold shiver down even Lamord's spine. 'Shouldn't be a problem. We'll scour the place until we do — find out if he knows anything.'

'Good. Thanks,' Lamord said, and nodded to Codlin to kill the call. He turned to Dower. 'You get down there with them and stay on it, Sean. When you find this guy, call me, I don't care what time. Find the girl. Okay? I want a lid put on this thing. Loose ends cost, and it's not a price you will want to pay.' A chill settled in the room.

Dower got up to leave. 'Sure, no problem, Roj. We'll find him, and if he knows where she is, he'll tell us.'

After the door closed, Lamord turned to Codlin. 'Good work Sam, you too, Rat.'

Balsamic & Olives was written up in the previous month's *Scoop* magazine as the most important new dining experience on the west coast. The reviewer described it as the first restaurant to bring the world to Australia. What Delmonico's did for Italian food in New York, the article read, Balsamic & Olives will do for world food in Perth.

The main image of the spread featured a beautifully framed photograph of Roger Lamord wearing jeans, a white open-necked shirt, and a jacket in warm grey with minute checks that perfectly offset the tempered grey of his hair. He was seated. His Chef de Cuisine, Alain Forstenheymer, stood behind and a little left, resplendent in tunic, hat in hand. Three of the five head chefs were seated at an adjacent table, with the remaining two standing behind, nearing the extremity of the lens's depth of field. On the right of the frame and forward of the feature tableau stood the restaurant's maître de cuisine, Jonathon Suter. The photographer had artfully captured the sense of substantial acreage between tables, the opulent simplicity of the decor that spoke to the revolutionary menu and the piquancy of the dining experience.

Balsamic & Olives was Lamord's pride and joy. It had celebrated its opening three months earlier with a Liberal Party fundraiser, attended by the financial luminaries and industrial heavyweights of the state. LOTO was guest of honour, a seat at his table fetching $25,000 for the coffers, the State Premier his host. Michael Bublé was brought in as the main event and all six chefs demonstrated what diners of the Western suburban élite could look forward to — culina mundi — food from all corners of the world, presented as though the diner were in those corners.

The restaurant's dining rooms occupy two floors, the kitchens one floor below, and a riverfront forecourt of a five-storey exclusive boutique hotel at the western edge of Northshore, a north bank enclave between the two bridges that cross the Swan River separating Fremantle from North Fremantle. The real estate prices are telephone numbers and the lifestyle infuses a sense of the Mediterranean more usually associated with Monte Carlo.

Lamord parked in the basement car park, but instead of taking the lift or internal stairs, he walked out of the car park around to the river side and up the steps to the forecourt, entering the restaurant through double glass doors. Max Glendinning sat in the reception lounge nursing a scotch and soda. He rose as Lamord came towards him. Jonathon Suter waited at a discreet distance while the two men shook hands, then led them upstairs to a private table at a window overlooking the river where leisure craft were taking rare advantage of a moment of beautiful August sunshine.

Three waiters were in attendance. A young man introduced himself as Alessandro and explained that the lunch menu was a choice of Tunisian, Caribbean or Baltic. The choice a diner makes at Balsamic & Olives is not reduced to individual dishes; it is a geographic gastronomy. A menu describing each meal was offered, but Lamord instructed Alessandro that they would be dining Tunisian.

He could see Glendinning squirm with unfamiliarity. 'Brik with egg and tuna,' he explained. 'Semolina flour turned and filled with capers and creamy egg with coriander and chili. Bernard is brilliant. You'll love his fish Chamoula — a speciality from Sfax on the eastern coast.' He gestured the wonder of what to expect with his hands as Glendinning paled. 'It's a steak of grouper cooked slowly and bathed in a thick sauce of glazed onion and raisins and spices.'

An older waiter with a thick grey moustache, bright blue eyes and an eastern Mediterranean accent approached with two small glasses and poured a shot of thick dark liquid from a green, long-necked bottle into each.

'T'ibarine,' he announced, 'a digestif from dates, 'erbs and grasses from Thibar, the valley of the Sun Kings. Perfect to prepare the palate for the brik.' He kissed the tips of his fingers. 'And after, a Distincto Magnifique Blanco, the aroma so perfect the Chamoula will taste like 'eaven. And to drink with the Chamoula we 'ave an oh-nine Selian Reserve; dark, ruby red, full and complex aroma with notes of caramel and black currants. It complements the raisins in the Chamoula sauce. And for dessert, vin de Paille — the flavours of apricot and peach in sweet syrup. And with your coffee, sirs, the unique rich flavour of the boukha. Perfect. A smooth fig brandy to complete the Tunisian experience.'

He finished with a flourish and a broad smile as Max Glendinning raised his glass and applied his nose to it tentatively. The medicinal pungency caused a reflex reaction that screwed his face up into deep lines, and he plonked the glass back on the table. The waiter laughed and walked away.

'Jesus, Roger, where the fuck did you get him from?' Glendinning was still reeling from the assault on his olfactory.

'That's Milorad. He's from Bosnia. Worked along the Baltic and Mediterranean for years — one of the best vintners alive. I guarantee he will not serve you anything he has not tasted, and he finds exactly the right taste for the moment.'

'That's all well and good, but how is he with beer?'

Lamord laughed. 'Sip the Thibarine. Once you get that first taste in your mouth, you won't even remember how beer tastes. I promise you, when you taste the brik, you will think you're in a Star Wars movie. It's that good.'

Lamord raised his glass and sipped. As the liquor hit the back of his palate it released its fire, clearing his upper airways and tracking its warmth down his gullet to settle like a hot coal in his belly. He took a second sip and leaned forward to discuss the business he had in mind.

Chapter Eleven

Lowdown

Saturday 10 August — 28 days before the election

Life slips by in such a way that I often feel as though I'm fooling with forces that care little about right and wrong. Perhaps that's why I'm thinking about making it through the night when I meet Kris for lunch. The wizened old poet with whom I sat and watched ducks on a lake a few years ago told me his name was Kris.

We're at Cicerello's, an iconic fish and chip restaurant at Fremantle's Fishing Boat Harbour that represents one side of the rivalry about control of the local fish harvest. When Captain Fremantle planted a flag the day after his ship ran aground, he posted a soldier dressed in the red tunic of the King's Arms before it. It stood until Captain James Stirling arrived a month later to formally claim the Swan River, and the eight thousand miles of coastline that comes with it, as an English colony. The thieves Fremantle was concerned about were not the natives of the land, or other members of his party, but the French navy. The claim for the colony was the result of a rivalry that began a hundred years earlier, on the battlefields of Waterloo, but there's a lingering contagonism that still spreads across Fremantle today like hollandaise sauce on battered whiting.

My forefathers and I are back-seat bogans watching from the safety of our Holdens or Fords as Greek and Italian migrants battle over fishing rights and markets, and Poles take on the wharves and Slavs the vegetable gardens. We rely on rumour rather than directly witness the hot-headed outbursts that spill into streets and onto football pitches. But that is the nature of Fremantle's Napoleon square of cultures. Much of the violence is done in the dark hours, the ghosts of intergenerational European wars stalking secretly in lanes and under bridges where the unsuspecting are caught out because they don't look over their shoulders. You can't walk more than a hundred metres in any direction without crossing the borderlands of one or another, and if you do, trouble is easily found. My home is far away in the foothills, and I cannot explain why I continue to come here.

I tell my companion that I'm feeling big trouble brewing and it's sweeping in on the back of a political contest with far greater intensity than the storms of the past few days. I can't explain the source of this apparition, but I begin by pointing out why I'd had a bastard of a week at work, and how a meeting with Lipschitz left my mouth tasting like the contents of a spittoon. I give him the lowdown.

I keep my head down, beg my way out of faculty meetings and pointless staff development get-togethers. I teach classes and advise postgraduates, but my absences have me fencing angry emails from Gardner and ignoring phone calls from her secretary. The backdoor to Lipschitz's communications reveals something new, but I worry about it being a trap, deliberately set to confirm smouldering suspicions. I tell him I've had it.

'You can't resign, Art.'

Now there's a word I am heartily sick of. 'Says who?' I ask.

He laughs. A dry cackle devoid of mirth. 'Your contract.'

'I have tenure,' I say, 'but that only means they can't sack me without proper cause — it doesn't mean *I* can't sever the relationship.'

'Not that contract, Art. I'm talking about the one that keeps you coming back to us.'

'Me coming back to you! That's a laugh.'

'Am I laughing?' He takes a deep pull at his beer, smacks his lips in appreciation before fixing a supercilious smile on me. 'You're in this for the long haul, Art. You are a guardian of state secrets. The way I see it, or at least how it was explained to me, you either took the oath or you took an indeterminate spell in gaol after a secret trial with a secret name in a secret court. Seems to me, you chose wisely. How are you getting on with Eli?'

'Wants me to talk about nineteen seventy-four.'

'I see. Well, I'm not sure doctor–patient privilege trumps the state secrets act. I'd keep my counsel on that one. Otherwise, we've got you fairly well covered there.'

'Right, so my mental health is all taken care of, then?'

Another pull at his beer. 'Of course. Got you covered all the way. Now, what about this plan of Lipschitz's?'

'I can see how it makes sense to them...' I start, and then pause, waiting for something to emerge from the depths of my despair. 'They have to be able to offer jobs at the end of the line — but they threatened me with irrelevance.'

'Yes, but it won't last.'

'How so?'

'Well they're doing this everywhere, you know, they've gutted other universities too, renaming courses to align with a job market that used to exist. It's all based on what your average corporate CEO is telling political pundits. And our politicians write a cheque on that say-so. They have no idea about the needs of the future. It doesn't matter how well connected your man is, he's out of his depth. Just ride it out. Any changes, if they happen, will be temporary.'

'It looks like Lippers has found himself a pretty high-powered consultant for this. They parade credits for brokering production partnerships with some Hollywood heavy-hitters. He's earmarked two parcels of land in the south-eastern corner of the campus — there's even a diorama sitting on a plinth outside his office. It looks legit to me.'

My colleague fists a stack of chips into his mouth and chews thoughtfully. Then he says, 'I think he sees a funnel of money coming the university's way if he gets this right. Our concern is how much goes sideways. Who's on the money-go-round. Who he's got lined up for those parcels of land. I think he's being pushed towards a lucrative international market that has slim chances of heading our way. I say again, he's out of his depth and it won't last. We need to know more about this Malaysian connection. These are big numbers.'

'If it's real,' I say. 'Names like these could be bogeys. The guy sounds like a movie star, with the yachts and penthouses to go with it. Lippers has a meeting set up with Roger Lamord next week. What's that about? I didn't take him as a Liberal man.'

He shrugs. 'He'll vote in the direction of the money. Maybe he's predicting the outcome. Also, look into some of these Chinese research connections. Could be he's doing deals that aren't in our interests.'

And then, an apparent afterthought. 'No going off the reservation again, Art. You can't get involved in other dodgy shakedowns we haven't sanctioned. There's one mission here, and it's low key. Are we clear?'

'Crystal,' I say, the cliché working its way around my head like a lonely sock in a tumble drier. I drain my beer and stare into the clouds that are absent from the bottom of the bottle.

Chapter Twelve

It Makes No Difference

Sunday 11 August — 27 days before the election

When you're issued a driving licence, you are given permission to navigate the roads with a vehicle. If you have a liquor licence, you can sell booze from a nominated outlet. With a marriage licence you can call your partner a spouse. But a poetic licence is more like a home-made fuzz box. Mine was issued in a backroom of a notorious hotel in Kalgoorlie in 1974 by some dodgy characters who said they worked for the government. What convinced me they might be speaking the truth was the close proximity of a ten-tonne ore crusher, a couple of cops of the brick shithouse variety and a guy who reminded me of Frank Zappa's *Willie the Pimp*, selling me what I didn't want to buy and leaving me an option I wanted even less.

My remit is to work outside of the accepted rules to get results that those who have to obey the rules can't. The limits of those acceptances are determined by others who choose not to share their secret with me, so apart from walking blindly into the wind, I spend my time trying to figure out just where the boundaries might be. And while I have a range of tools at my disposal, the other party has absolute deniability.

I have long learnt to disregard warnings about going off piste. The plan Hunter and I devise for Fallulah's safety takes me a long way from it and draws another person into the web. Lavender Jensen came into my circle of trust after she shared an experience with me that she went through when she was just thirteen years old. She's twenty-three now, an attractive young woman, an outstanding scholar and researcher, and a person of overwhelming compassion. Ten years ago she spent a long cold November night, lost, deep in a southern forest where she discovered the existence of ancient Australian spirit creatures. They warned her about the end of the world. No-one believed her. Except me.

It wasn't Lavender Jensen's first time at St Pat's. She'd been there twice before, conducting interviews with older homeless people. Her ebony hair was pulled back in a ponytail, her blue-framed glasses perched on her nose. She wore a pair of jeans and a woollen jumper under a grey, rain-resistant jacket. She was on time, but Hunter wasn't waiting where she expected him to be.

Interview three before you get to me, his note instructed. She had dug the note out of the ticket dispenser of a parking machine in the car park on Parry Street and threw it into a bin along the way. She was alerted to the note by a strip of masking tape stuck to the lower part of the machine. A second strip crossing the first would have been a sign to abort the meeting. Hunter had instructed her in the tradecraft in the early hours of Saturday morning when she had come to spirit Falullah away to her apartment in Applecross.

Lavender worked her way down the room and introduced herself to an older woman who was finishing her meal with a cup of tea. Lavender explained that she was from the university and asked the lady if she would speak about her circumstances. The woman agreed. Not all do. Sometimes she is told to fuck off, precisely what the next person told her when she approached him about ten minutes later.

He appeared to be about fifty. On reflection, he didn't look all that disadvantaged: his clothes were well cut and had the appearance of a styled shabbiness. He toyed with food. And when she approached him, he lashed out.

'Not feckin' interested in yer shite research, girly.'

The old fellow at the next table welcomed her. He brightened on her arrival, told her his luck must be running and joked with her while she engaged him in a discussion about why he was homeless. His name was Clifford. He'd been a corporate manager, high earning and hard working, but his company went broke and he'd lost it all. The shame of it drove him to hide it from his family, and he drank, until one day he realised they were no longer there. The only thing left was the street.

Hunter tramped in from the front door while she was engaged with Clifford. She followed his approach with her eyes without raising her head. Past Clifford she could see the Irishman showing more than a casual interest as Hunter dragged a chair out, sat heavily, and drew a tattered notebook from a briefcase that he shoved under his chair with his foot. He opened the notebook with one hand while a pen magically appeared in the other and spent the next few minutes scribbling rapidly.

By the time she approached he was well into a meal of roast lamb and vegetables, with a mug of tea. He looked up with a blank expression.

'Can I ask you some questions about your circumstances?' she asked, hoping a measure of earnest sympathy was evident.

'My circumstances are all acalistic,' he replied, forking a piece of lamb into his mouth.

'Does that mean you write about them in your books?' Lavender asked.

'No, it means my circumstances are all good, they're agreeable.'

She'd never heard of it, and briefly wondered if it was even a word. 'Will anyone ever read them?'

'Of course not. Why would anyone be interested in anything I write?' He stared into her eyes to get a measure of how she might respond, shovelled up a load of lamb and vegies and then, suddenly, stood and pushed a chair out for her. 'You've got ten minutes, then I'm gonna piss off and find a high cliff above the sea and throw myself off. You can write that if you like.'

'That's lovely, thanks.' She waited for him to sit again before continuing. Then she said, keeping her voice low enough to skate just across the surface of the room's susurrus, organising her materials in front of her, 'Why all the cloak and dagger?'

A young volunteer topped up Hunter's tea from a large urn on a trolley and poured one for Lavender. When they were alone again, he spoke in low tones.

'We can't be connected, can't be seen to know each other — you gonna write this down?' She looked at him, knowing there was more, waiting on him, allowing a reproachful scowl to spider across her forehead, daring him to state the obvious. Which he did. 'You're supposed to be interviewing me for your research. At least look as though you're doing it.'

Lavender refused to glance at her question sheet, taking an attitude to make her feelings felt. 'Why am I here? Do you want to know how Falu—'

'Hey!' His sharp rebuke caught her by surprise. 'No names.'

'Sorry.' She took a moment to rein in her feelings. Her eyes, tinted in the hues of the flower after which she'd been named, glistened behind the dark blue frames of her glasses. 'I didn't know an interest in elder homelessness would get me into the spy business.'

'Can't be too careful,' he rejoined. 'Tell me about your research.'

'The causes of elder homelessness? For most I've spoken to, it's not just a lack of shelter. It's more like snowballing disadvantage. People lose connections, their social resources fray, their personal economy disintegrates, the issues pile up and bury whatever real thing started it.' Seeing his interest was piqued, she continued. 'A particular form of life dies away, then the spirit dies. Once the spirit is gone, it can never come back. Our society hasn't learnt this, but it desperately needs to. If you're not successful, you're a failure. I mean' — she cast her arm around — 'this is failure on a grand scale. No-one understands it. Governments and do-gooders try to solve the wrong problems.' She looked him in the eye and asked, 'What's your story?'

Hunter returned her stare for a long moment and then shook his head. He looked past her. She could sense he didn't want to disappoint her, but there was nothing he could tell her.

Yet he could fill her book.

At length he turned back to her and countered, as if he felt it best she let it go. 'You might be better off worrying about your own generation.'

'I think there are plenty of people worrying about my generation. I'm more concerned with why someone like you ends up on the streets — eating in a soup kitchen.'

'Some of the best meals I've had in my life, I've had right here.'

'That's the reason? The food?'

'If I told you the real reason, it could cost us both our lives. It's not because of any snowballs though, I can tell you that — you don't get them in hell. You want to do something real with your research?' She nodded, anticipating a pearl of wisdom about to shuck its own shell. 'Get people talking about asylum.'

'Asylum?' That was out of left field. Somehow the dots must connect, but she didn't see it. She felt him watching her struggle.

Then his eyes popped forward in their sockets and he zeroed in on Lavender's, boring deep into her mind.

'You're right,' he said, 'it's not about loss of shelter. A homeless person isn't just left out in the cold – they're running away from what they can't go back to. Figure that out and your research is done.' His voice cracked. She thought his eyes moistened. Then a change of subject. 'Did you talk to that smug-looking prick over there?'

He held her eyes, a sign not to look. 'Told me to fuck off. Doesn't look homeless to me but he does seem interested in you.'

'He's been sniffing around for a few days.'

Thought lines above the bridge of Lavender Jensen's nose fanned out into a little frown — a sign her curiosity was aroused. The deeper they go and the farther they spread, the greater her interest. Hunter picked it up straight away.

'Some of us are lost,' he said, his voice low and earnest, 'and don't want to be found, and others have found what they don't want to lose. But that guy — he's looking for what he's lost. Understand?' She nodded. 'His name's Sean Dower. Runs a large, highly profitable security concern owned by Roger Lamord. Heard of him?'

'Don't think so.'

'It's funny. Well known among a select few, hardly known among the masses. He's an arsehole. The sort of bloke who assumes everyone is for sale.' Hunter directed a quick gaze at the nearby table and dropped his voice even further. 'This guy, though, he's a real cunt. He wants to get his hands on your guest. So, what I want to know — and intend to find out — is what would a fucken king-maker like Lamord want with a young asylum seeker?' She made a note on her page.

He continued, more animated, more effusive. 'You know, these pricks, they all still think asylum is that building on the other side of the park. They can't imagine — sitting in their little worlds with their secure salaries and safe suburban addresses — they can't imagine what it's like to be talked about as the product of a sick society that they refuse to admit being part of. They watch the news on their big screen TVs, hear stories about child molesting, domestic violence, workplace abuse, wars on drugs, on terror, on gang violence and they believe that they'll never have to confront it. If they stopped for one moment to think, they'd see they're equally guilty of the same violence. No wonder this country treats asylum seekers like shit, it's part of our DNA.'

Lavender thought about that. 'But homelessness and asylum seekers — it's a bit much to wrap them in the same package isn't it?'

'You think so? What was it you said earlier? Snowballing disadvantage, fraying social connections? It's the same cause. If the state doesn't want homeless people on its streets, it shouldn't support the violence that causes it. Greedy corporations, abusive institutions, land grabbing, unfair gender laws, inability to police domestic violence — it's the same for asylum seekers, just on a different scale. If we're going to fight wars in other people's countries, we could at least make sure the refugees we create have somewhere safe to go. Sending in soldiers and guns might settle the matter for the moment, but the job's not finished when all you've done is left a smouldering ruin in your wake. It is so fucked up. I mean, how is that different from domestic violence?

'And don't get me started on the language they use. This election will be decided on asylum seekers. Both sides will play to the xenophobia that makes up the most part of this country. They'll trot out their absurd ideas branding anyone arriving here on a boat illegal and criminal — and give the average Joe every reason to suspect they are terrorists. We don't want Muslims, we don't want dark-skinned people from other lands. Shit — we don't even want our own dark-skinned people! Fuckers!'

She put her pen down and smiled at him. 'So, where does that leave us?'

'I'd say you've had your ten minutes.' He stood, leaned down in front of her and said, in a low voice, 'There's a key stuck to a swab of chewing gum beneath this table. It's to a storage unit. It's for Lazaar. Close your book.' She shut her notebook and Hunter continued. 'You need to drop your pen on the floor, scramble around to retrieve it, bang your head on the table when you do — hard! Got it?' She nodded. 'Tell Lazaar the confederates are combobulating — exact words, got it?' She nodded. 'We won't meet again.'

He pulled his coat tight around him, lifted his collar and, as he bent to retrieve his briefcase left her with final instructions. 'Do more interviews before you leave. Bo Peep over there will follow me. Under no circumstances are you to follow him. Burn his face into your memory and if you ever see him sniffing around — ever — tell Lazaar, and fucken hide. Above all, keep our package safe.'

He tucked his briefcase under his arm and lurched off, just as her pen clattered to the floor.

Instead of heading for the door, Hunter walked towards the kitchen. He slipped through a door on the right which took him into an anteroom. Several doors led off the room and through one of them the bustle and hum of the kitchen could be heard as returning crockery was scoured and stacked and new plates set forth with a clatter of cutlery and production orders barked out at a furious pace. Against the western wall, a roped-off balustrade surrounded a set of stairs that descended through the floor. Hunter straddled the rope and dropped down the stairs two steps at a time. At the bottom, he unlocked a door with an old Bradley key, went through it and relocked it from the other side. He was in a small limestone cellar that had been hollowed out when the building was constructed in the late eighteen-hundreds. Back then, it was a seafarers' hostel.

At the far end of the cellar, another door let him into a tunnel once used to transfer goods from ships docked at the wharf, but now terminating just before Beach Street. The alley he emerged into ran alongside the building he'd just left, connecting Beach Street to Queen Victoria Street. He kept to the shadows, moving quickly, exiting into Beach, where he turned left in the direction of the train station.

He hadn't gone fifty metres when his passage was blocked by four younger men. The mouthpiece he recognised as a member of The Brotherhood, a vicious gang of dope dealers and thugs who coerced the younger and vulnerable of the street to join them. Hunter had seen the guy around, knew him by name, but avoided having anything to do with him.

'What can I do for you, Tor?' he asked, feeling around in his briefcase, readying his taser to deal with physical threat. He got a feel for where the other three were positioning themselves.

'Man lookin' for you, Hunter. Says I should bring you to him.'

'That a fact? What's he offered you?'

'Thousand bucks.'

Hunter whistled. 'That much.' He took a step closer to Tor. 'Want to double it?'

Tor laughed. 'What? You saying you'll give me two grand?'

'No, I'm saying you can collect your grand from the guy looking for me, and I'll give you a grand if you lead him to where I tell you. In fact, I'll pay you first.'

'Where the fuck you' gonna get a grand?'

'Don't worry about that.'

'I don' know, Hunter. These are pretty serious guys.'

'They paid you yet?'

'No. They've offered a thousand bucks to anyone who brings you to them. The whole street's lookin' to collect. But I aim to get it, see?'

'I do. And you're saying they're solid for the dough? You know them that well, huh?'

'Well, no. It's like a reward, dude. You know, "captured dead or alive" — I capture you and bring you in, I get a reward.'

'Doubt I'd be worth a thousand bucks dead, Tor. All the same, I'd watch my back if I were you, it could be you who ends up dead. Like you said, they're serious guys. What if you take me to them but they don't pay you, what are you gonna do then?'

'What do you suggest?'

'You come with me now, I'll give you a thousand bucks. Then you go find those guys and tell them that you'll take them to me, and they give you the thousand bucks when they see me. Don't worry,

I'll make it easy. But here's the thing — you have to get your money before they get me, understand? 'Cos after that, you won't be able to get it. Of course you could just stiff me, take my thousand and go blow it on dope or whatever and not bother telling them. But there's one difference isn't there?'

'What difference?'

'I know where to find you.' Hunter waited while his words sunk in.

Tor still didn't seem convinced. 'Yeah, but if they get you, you're dead, man. These are serious lookin' fuckers — special forces or somethin'. You musta' done somethin' real bad against them.'

'Maybe. But you'll still be a thousand dollars better off. Do we have a deal?'

After handing Tor the money, Hunter returned to his hideaway. This time, he used a hidden access near the old warden's house. It took him down a storm drain and through a manhole that opened in the ceiling of the collapsed tunnel on the gaol side of the room. He left the cover off the opening. This would be his escape route.

He'd instructed Tor to find the pursuers and keep tabs on them for the following hour, and then approach them and lead them to the car park.

'Tell them to park where the witches' hats are,' he said. 'They'll see a small gate in the embankment in front. The gate will be open. Tell them you watched me go in there — have one of your boys say they've been watching — and when you checked, it was still open. It will be, don't worry. Then ask for your money and get the fuck outta there.'

Tor laughed. 'What you gonna do, old man?' The derision was unmistakable. 'There's like a fucken army of them, and just one of you.'

In the north of the city, along the waterfront from the Stirling Bridge, a black Range Rover crawled the streets, stopping occasionally against kerbs where no streetlight fell, its passengers, dressed in black, alighted and walked the alleys and underpasses, peering into doorways and boltholes, searching for a face among the homeless who had settled in for the night.

Swaddick, Dosek and two German Shepherds moved stealthily, coming up on exiles like apparitions from the mists, their silent presence inspiring the dread of an executioner, deliberately played in sharp contrast to the promise of a thousand dollars for anyone who could produce the evasive Hunter. None were able to help. The car kept cruising.

During one of these stops, one of Tor's boys crawled beneath the vehicle and attached a device using a magnetic pad. Hunter followed the vehicle's movements on a hand-held GPS tracking device. It was just after ten-thirty when the vehicle arrived at the car park. Hunter was ready.

It took several minutes before the smell of a man's sweat swept into the room; Hunter caught it at exactly the same time as a hidden motion sensor activated the solenoids of a series of fire sprinklers. A wall of fine spray showered from the roof above the rockfall in the entrance tunnel, behind the intruder.

Hunter flicked the switch on the one and only power point. A bank of work lights lit the tunnel entrance in full glare. The man wore night-vision goggles and held a handgun at the ready. The sudden intensity of the glare momentarily blinded him, but as he raised his hand to tear the goggles from his eyes, Hunter was already on the move. He brought an axe handle down on the intruder's gun hand. As the weapon clattered to the floor Hunter's waddy was in motion again. This time it struck the man's knees. The crack of bone cut through the air as he sank to the floor. A third blow followed, striking the victim across the shoulders. He never once cried out.

Hunter picked the weapon off the floor and sat on the far side of the small table in the dark, and raised a revolver which he aimed at the figure on the floor.

'Just for your information,' Hunter said, 'that spray behind you is live with two hundred and forty volts. It's earthed to the sluice that runs along the wall. If you try going back, you'll be fried. Anyone who attempts to follow you will be fried. I've got your weapon, but the one I'm pointing at you is a standard issue world war two Webley forty-five. It's perfectly maintained, fully loaded, cocked and, right now, aimed at a point between your eyes. I have no compunction in pulling this trigger. If you follow me it will be all acalistic.'

'It what?'

'Fucken acalistic, you moron. Do you understand?'

'I would if you talked English,' the man said, blinking rapidly and holding his hand up to shield the intensity of the light.

'Okay, I'll try to be as plain. Play nice and make sure all my questions get answered before that water flows down here, which it will do, eventually, and you just might get out of here. So, hit your communicator button and let your mates out there know I'm here. Any code words and you get a bullet between the eyes.'

'You know you won't be getting out of here, old man.'

Hunter pointed to the ceiling. 'You hear that song? That's The Band singing *It Makes No Difference*. Communicate.'

'Jesus Christ, mate. What fuckin' era are you livin' in? My partner's heard every word since I got in here. I don't hear no band.'

'Then he'll know what to expect if he tries to come down that tunnel.'

Hunter rose from the table and stood over the man on the floor, the gun in his left hand and cudgel in his right. 'Where's your communicator?' The man didn't respond. Hunter briefly inspected his gear and swung a vicious blow at the man's kidneys. The resounding *crack!* cut the air like a shattered window. Hunter swung again at the other side, but the man doubled up and the axe handle landed on his ribs. This crack did not sound like splintering plastic.

Another blow and Hunter found his mark. The electronic device disintegrated, and a spray of fine pieces spread like midges across the light. Hunter reached down and tore a tiny lavalier microphone from the collar.

'This is pretty hi-tech gear you've got here, soldier,' he said as he backed away to his table. 'What's your name?'

'Don't use one.'

'Really? Your mates out there must call you something. Dickhead, Arsewipe, Jack the Fuckin' Ripper. What about your boss? Wouldn't be that Irish fella would it? What's his name?'

'I'm not answering your questions.'

'Sean Dower. That's his name. But that's okay, you don't want to talk — macho soldier bullshit, take one for the team and all that crap. Now who's the one living in some fucking warped era? What do you want? I've heard you've offered some junkies a thousand bucks for me. What's that about?'

Silence.

'Time's up. See, I'm guessing that water will reach you in about ten seconds. I'm leaving this way.' He pointed behind him, and then swung a double handed blow that shattered the man's right kneecap. 'There'll be a minor rockfall down here after I leave. Good luck.'

Hunter picked up a small backpack and disappeared into the tunnel behind him, climbed up to the manhole and pushed the backpack into a crevice beneath the ceiling. As he was about to drop the cover in place, a scream reached him from the other tunnel. Someone had decided to test his electrified water trap. If there was one thing his war with the Gordionis had taught him, it was not to bluff.

Chapter Thirteen

There is a Reason

Monday 12 August — 26 days before the election

Boulter arrived at the site just before 7 am. A crime scene perimeter had been taped off, the electricity services rerouted and restored, work lights blazed, and an excavation crew was clearing the collapsed limestone. The unsettled weather corresponded with Boulter's constitution as she mounted the steps of the mobile command centre.

McPherson had called her early with instructions to coordinate the investigation. Before she arrived, she knew it would be a messy, multi-agency affair prone to the kind of ego stress that leads to investigative constipation where nothing happens because *somebody*, *anybody* and *nobody* are all present and accounted for. The one redeeming factor was the forensics lead. Sergeant Greg Chapman had no personality to speak of but he was thorough, methodical — all business.

She leant against a bulkhead, in preference to sitting among a wild festival of early morning testosterone. Coffee, poured from an urn, was bitter and stale and strong, and handed around as though it were the elixir of life. For some of these poor sods, it probably was, given the stony faces and deep soot of tired eyes.

Chapman opened proceedings by running through the timeline of events as they came to the notice of the investigative team. Nothing struck Boulter as out of the ordinary. There was an explosion a few minutes before eleven o'clock the previous evening — eight hours earlier. It caused a collapse of limestone.

'Although there's no certainty at this time that the rockfall didn't cause the explosion,' a city engineer announced.

'Quite,' Chapman said, and continued with his summary. Boulter jotted one or two salient details in her notebook and when Chapman had finished she drew a short summary.

'So, electricity, water and gas...' it wasn't quite a question, but it wasn't a statement either. 'Thoughts on cause?'

The fire expert toyed with his mug for a moment or two, leaving rings of coffee to stain the lacquered surface of the table. He looked at Boulter, his expression serious and his tone reserved. No-one wants to make any proclamations this early in an investigation, it only makes them look foolish.

'Whatever happened in there,' he said, 'it happened quickly. Fortunately, the gas shuts off at the junction valve as soon as there's a pressure loss, so only what was in the pipe combusted. It will take some time before we know what caused the rupture, and what brought electricity and water into the mix.'

'We don't know if there are any people involved,' the city engineer said, and he rolled out a large plan, with recent markings in red and blue and green. He traced a line with his finger as Boulter leaned across the table to see.

'A tunnel ran along here. The roof at the bend here collapsed some years ago and we considered it a public hazard so the tunnel mouth, what there was of it, was boarded up. More recently a locked wire-mesh gate was fitted. Our surveyors have marked earlier rockfalls up the top here, which appears to be around where the explosion happened. There's a lot of water runs beneath here, and with this rain we've been having, it's just possible that this was another rockfall, but somehow with a gas line and power line caught up. We won't know until we excavate back into this area.'

A knock on the door caught Boulter's attention. She opened it and peered out. A young female uniformed officer stood with a scruffy looking teenager by her side. Boulter stepped outside and closed the door behind her.

'I'm sorry to barge in, Detective,' the constable said, 'but this young man has some information that might be helpful.'

Boulter studied him. He was dirty, his clothes unwashed, sores littered his arms, and his face was a mottled patchwork of crimson and chalk-white pocked with pustules of late adolescent pimples. He wore a torn and threadbare woollen jumper, olive green dungarees and white Volleys riddled with holes. He was malnourished and, she guessed, not more than seventeen. She led him to her car and opened the passenger side door for him. He baulked.

'It's okay,' Boulter said, 'we can talk in here because there's a meeting going on there' — pointing to the trailer she had just left. Then, as if a thought occurred to her, she added 'Why don't we go and get some breakfast?'

'So what's your name?' She'd driven to a cafe in Essex Street, and they were all but alone. She'd ordered a coffee and croissant for herself, and a breakfast of sausages, bacon, eggs, tomato and baked beans, with toast and tea for the boy.

'Spider.'

'Spider? Is that it?'

'It's what my mum called me.'

'I see. Who's your mum?'

'A junkie whore named Alice Webb.'

'So you're Spider Webb?'

'Nah, jus' Spider.'

The tea and coffee arrived. Boulter watched him dump five packs of white sugar into his tea. He splashed it with milk and stirred noisily. 'What about your dad?'

'He's in gaol. Good thing too.'

'Why's that?'

'Violent prick.'

'How old are you Spider?'

''Bout seventeen.'

'How long have you been on the streets?'

'Since I was ten.'

The sudden image of another young man flooded Boulter's mind. As though it were yesterday, she saw a frozen moment at two o'clock on a freezing Friday morning six years ago in a Northbridge lane.

A son she'd given birth to seventeen years before lay unconscious with a belly full of gutter drugs and cheap wine; a son for whom she'd been searching since he was ten; a son she'd given up nothing for in those first ten years; a son for whom she would have given up everything since that night. A son who had every right not to trust those duty bound to love him.

It was touch and go, the paramedics said. One minute he was gone, the next he was still breathing. Boulter held that icy hand and begged him to stay and fight. He scraped through and she swore that she would protect him, nurse him, make him whole again.

She was only seventeen when he was born, conceived just three months after she joined the navy. Her superior officer at HMAS Leeuwin, a lieutenant who believed he had a God-given right to her body, raped her. She took leave and gave birth in her mother's Housing Commission home in Bentley, cheap vodka for painkiller. She suffered and ran, seeking and accepting postings in the far corners of the world — active duty wherever it was to be found — leaving her mother to raise the boy.

She was in the Baltic for the boy's first birthday, the Timor Sea for his second and the Gulf of Arabia when he turned seven. He was ten when her mother suffered a stroke and died. She left the navy, deciding to make a go of parenting. But less than a month after her return he disappeared one night. She searched but turned up nothing. It was then that she turned to forensic science, for which her naval training in medicine proved a solid foundation. She applied every theory, tested every angle, scratched at the remotest clues, followed threads so fine they threatened to snap at the slightest tension.

When she found him, he was close enough to death for her to feel her own life force falter.

She nursed him, brokered a kind of peace and began to share something of his life. Lucas's story is still a work in progress seven years on. He's no longer living with her, having struck out on his own three years earlier in what appears to be a loving relationship with a nice boy called Tom. But at least, she thought, when he needs it, he knows I'm there for him.

But who's there for you, Spider?

His plate was piled high and the attack frenzied, wolfing down shovelfuls at a time.

'Whoa, whoa,' Boulter said, laughing, 'take your time, there's no hurry. Chew it. Taste it. Enjoy it.' Her eyes flashed a warmth she hadn't felt in a long time. She watched as he bit off a chunk of toast and forked in a crispy bacon rasher bathed in the golden yellow of a soft egg yolk.

She let him finish and ordered a refill for his tea. 'Tell me about last night,' she urged, bringing the professional cop back to the table.

'Don't know a lot,' he replied. 'But we was jus' leavin' the railway bridge — musta been about seven, seven-firty, ay? — when this big guy, military lookin' guy, comes up to us an' arks if we seen Hunter. There was four of us ... yeah, Tor an' us free—'

'Tor?'

'He's our leader, like.'

'So, what — you're in gang?'

'Nah, not really a gang, more like a bruvvahood, yeah, we're like bruvvas. But we says "nah, aven't seen 'im"'cos even if we had, you don't tell some fucker you never seen before where someone is, right? But then this guy says he'll give us a fousan' bucks if we can find Hunter and bring him to the guy. Well that changes fings ay? I mean a fousan's a fousan'.'

'So did you get your thousand?'

'Nah. We was 'sposed to, but nah ... didn't.'

'What happened?'

'Hunter ... see he's smart. He offered us anuvver fousan' if we'd bring the guy lookin' for 'im to where 'is crib's at.'

'And where's that?'

'Well, we didn't know 'till he tole us, but it's right there, where the explosion was.'

Boulter shook her head. 'I don't understand, Spider. In the old warden's house?'

'I dunno, really. Don't fink anyone knew, ay — but I fink it was under there somewhere. Anyway, first Hunter took us to a ATM on Market Street an' he gave Tor a fousan', jus' like that. Fucken amazin'. And then he left and we waited a while and then went an' found the guy and tole him to meet us up at the car park ay — near the turn where all them bushes are.'

'Right. Where the explosion happened?'

'Yeah.' Spider took a sip of his tea.

Boulter had to break the silence. 'So this guy, Hunter, paid you a thousand ... but what? You were expecting to get a thousand off the other guy as well?'

'That was Hunter's idea, ay? He said for us to bring 'em up to where his crib was, like I said. There were free of 'em in a big black four-wheel drive, ay — but the guy wouldn't give Tor the money until he knew for sure.

'So one of 'em, fucken' big bloke, real soldier lookin' bloke, wearin' a gear belt an' torch an' gun ... 'e gets out an' Tor points to this spot behind the trees. There's a wire gate in the side of the ground. You couldn't see it normally, but this bloke goes to the gate, pushes it and goes inside. He's talkin' to the uvver one over the radio frough their shirt collars and earbuds, freaky shit man, these are fucken heavy dudes. And then after a while it's all quiet — like the bloke inside's not answerin' his radio, ay? It looks like somefin' heavy's goin' down. So Tor arks for the money so we can get out of there, but the bloke tells 'im he still hasn't seen Hunter so he says for Tor to go inside an' see what's happened to 'is mate.'

Spider fell silent and took a long drink of his tea. Boulter nudged him to continue, 'And?'

'Yeah well, he went in, ay.... An' then there was a loud crack like a lightning bolt and the whole ground just fell in. Me an' the rest of us fucken' ran. I didn't see what happened to the car.'

'So, you think there are bodies in there?'

'Well, yeah. Fuck yeah. Tor didn't come out and that soldier bloke... Fucked if I know about Hunter. I fink there's somethin' goin' on here, ay. Tor used to tell us that the guvmint was doin' all this shit to get rid of us — to kill us who live on the streets. Hunter said, compared to the guvmint, these guys could make all the fish in Fremantle smell bad. They were huntin' Hunter—'

'Wait. What was that you said about the fish?'

'Yeah, it's what 'e said, ay ... about them guys, that they make the fish in Fremantle smell bad. Anyway, you don't get all that soldier gear ... guns and night goggles and shit like that unless you're the guvmint, right? They looked like fucken' soldiers, tell you...' And at that point, he just ran out of story and energy.

Boulter drew her phone out and punched in a number. Chapman came on the line and she told him what she'd just learnt.

There were three big questions in Boulter's mind as she mounted the stairs to her office: Who was Hunter? Why were these soldier types looking for him? And was the explosion an accident or deliberate? She didn't buy into coincidences, which is why she felt the last point was a direct result of the first two. It couldn't be an accident. And why the sight of Max Glendinning leaving McPherson's office as she crossed the situation room sent a bead of cold sweat rolling down her spine.

At her desk she logged onto the central records system. There was already a file on the Parry Street car park incident — with Greg Chapman involved, she knew there would be — so she added a new record, typing up her interview with Spider — *Witness#1* — as quickly as words could form. She uploaded the picture she'd taken of him from her phone and flagged as 'urgent' the possibility of as many as three persons buried in the rubble. She flicked through the reports that had been uploaded from the mobile command centre, but at this stage no new details were available. She opened the timeline file and added *Witness#1* to it and the possible time frame of activity at the site. This would be useful information to the pathologists if bodies were recovered.

While she was logged on, she pulled up the file from a couple of years ago involving Glendinning and Lazaar — the one called *Operation WTF* — which actually did not stand for 'what the fuck'. What triggered her interest in revisiting the file was what Spider said about Hunter's comment on the fish in Fremantle. She typed in the search terms and was immediately rewarded. Several years prior to the investigation, suspicions involving the Gordioni family and drug trafficking through the port were raised by a journalist in an article that ran in *The West Australian* entitled, 'Why Fremantle's Fish are on the Nose'. The by-line, Calvin Bishop.

'You gotta be kidding me,' she said under her breath, clicking on the link for Bishop, bringing up another file in the context of the investigation. Bishop had disappeared, date unknown, thought to have gone missing at sea, no foul play suspected, but no body ever found. There was a photo. She could print it and ask Spider for an ident. She dug further back into Bishop's history as a journalist and snapped on the Kalgoorlie connection. Lazaar, you fucker. You've got a deep cover asset, and he was there. Hunter is Calvin Bishop. 'Bet my fuckin' badge on it,' she said.

'Bet your badge on what?' Parker stood in the doorway a printout in his hand and a silly, boyish grin across his dial.

Boulter closed the browser window and looked up. 'That you would walk in here any minute now with really good news.'

'Jesus! Sergeant, you're a bloody mind reader. It just so happens we've caught a break on the paint.'

'The paint?'

'Yep' — he looked down at the page in his hand — 'the batch was made at Dulux in O'Connor and sold to three panel beaters — one in Midvale, one in Kewdale and one in O'Connor.'

'O'Connor. Fits the location. Any word from Baxter on the bin?'

'Uh, yeah, he called in about half an hour ago. Said there's no way he can pinpoint the location or the time of the theft. Mystery, he says.'

Boulter said, 'The only mystery is when he'll do any actual detecting.' She took a beat while she thought about the next line of action. 'Right ... need a document package on all three panel shops. I want to know everything about them before we go knocking on doors — name of business, how long in business, owners, landlords, whether they pay their rent, tax records, types of insurance jobs they do. And check with MV for any history as chop shops. Do it this morning; we'll go toot their horns this afternoon — at least the O'Connor one.'

'Will do. Oh yeah, Super said for you to go see him.'

Boulter logged out of her computer, picked up her notebook and pen, and headed for McPherson's office. She knocked and walked in, unbidden.

'Want to see me, Sir?'

'Yes, lass. Come in, close the door, have a seat. I'll be just a moment.' He busied himself with some handwritten notes on a file, scrawled a hasty signature, punched the intercom on his desk phone and called his personal assistant in to take the file.

He reprimanded the girl. 'Last week's figures are wrong. A bit more care checking my notes, please. Get them in order and send them through. The brass are waiting on them.' He nodded his dismissal.

Boulter couldn't help but feel the show was for her benefit.

'We have a breakthrough,' he said when they were once again alone.

'Yes, Parker has just filled me in on the paint.'

'Paint? What are you talking about?'

'The paint from the wheelie bin, Sir, we've identified the batch and its distribution. Parker's backgrounding three panel shops this morning.'

'Oh, good. Yes, that's good. But I'm talking about a tip-off we got. We'll raid at dawn tomorrow. You can do the panel shops after if you need to. I want a full briefing at thirteen hundred — the full team — and involve the Tactical lads too will you? Can't be too careful with these jihadists. Oh, and talk to media relations will you? We want the lid on this locked down tight for the time being. Need to know only.'

'Jihadist, Sir?'

'I think so. His name is Mahmoud Khalil. I'll take the lead on this one Detective Sergeant.'

'Of course, Sir. Can I ask where the tip-off came from?'

McPherson appeared to consider the request for several moments. 'I don't think that would be appropriate at this moment, lass. It's bit sensitive.'

There was a lightness to her step as Boulter returned to her office. With a murder suspect in sight and the potential of a high profile result, the posting back to Major Crimes looked closer.

Chapter Fourteen

Only You Know and I Know

Boulter hasn't returned any of my calls over the weekend. I grow anxious that I don't have any kind of agreement with her to secure Falullah's safety. I grow anxious that Hunter has vanished after placing Lavender in peril and apparently leaving nought but a key and a cryptic message. Killers are on the loose and I have no way of knowing who they are or where to find them. From first thing Monday, I feel Friday closing in like a garbage compactor.

I buy some extra time from Gardner in a brief meeting on Monday morning arguing my need to digest some recent research. I ask what it is she thinks Lipschitz is up to. Her answer is cryptic. I leave that meeting more unsettled than when I went in and head to the university's club cafe for another one with WiFi. He tells me everything is in place for Falullah's enrolment. All he needs is the legend — a name with an academic history that he can slip into the system. Then Falullah will have a new identity, her studentship, and accommodation in the student village for six months. Hidden in plain sight.

But finding a legend is like finding water in the desert and the

Friday deadline for Falullah's enrolment looms.

'Can't you just make up a name and enrol her?' I ask.

'No, man! Two people have to sign off on the enrolment. They check the application history and if it's not all there they will ask questions. If they do that, we're history. The enrolment has to be genuine. A confirmed hundred point identity, a history of education with accessible transcripts — a verifiable legend all the way through. Without it we'd be done before she started. We'd both be out of a job and you'd be in gaol, man. Fuck that!'

'Where do we get this legend from?'

'The Registrar General's office.'

'Well that's a bit of a worry isn't it? Do we happen to know someone?'

'I don't. Do you know anyone at ASIO? They use false identities to protect their spies. Or the Attorney General's Department? They use them mainly for witness protection, but sometimes they grant them to Community Services to protect women at risk. What about the cops? State and feds use them for undercover operations. You with me?' I nod. He continues. 'Identities have to be based on an original and authentic birth certificate.'

'Birth certificate?'

''Fraid so. That's the only evidence that someone actually exists. All other identity documents arise from the birth certificate.'

'I thought they just made up a name.'

'Can you imagine how risky that would be for an undercover cop? Or a woman on the run from a violent husband? What if they had to open a bank account, get a Medicare number, a working with children check? No, the identity has to be the real deal.'

'Can you hack them?'

'Hack them?' His laugh is unkind. 'You watch too much science fiction, Lazaar. Creating an identity is fucking complex. Identities they use for legends are birth certificates that are no longer needed.'

'How can it be no longer needed?'

'They're dead. They choose deceased identities born within a range of years that might match the subject and died young. The death certificate is suppressed by an executive order, and a deed of name change is registered against the birth certificate. Once a deed of name change is registered, the identity is new, and the deed serves as the originating document. These new identities are flagged and highly protected.'

'Jesus. That's a lot of paperwork. How many of these are around?'

'A lot. And they're protected under a classification system — the paperwork is necessary to protect the decision makers, not so much the subjects, and against original family members making enquiries. The different agencies can apply to the Registrar General for "operational identities". Obviously the real person's identity remains secret, but they build up the components of the operational identity before putting it in play, so they will have bank accounts, a driver's licence, passport maybe, federal police checks, a real address, energy bills — whatever might be needed for the legend to be authentic. The trick is to get one that roughly matches your girl's age and has the right educational history. The photographic details and any change of address — stuff like that — are applied to it later.'

'Fuck me. How are we going to do that?'

'Shame you don't know any female undercover cops.'

'As a matter of fact I do know one who was undercover a couple of years ago.'

'Oh.'

It is a flat sound. 'What does that mean?' I ask.

'If she's no longer undercover, the legend will have been burnt.' Any chance of Boulter being the solution pretty much vanishes. I hadn't realised the complexity of it. But there is another avenue...

Chapter Fifteen

Standin' on a Mountain Top

Wednesday 21 August — 17 days before the election

I spend the day at home in Roleystone on the slopes above Brookton Highway, surrounded by tall thick jarrah and marri trees, an understorey of myrtle and grass trees and prickle bushes. The house is new, rebuilt after the fire, with furniture still squeaking of newness, nothing hanging on the walls, and bare bookshelves. I've been back for about six months. It's a strange feeling, like entering a parallel universe.

The house is set back from the highway behind a stand of low trees, backing into the slope, a front verandah raised on stilts offering splendid views straight down the Araluen valley. From the western end of the verandah, I can see the smokestacks of Kwinana. Beyond, the ocean and Garden Island. I spend the morning marking assignments, my thoughts accompanied by the elegant virtuoso of James Taylor and the remastered collection of *Sweet Baby James*, birdsong in the jarrahs outside, and the occasional whine of a motorcycle cutting up the highway below like a Bamix through a load of frozen blueberries. It's a sunny day with moments of cloud.

Cold, but I'm glad of the respite from the rain.

Later in the afternoon, I set out on a walk along a trail behind my house that takes me up the slope to a spot where I can gaze directly across the city to the Fremantle coast. Bursts of blue from devil's pins and blind grass colour the city side of the slope as I climb, with the occasional boronia and macrocarpa adding their red sunbursts to the canvas. A low and heavy cloud bank forms on the distant horizon over the ocean, and as I reach the lookout a hundred metres or so above my house, I watch the sun drain into it. I am deep in thought, lost in the way Louie Shelton's guitar solo in *Standin' on a Mountain Top* left me feeling after hearing it for the first time many years ago. It's not one of his most talked-about pieces, but for me it was a defining moment in music that returns to me every time I catch a view from a place like this.

Footsteps sound on the gravel behind me and a large man walking a terrier comes to rest on the bench beside me.

'What is it the flame trees do to drivers?' he asks, wheezing a little from the exertion of the climb.

'Blind them,' I say.

When you don't know with whom you are talking, it pays to have a mechanism for making sure. A lyric from a song that is barely recognisable from the way it is sung, answered correctly and chased with another is one way of doing it. We've already got it sussed.

'And how is her mind twisted?'

'Tiffany.' That sorts out his bona fides. I check him out more closely. He's heavy-set, I'm guessing mid-fifties, grey hair pushed back under a brown fedora, and bright hazel eyes sparkling behind gold-rimmed glasses that sit low on a long nose. He has the demeanour of one who has been passed over in his career one too many times. 'My name's Nicholas,' he says.

'First or last?' I ask, knowing it doesn't matter because it is neither.

'Alex said you asked about people smuggling?'

I'm thinking that this is an odd way to frame a question. Alex is the moniker given to the top person — man or woman, who knows? — and this is a way of saying the question has been received, but more explanation is expected before engaging.

'If you don't have the answer, why are you here, Nicholas?'

'Didn't say I don't have the answer. Curious about your interest is all. Alex says your target is a long way from people smugglers.'

'Can't say that's so. There's something strange going on.'

'There's an election looming. Things are always strange when there's an election looming.'

I gather my jacket around me as a cold wind whips up the slope from the south. 'How is that connected to people smuggling?'

'I'd say the election will be decided on it.'

He's voicing what I already know. 'Can't be that simple,' I say.

'It's not. Takes a lot of money to run a people-smuggling operation. Money has to come from somewhere.'

'Don't the smuggled people pay?'

He laughs, a dry cackle which finishes with a cough. He wipes the spittle from his mouth with a handkerchief and leans down to pat the dog. 'Oh yes, they pay,' he says, rubbing the dog's ears. 'They pay through the nose.' He straightens up and looks me in the face. 'You better know what you're getting into here Lazaar. The stakes are high when people are using ASIO assets for personal gain.'

If you know how politics works in this country, try to outdo that statement.

I visit Falullah at Lavender's. I want to know more about how she came to know of her brother's murder. As much detail as she can recall.

'I was on the bus when Mahmoud sat down in front of me,' she says, dredging up the memory. 'He said he had something to show me, but no-one else could see it. I was right next to the door. He leaned over the seat and had this little camera in his hands. He says, "That is Ishmail hanging from the chains." All I can see is a picture of a body. I can't see for sure that it's Ishmail because the picture isn't that big, and the face is not clear. The shape, it looks like Ishmail, but I haven't seen him for a long time, so I have to take Mahmoud's word for it. I don't get to look at it long, but I can see whoever it is, the head is hanging at a funny angle. There are some reflections from the camera's flash in the background. That's all I remember. Mahmoud tells me Ishmail wanted to go to the authorities because Yusuf hadn't kept his promise. "That's what happens if you cross these people," he says. I remember looking him in the eyes and asking, "Is this really Ishmail?" He places his hand over his heart and says "Upon Allah", meaning that it is a God's truth. I want to look again, but he takes it away and puts it in his pocket. It was just a photo, but I'm sure it was Ishmail. Mahmoud wanted to warn me. So, when the bus stopped at the traffic lights, I opened the door and ran.'

'Okay, so apart from the body and some reflections from the camera's flash, you can't recall anything else in the picture?'

She says no and asks what I'm looking for. I say I'm not sure, because that's the truth. I leave it at that. I ask what she's been doing, hoping for some levity.

'Reading the university handbook,' she replies. 'I think I will enrol in international politics and security. When do you think I can?' I assure her that all will be in order by the end of the week. I hope that won't turn out to be a lie.

She has also been writing, Lavender insists I read her work.

It is extraordinary. Her expression lends her a voice that transcends the pain of loss and grief and enters an entirely new plane. It is angelic, soft, understanding and forgiving. A kind of poetry that is found at the root of all prayer. A healing I had rarely encountered.

```
I must face my inner demons before I face
those on the surface. So I will write for you
```

about the things that happen inside when, one by one, those whom I love are plucked from my world to become scores on the boards of men who do not value a touch, a smile, a whispered endearment. Such scores do not scar me; they embrace me, they fulfil me, for they are no measure of achievement to those who would rob the world of love and compassion. They are a measure of my faith; spirits held in my heart, near in the hope that they will not leave me without the courage to not be vengeful. These men will not rob me.

That evening's news reports a capsize, 120 nautical miles north of Christmas Island.

Border Protection crews have suspended operations after rescuing one hundred and six passengers from the scene. Survivors report that five people are still missing, believed to have gone down with the vessel.

Grist for the mills of the political campaigners. Four asylum seekers died on Saturday from a capsized vessel, one last Tuesday and now another five are believed drowned. Almost two hundred people in all — men, women and children from the Middle East and Sri Lanka. The media is full of it, and the resulting political rhetoric deafening, the incumbent government obvious in its impotence, failed 'solutions' and national inhospitality. Words like 'illegal immigrants' and 'queue jumpers' buzz out of the Opposition camp like bush flies from the outside toilet. One of the party's leading lights makes a brief appearance on the news.

'The people smugglers continue with their daily ferry service,' he says, his quarry-faced expression panning, precisely, a rehearsal from earlier in the day. The religious fervour is unmistakable. 'The facts are what they are — twenty-five boats carrying almost seventeen hundred people have arrived this month alone.' Where, I wonder, are these guys getting their media training? 'Only tough border policies can break the people smugglers' business model — that's what the Coalition will do...'

I zone out.

Ever since LOTO announced his proposed militarised border protection scheme on the 25th of last month a soundbox of contagion has spread thicker than Vegemite on a fresh horseshoe roll. Most notably, the Coalition release their media statements through the one news source that has the most to gain from a change in government, a fact that has the unavoidable consequences of the public broadcaster having to pick up the slops. I vividly remember that appearance.

Flanked by dark-suited apparatchiks, each a head and shoulders taller than LOTO, posed before a blue backdrop with gold writing urging Australians to *Strengthen Australia,* the camera operator using the flanking to frame the image, its mis-en-scène belonging entirely to the character at its centre. LOTO's expression of faux concern had said most of it, his words merely the colour. He began by foreshadowing a major announcement: an important development of the Coalition's border policy.

A deep breath to illustrate the gravity of what is to come, that shifty little look left then right as though stepping into the ring — a small oblong of paper in his right hand that never scores a glance, and he launches into it.

Our border crisis is now a national emergency. Almost fifty thousand illegal arrivals in almost eight hundred illegal boats have come to our shores under this inept government. There have been a thousand or more deaths at sea, and there's been ten million dollars plus in spending blowouts. This government can't fix it; the Coalition will.

I make a quick mental analysis of the speech. Fifty grows to eight hundred, the thousands into millions; an image of five ratchets to eight before it becomes a thousand or more. Then there's the repetition — illegal arrivals, illegal boats; borders, problems. The aim is fear followed by what's the unimaginable horror of deaths at sea. It doesn't matter that we have three thousand deaths a year on our roads, but deaths at sea ... that's not tragic, it's unimaginable.

I feel for Falullah seeing the plight of others in circumstances she has lived through. How it must be to have all you have known taken from you at gunpoint. And then to arrive in a foreign land, the hollow ring of the people smuggler's promise in your ears, only to find the welcome mat pulled sharply out from under. Imprisoned by those charged with your welfare, branded 'illegal' by a would-be prime minister. I have never imagined my country to be so cruel, so harsh, so final.

It was all too perfectly timed, with the arrival of another two boats bringing the number seeking asylum in less than five days to almost four hundred. And the media frenzy grows right alongside with increasingly improbable headlines that take the discourse from 'illegal immigrants' to an 'invasion'.

LOTO pushes on. Arrivals of the few days past an example of a weak government, soft on people smugglers, he claims, out of its depth. Tougher measures are called for. And, as if to ice the cake, he argues that his proposed policy is necessary to save lives at sea. Lives, he says, the current government has no regard for.

On the same day, and as a strange aside, another announcement comes to my attention. It does not garner a lot of press, and nor does it seem in any way connected to anything else going on in my life, but Hunter's odd comment to Lavender that the *confederates are combobulating* heightens my senses to happenings that are both out of the ordinary and connected by thin threads. Back in Kalgoorlie, Bishop had asked one day, 'if discombobulating is a word describing the feeling of being thrown into confusion, why isn't combobulating used to describe the feeling of coming out of confusion?' Hunter is suggesting I should look for situations where the Liberals were showing those signs, only it wouldn't be obvious because combobulating isn't a word.

This is one such news item.

Local billionaire Roger Lamord today announced the establishment of a ten million dollar fund to help returned armed service veterans. He called the fund the Lamord Living Foundation, named, for a man he knew who died at the weekend. His name was Mick Dosek, a returned SAS soldier who had served in Iraq twice and subsequently in Afghanistan, and was removed from active duty suffering post-traumatic stress disorder. With no family support and little professional treatment, a spokesman for Lamord claimed, he was left homeless, living on the streets, and he died alone in a limestone cave collapse in Fremantle following a gas line rupture and minor explosion. The fund would provide for research into psychiatric treatments specific to the disorder, and housing and counselling for veterans at risk.

Rising Liberal Party star Noah Carter addresses the cameras on Lamord's behalf. Carter is standing as a candidate for a safe Liberal seat in Lamord's own Swan Valley electorate.

'Our armed services personnel are an important part of this country's protection against world terrorism and threats of invasion,' Carter tells the television audience. 'If we don't offer our service men and women and their families the highest quality of care after they have given more than any reasonable person would ask, how can we expect to attract the fighting talent we need in these dangerous and difficult times? A successful Coalition campaign will see matching government financial support for the Lamord Living Foundation fund.'

What is less well known is how much Lamord's enterprises profit from the armed services. For several years, SANCAT, the catering division of SANCO, has held contracts to supply all armed services with active service rations and mess services at home bases. His company's catering reach now extends into a great many remote mining sites, detention centres and prison populations. His ten million dollar fund is small cheese by comparison, but the media laps it up.

It turns out that my university does too, with Vice Chancellor Lipschitz offering up radio commentary later the same day, applauding the investment into a much needed area of health sciences. It's pretty clear which university stands to gain the most.

Chapter Sixteen

You've got a Friend

Thursday 22 August — 16 days before the election

The following morning, I leave two messages on Boulter's voicemail before heading out from my office for Fremantle. I am baffled at being shut out by her, but more concerned with the pressing problem of obtaining an identity for Falullah. The window is closing, and I have nothing. I take the key Hunter gave Lavender and investigate the threads he left in his wake.

The lockup is easy enough to find — top floor of the wool stores, locker 989 — and it yields a small notebook computer, a USB drive and a scrap of paper with incoherent scribblings including two lines of verse I recognise:

Rover, rover, cattle drover ...

... that you do not often spy

I clear the locker, stuff the items in my briefcase and take them back to my office where, behind a locked door, I plug the USB into my laptop. It's protected by a TPM code: only the computer used to store the data can access the files.

I power up the notebook computer. It is password protected

but the clue to access lies in the lines on the scrap of paper: both from CJ Dennis. The first line suggests the first half of the title, *Cuppacumalonga* and the second line, the second half of the title *Triantiwontigongolope*. But there is a third clue that I almost don't see: the 's' on 'spy' is inverted, as though written in a dyslexic hand. Clever that. Arse about. Therefore, the password: *gongolomalonga*.

I type it in and snap the USB drive into its socket. There are two folders. One called *Boulter*, and the other called *Confederates*.

I start with the one called Boulter. It contains a number of subfolders and documents. I work quickly through the documents, reading snatches to gather the gist. I will come back later to those I need to study in further detail. But what catches my eye is a subfolder called *Kedma Boulet*. The documents reveal an enrolment and academic transcript of a French exchange student whose enrolment at Curtin University is temporarily in hiatus for family reasons.

Hunter left a note explaining that it is a legend Boulter had used to infiltrate an examination fraud involving international students and English language testing three years ago. The investigation uncovered a high-level fraud and resulted in the prosecution of twelve people over seventy-three charges. The police considered the action closed but according to Hunter's notes, the legend is still live. Boulter must still have the package. This could mean they are still after bigger fish, or she's retained it for some other reason.

Either way, it is a perfect solution for me. All I need to do is separate her from it. The way I see it, I can either get her to do this willingly or — as a last resort — exercise some poetic licence. Tricky to get her to hand it over willingly if she's refusing my phone calls.

Another subfolder catches my eye, this one called *Lucas*. A quick scan alerts me to two facts. First she has a son who is now twenty-three years old, a fine arts student at Curtin University — that could explain why the legend is still live — a useful way to keep tabs — but more important are the series of charge sheets that seem to be unactioned. Lucas Boulter's life obviously has been challenged. He has a sealed record of juvenile offences dating back to when he was about twelve, a string of petty crimes including property and drug crimes. How had Boulter gained access? Or Hunter for that matter?

In July 2011 he had been arrested for methamphetamine possession, manufacture, and intent to sell and supply. But the charge has no follow-through, and the arresting officer's name, along with several other lines, especially the 'known associates' have been redacted.

It could have been an undercover operation. Or had Boulter leaned on someone? And how had she paid for it? Most people I know will cross almost any line for their kids and the price of an inside trade can be steep. As Nicholas reminded me just yesterday, I'm still paying for mine. But I have found my bargaining chip. All I need to do now is to get to Boulter—

There is a loud rap on my door.

'Just a minute,' I call, snapping the computer shut, dropping it into a desk drawer and turning a key. I slip the USB into my pocket.

When I open the door I look into the clear blue eyes of Detective Sergeant Kelly Boulter. By her side, a young man with as classic a Teutonic shaped head as ever I'd seen — square jaw, steel-blue eyes, blonde close-cropped hair, and he stands a full head and shoulders taller than me.

'Detective—' I barely have a chance to express my surprise when Boulter cuts me off.

'Detective Sergeant Boulter.' She has her warrant card out 'This is Detective Parker.' I cock my head and raise my eyebrows at this show for the young cop. Boulter continues, 'We'd like a word. Can we come in?'

'What — in my office?' I block the door and indicate over my shoulder with my thumb. It is hardly a welcoming place at the best of times, and there was nowhere to sit, certainly not enough space to accommodate young Giant Parker and all breathe the same air.

'If you don't mind,' Boulter says, taking half a step forward.

'Ah ... look, there's a small conference room just down here,' I say, taking my keys from my pocket. 'We'll be more comfortable there.' I step out, pull the door closed behind me, and lock it.

The problem with cops is, if you invite them in, they can look at anything, search anywhere. If you don't, they have to get a search warrant and specify exactly what it is they're looking for. Boulter's expression tells me they are looking for something. And I have something I prefer they don't find.

We sit around a large table, Boulter and Parker closest to the door and me opposite, my back to a window. I pour each of us a glass of water from a jug I fill at the kitchenette off one end of the room. I maintain the civil distance Boulter established.

'What can I do for you, detectives?'

'We think you may be able to help us.'

'Always like to help, Detective.'

'Detective Sergeant. Ever met a homeless man who goes by the name, Hunter?'

'Hunter? No I don't think so.'

Teuton-face Parker weighs in. 'You're sure about that, Doctor?'

'Just Lazaar's fine. But yes. Pretty sure.'

The young detective screws his face up and leans forward across the table. 'Well now, that's strange *Doctor* Lazaar, because people we've talked to describe someone who looks a lot like you being seen with him.' He lays a grainy photograph on the table, then another and then a third. The pictures are stills printed off the CCTV at an ATM machine, the time codes stamped across the bottom. I study them closely, shake my head.

'This is the guy? Hunter?'

'Yep.'

'Looks a bit rough. What makes you think I know him?'

Boulter takes the lead again. 'Oh you know him, Lazaar. Only, you know him better under a different name.' Her eyes burrow into mine.

I try to make sure there is no imprint back there to read. 'That a fact, Detective Sergeant? Then your question's answered isn't it?'

'My question?'

'Unless you have another question. I'm sorry you've wasted a trip.'

The silence that falls over the room could stop freeway traffic. Boulter doesn't speak for a long time. When she does, it is two words. 'Calvin Bishop.'

She leans forward and taps the picture in front of me. 'Look closely, Lazaar. This is Calvin Bishop.'

'Cal Bishop died ten years ago, Detective Sergeant. Lost at sea, presumed drowned. This isn't him. I don't know this man.'

'The coroner ruled an open verdict. This photo was taken last Friday night at nine fifty-two. It's a man who goes by the name of Hunter, drawing twelve hundred dollars out of an ATM in Market Street, Fremantle. One of the boys who was with him, one who he gave the money to, said this guy made a comment that the "fish in Fremantle were on the nose". That phrase was coined by Bishop in a headline he wrote years ago, triggering an investigation into the Gordioni family's waterfront activities. Calvin Bishop, your ex-boss from Kalgoorlie, and Hunter, your homeless friend, are one and the same. We don't know for sure, but right now he could be buried under a pile of limestone at the top of the Parry Street car park, or he could have triggered the explosion that buried the two we do know of. What do you have to say to that, Doctor Lazaar?'

'Not much, Detective Sergeant. I don't know this man.'

'Okay, have it your way.' She stands and ushers Parker to the door, before she, too, turns to leave. I remain seated, waiting until he is out the door.

'Oh, Detective Sergeant—' She turns back, the door held ajar in her hand. 'If you'd care to leave me your number, I'll call you if anything comes to mind ... unless of course, you're not taking calls.'

She hesitates a moment and then calls out through the door. 'Parker, I'll meet you at the car in five minutes.'

She returns to the room, closing the door behind her.

'You're lying to me, Lazaar. I don't like being lied to. I'm going to find your friend Hunter. I'll get to the bottom of this. I have a witness says two people are dead because of him.'

'Two people eh? Boulter, I don't know anything about that. But I've left messages all week. Why haven't you returned my calls?'

'When I realised you lied to me, I didn't see much point in talking to you. You're still lying to me. I'm going back to the office and I'll be getting McPherson to authorise a warrant to arrest you for obstruction. I'll give you two minutes to convince me otherwise.'

'I told you I need protection for a witness.'

'A witness to what, exactly?'

'You have an unsolved murder, Boulter. The guy in the wheelie bin. His sister is at serious risk of suffering the same fate unless she can be protected.'

'I don't think so, Lazaar.'

'What do you mean?'

'The person who committed that crime has been arrested. So there's no need to protect her. Why don't you hand her over to Immigration and, if I need her, I can get in touch with her there.'

'Are you nuts? They'll put her back in detention or deport her.'

'They won't deport her while there's an active investigation into the murder of her brother — assuming she can prove he is her brother. But in any case, she's an illegal isn't she? No identity, no legal reason to be here.'

I leap from my chair and lean forward across the table, like an ape, resting on my knuckles. I'm sure my face is a pomegranate shade of purple. 'She's a fucking *asylum seeker*, Boulter. Last time I looked, it wasn't a crime to seek asylum in this country and lodge a claim to be recognised as a refugee.'

'Yeah, but it is a crime to withhold information from the police about an active investigation, Lazaar. I intend to charge you with that. If you want to avoid the same charge being levelled at this girl, you would be wise to get in touch with Immigration.'

I bite my tongue. I don't want to play a card from my new deck just yet, I need more time to think about it, so I try for a hedge. 'Are you sure you got the right guys?'

'Guy, Lazaar. The one who did it. Yeah, I'm sure.'

'What makes you so sure?'

'Look I can't discuss an ongoing investigation with you, okay? I got the guy, he has identified the victim, end of story. I don't need the girl. What I do know is that two people are dead because your friend led them into a trap — which has nothing to do with this, by the way. But you're obstructing that investigation.'

She cocks her head to one side, gives me a thin smile, pulls the door open. 'I will get a warrant for your arrest. Don't leave town.'

After she has left, I stand rooted to the spot. My options are dwindling at an alarming rate.

Things are falling apart faster than a timber hut in a bushfire, and it takes me some time to recompose. I sit alone in the conference room for ten minutes, thinking about what has just happened and what to do next. I am curious. Why have I seen nothing of the arrest she's made, and how did she twig Hunter's identity and my connection to him? And why does she think the blood of two lives might be on his hands? I can't shake the feeling that it is all connected, but none of the threads tie up.

What I know for certain is that Hunter's notebook computer and USB aren't safe in my office. There's every likelihood that my communications are compromised. Boulter will have phone tapping and email harvesting in place by the end of the day if not already. I go to a colleague's office, use her phone on the excuse that mine is out of commission and call WiFi, suggesting a meeting in the cafe. I also call Lavender and ask her to meet me half an hour later.

I hand WiFi the documents from Hunter that confirm Boulter's existing legend and ask him to use it for Falullah's enrolment. He explains that he has to expunge the Curtin University transcripts and originate her enrolment as an international student on exchange. There is a substantial risk attached to this, but I have a plan and think we may just get it through.

I hand him the notebook and USB, asking that he check it for security and ensure it has no trace back to me or anyone else. Among the protocols for my communications, I am to refrain from using the campus wireless internet system. He will route my office IP address through a TOR connection. He asks for my mobile phone, strips the SIM card from it, produces another, older model — gsm he calls it — inserts my SIM card into one of its two slots. I am to use my usual number for normal business, but secure contacts should go through the second SIM. He gives me a quick lesson in its use, assuring me that the phone has firmware installed that leaves a smoke trail of mobile phone routers on every call, which means it can't be traced quickly or accurately.

My final request is the tricky one. I have just finished convincing him of its necessity when Lavender arrives. He leaves without introduction.

I spend the next thirty minutes explaining the situation to Lavender. Falullah has about two weeks to become familiar with her new identity. This means purchasing a suitable wardrobe, speaking mostly French, and whenever she speaks English, to do so with a modest difficulty and a French accent. It is Lavender's job to acclimatise our new French exchange student to campus, including introducing her to her fellow students at the student village. Her student documentation will be processed over the following week to ten days, after which she will be able to collect her student identity. Lavender's campus address and phone number are the contact points for student services.

I have decided to disappear for the next week and I leave campus to Carole King reminding me of what it feels like to be on the outer bearing the weight of the world. I drive home to Roleystone, make a show of collecting some papers in case anyone is watching, or the house is bugged, throw some clothes into a duffel bag and head to Fremantle, where I book into the Esplanade Hotel.

Chapter Seventeen

Wartime Prayers

Friday 23 August — 15 days before the election

Mick Dosek's funeral at Karrakatta was a sombre affair attended by a handful of SAS mates, a former commanding officer, Sean Dower, Swaddick and a small group of supporters. There were no family members — Dosek had no record of next of kin — but a contingent of press were on hand, marking the event as the first formal activity of the Lamord Living Foundation, a generous attempt to bring dignity to the sacrifices of our veterans, one TV presenter stated. Sam Codlin directed affairs and, following the service, a small lunchtime celebration was held in a private function room at Balsamic & Olives, which Lamord also attended.

Lamord left early for his Cottesloe office, where he led Max Glendinning to his boardroom for a private meeting.

Glendinning placed a buff manila folder on the table in front of him and sat forward in his chair. The folder, with no title or label, contained several photographs and printed sheets.

'Your boy did well at the weekend conference,' Glendinning said. 'Noah has a bright future.'

'Leadership?' Glendinning enquired.

'We could do worse, Max. But we need to knock off the old-boys attitude in the East. They seem to think it's their party and we're Cinderella.'

Glendinning emitted a short laugh. 'Well, good luck with that one Roger. That sort of talent needs looking after, though. How are plans?'

'I'm told there will be an immediate opening in Border Protection for a man of your experience. I've put your name forward and it was well received.'

Glendinning nodded. He turned to the pages in his folder. 'Fremantle detectives will soon be charging Mahmoud Khalil with the murder of an unidentified person found in a wheelie bin in Hamilton Hill. Thought you'd like to know.' Lamord nodded his thanks. Glendinning continued. 'Unfortunately, there's no sign of your missing girl. But there is an interesting connection. Fremantle detectives seem to be interested in talking to the same fellow Dower's people were looking for earlier last week.' He placed several large, but grainy, prints on the table. 'This is a picture taken at an ATM in Market Street last Friday night. As you can see, they're a little grainy, but this is the guy known as Hunter — your people believe he's the one spirited your girl away.'

Lamord studied the images closely, one by one. 'Looks familiar...'

'I'm not surprised,' Glendinning said. 'The detective leading the investigation thought so too. She had forensics run the image through facial recognition software. Turns out to be a guy named Calvin Bishop.'

'Bishop?' The name struck a chord. Lamord creased his brow in an effort to place it. 'The journalist? Investigated Bondy? I thought he died years ago.'

'Lost at sea was the word,' Glendinning said. 'Poked his nose into a drug racket he alleged was run by Enzo Gordioni. Wouldn't have had much choice but to disappear once Gordo'd caught wind of it.

But hiding among the homeless — I have to give it to him — that is clever. Gordioni would stay upwind of a homeless person.'

Lamord sympathised. Nothing like a beggar to blight the landscape: an unsightly brown smudge on a pristine postcard. Society would be better served if they were all rounded up.

In a measured, even tone, he asked, 'Do they know what caused the rockfall?'

'The fireys are still looking for traces of explosives. They think calcium nitrate may have been used and some water-soluble agent. It's hard to isolate because it's limestone. It's a matter of finding a spot that burnt hotter than the rest. In this case it's doubly difficult because water and electricity were both present and the forensics people can't tell in which order. Either this guy, Hunter — or Bishop — has the luck of the gods, or he's resourceful.'

'Sean Dower says it was booby trapped with electrified water.'

'Dower would be best advised to keep his bloody head down and his thoughts to himself. The investigation has confirmed that the space was lived in. Electricity was supplied from the old warden's cottage — the wiring was at least seventy years old. Water flowed through there from an underground source. It was originally part of the tunnel system that ran between the harbour and the gaol, but there have been collapses in the past and the city put up grilles to bar access. I guess this Hunter found a way in and, if he's had ten years to work on it, he could have set up anything down there. All the same, the geologists reckon it's possible the cave-in was a natural occurrence. Won't know definitely for a few months.'

A brief silence settled between them as Lamord stared out the window. The sun's rays struck laser-like bars through a bruised cloudbank rolling in from the west, trying to muscle through, rearranging the sky's stuff. At length he said, 'The girl still has to be found. How sure are we this fellow Hunter is hiding her somewhere?'

'Dower's boys and Codlin have done a top job,' Glendinning replied. 'They found him and determined that he was the last person seen with her. But nothing definite ties his actions to your search for her — he could easily have mistaken Dower's boys for Gordioni's goons — and maybe it's not a bad idea to float that thought. But if he did get her into hiding' — he paused while he extracted another photograph from his folder — 'he's not the worst of your problems.'

'A fucking poet?' Lamord looked across the table at Glendinning whose return gaze was dubious. Jesus! he thought, what is it with people like this? As though some hack writer can have any real influence on events under my control.

'Well in a manner of speaking,' Glendinning answered at length. 'Art Lazaar was a middleweight entertainer in the eighties and nineties with something he called performance poetry — a singer who can't sing writing about social justice and political entanglements. He's a lightweight academic now. Those who can, do. Those who can't, teach.'

'Yes, I know what you mean. But I don't see the issue — if he was never really anybody, and he's even less now, what's he got?'

'It might be more about what he hasn't got.'

'What hasn't he got?'

'Money. Fame. A wife. He's hardly even got a job from what I hear.'

'I don't get it.' Lamord's bewilderment was genuine. Glendinning allowed himself a laugh on the inside.

'Let's look at it this way, Roger. Who would you say is the most well-known member of your party in this state — the person most people think holds the power?'

'The Premier, of course.'

'So, does he hold the power?'

'Of course not.'

'Who does?'

'You know damn well.'

Glendinning took a beat. 'It's you of course. But no-one knows that. I mean Joe Public.'

Lamord looked into Glendinning's eyes, his face passive, accepting of the honour the other had afforded him. 'That would be the quickest way to lose it.'

Glendinning, nodding agreement, said, 'Art Lazaar was a journalist. He's had a string of low-level gigs since — performance poetry, satire, that sort of thing. When there's a sniff of official corruption, or an undercover cop is threatened, somehow he's there. There've been rumours about him for years. He appears like a ghost who walks between the law and the lawless. He digs in and he doesn't let go. He's worse than a fucking bobtail.

'No-one knows how this guy knows what he knows, where he gets his information — or his instructions. No-one fronts for him. He doesn't have a premier. And he's got nothing to lose.'

'Which university?'

'Sorry?'

Lamord rose in his seat and a flash of ice passed through his eyes. 'Which university does he teach at?'

Glendinning told him.

'Good. The vice chancellor is a good friend. This Art Lazaar is as good as gone.'

Glendinning sat back, thoughtful. 'I wouldn't bet on it, Roger. I'm telling you, this guy has a remit that is outside of anyone's reach.'

Lamord got up from his chair and walked around the table. Glendinning rose as Lamord extended his hand and shook the other's. 'Thanks for coming, Max.' He waited while Glendinning gathered his folder from the table and lifted his coat from the back of his chair before guiding him towards the door. 'I'd like to meet this poet. I'll invite him to lunch.' He opened the door and ushered Glendinning through. 'I would have thought that you, more than anyone, would know that nothing is beyond my reach.'

After escorting Glendinning to the lift, Lamord returned to the room and picked up the 10x8 from the table. He studied the image before him, looked directly into the eyes — clear, hazel in colour, with that little reflected square in the top near-side that is often—

'Mistaken for the window to the soul,' he murmured. He looked for a long time, and then came to a decision. 'A Columbian lunch for you, I think Doctor Lazaar.'

He dropped the photograph onto the table, went to the bar and poured a glass of his own estate's Shiraz from a crystal decanter. He took it back into his office where he stood before the plate-glass window and allowed the spicy black current and hint of cinnamon to fill his nostrils and whet his palate. As the black belt of clouds tightened its grip on the ocean before him and swallowed Rottnest Island, an ancient refrain drifted into his mind like a wartime prayer.

At first it seemed a little speck,
And then it seemed a mist;
It moved and moved and took at last
A certain shape I wist.
A speck, a mist, a shape, I wist!
And still it neared and neared:
As if it dodged a water sprite,
It plunged and tacked and veered.

What poetry could you possibly have that stands up to those of the great seafarers, *Art Lazaar*? If that is even your name. You will know, firsthand, tack and plunge, my friend; and you will veer on and return to a shape, a mist, a speck. And then you will veer out of sight. You will be no more. Fucking poets. Who needs fucking poets?

He filled his mouth and let the wine flow across all the taste buds on his tongue, rolling it like a wave — forward and back, side to side. And then he swallowed. He let the moment pass, reached for his phone, and dialled a number. A voice answered.

'Enzo, please,' he said.

Chapter Eighteen

An Innocent Man

Monday 26 August — 12 days before the election

Kelly Boulter was up at five after a restless night. She set out on her morning run into a bitter and miserable dark from her Como apartment in Lockhart Street, the rhythm of her footsteps falling in time with Glen Frey's *Smuggler's Blues* loud in her earbuds. She crossed the freeway and then the river at Canning Bridge before turning south along the Mount Pleasant foreshore. An icy wind barrelled up the Canning River. It drilled through her and spat fine shards of rain in her face as she ramped up into a spanking pace towards Mt Henry Bridge. She recrossed the river along a dry path beneath the bridge and with the wind and rain now at her back, pounded her way back to Canning Highway and home. The ten-and-a-half kilometres took just on thirty-five minutes — close enough to a record — and time enough to think on issues plaguing her mind.

A recent habit of Boulter's has been to spend some of Sunday evening logged into Oasis, the Curtin University Learning Management System, where the credentials of an undercover legend gave her access to a wide range of student bulletin boards and topic discussions on the system's Blackboard. It was a way of following Lucas's progress and gave her an insight into his state of mind. She'd been pleased with his recent activities and discussions. But last night, when she tried, her access was denied. She had made several attempts, only to be advised that her credentials were not valid.

Normally this wouldn't be cause for concern, but something about the finality of the system message prickled the hairs on the back of her neck. It was that her *credentials* weren't valid, not that the system was somehow down and unavailable. *Her* credentials. According to COPs — the Covert Operations management team — the credentials she had been handed were foolproof. And even though the job had finished, she had managed to persuade a contact there to keep the identity live on the pretence that there might be follow-up enquiries. It wasn't strictly legal, she'd been advised — could be cause for abuse of government property — but they'd placed her university identity on a leave of absence, still enrolled, still *credentialled* beyond usual student access. She would check in with her contact later.

As she took control of her breathing and synchronised it to the rhythm of her footfall, her thoughts flipped through her case data as though her mind were a filing system of index cards, pausing on each mental image before slipping it back and bringing the next into focus. The wheelie bin murder was perplexing, as was the Parry Street explosion, from which two bodies had been recovered. Assuming he was there to begin with, this meant Hunter — or rather Calvin Bishop — was either still buried in the remaining rubble or had escaped the blast and disappeared. Something he's good at, it seems. Interesting how the soldier's body had been claimed by his ex-unit in double quick time, then cremated and made news of by this Lamord Living Foundation — hardly time enough for the coroner to reach a conclusion and release the body. The coroner's report on Tor, the homeless lad said he'd been electrocuted before being crushed. Nobody had come forward to claim that body.

The nature of crime is that someone has to lose. Whose were the losses here? Whose losses?

The cards kept flipping. Interviews with Mahmoud Khalil had led to nothing. He said the victim was his friend. He had no identity papers. The transporters wouldn't take you unless you destroyed your papers.

Talk to Yusuf, he said. He has my new papers.

Who is Yusuf?

Yusuf gave me the camera with the photo.

What photo? Who is Yusuf?

Yusuf knows who did this.

What is your connection to the panel-beaters shop?

I help Channa sometimes. Yusuf arranged this.

Who is Yusuf? Your fingerprints were found in the tow truck. A green wheelie bin containing a body was transported on that tow truck. Do you want to tell us about that?

I drive the truck to move vehicles around the yard. I don't know anything about a wheelie bin. I need to talk to Yusuf.

Who is Yusuf?

The cards came and went quickly, in rhythm, and increasingly the cards that flipped through her mind had a connection which grew more intense. Lazaar. Could Lazaar be the link to it all? Lazaar who betrayed me. Lazaar who knows something. Lazaar who taught me about the poetry of murder. Not that which rhymes, he'd said. More the way Aristotle thought of it — is it tragedy or comedy? Ari-fucken-stotle; Art La-fucken-zaar — that's poetry. It all depends on who's lying, and to whom.

Whose losses?

Are you lying to me Mahmoud?

I'm not lying. Ask Yusuf. Ask Channa.

Who is Yusuf?

Maybe that's it, she thought. A blast of wind from behind released a sudden shower that soaked her through. She pounded harder, focusing on her breathing, keeping it in rhythm. Rethink the poetry.

By the time she reached home she had a plan for the day. Find out whose losses add up.

Boulter passed through the station security at eleven minutes past seven. Part one of the plan was to attack the objects that made up the evidence she had to hand. Even though she had a feeling the wheelie bin case was somehow linked to the Parry Street blast, she was determined to work systematically as though there were no links. The networks would find their own paths if they were there to be found. They form their own rhizomes. Parry Street can be planted in a different patch for now.

She heard Lazaar's voice in her head as she entered the situation room and began to re-arrange the pieces on the board. *Drawing conclusions is for novelists. You know the conclusion, that's where you need to look back from — the totum simul. First is to decide whether it is tragedy or comedy.*

Jesus! That man is like an original sin.

To exorcise Lazaar's presence, she sent a series of text messages and logged a calendar entry for a team briefing at 10:00. She intended to create a history of the murder from the end that she already knew, back to its beginning. Its narrative. A compression of time that she visualised from outside the events, standing like a general on a high ridge overseeing a campaign. The totum simul.

Boulter saw each material object present at any point along a timeline as belonging only to that object, with its own small story. The tendrils from those small stories generate the Narrative of God, from which she will come to understand motives, intentions and beliefs of those involved. Why did the wheelie bin get moved to that location? That *specific* location? Why did the killer mix red paint with the victim's blood? To see all as a single, timeless whole is to see the way the material objects that make up the murder lie in relation to each other. No murder is a single event. This is what determines whether it is tragedy or comedy. Whose losses?

Tragedy, Lazaar told her, is the story in which the liar is lying to himself; in comedy, the liar is lying to everyone else. What about you, Lazaar? Tragicom?

But his thinking is useful. Especially when it comes to piecing together the small stories that comprise the bigger narrative. Using timeline software, she created three arcs: The wheelie bin, the body, and the paint — the primary objects. She assigned the main points to critical times along these, and then added a master arc, the *investigation*, and another called *locations*. Each entry linked to detailed information held in IIS — the Incident Information System (pronounced 'eye-is') and established relationships between the objects, events and actors. These last she divided into crime-involved and investigator.

At nine-thirty she was interrupted by a call from a voice who identified himself as Agent Jones, from the AFP, Perth Crime Operations.

'Yes.' Boulter's response was a clear signal that she was being interrupted.

'I head the people-smuggling team here in Perth. Your boss has requested assistance relating to a suspect you're holding. Would you be willing to meet us over lunch today?'

'Us, Agent Jones?'

'Me and my partner, Agent Smith.'

'Smith and Jones?'

'That's right, Detective. You're holding a guy who says he is Mahmoud Khalil, right?'

'Why lunch?'

'Because it's sensitive. Balsamic & Olives, one o'clock.' The line went dead.

Boulter tapped the details into her calendar and went back to her task, determined to have the picture as complete as possible by ten, and any questions about missing information or holes in the

narrative clear and highlighted. She was interested in whose losses
rose to the surface.

The team filed in a few minutes before the appointed time. McPherson
was the last. He handed Boulter a piece of paper.

'Before close of business today.' The instruction was clear, but
she wasn't to be side-tracked. She noted the Police insignia on its
header, folded it without looking further and stuffed it under the
cover of her daybook.

The projectors were directed in high resolution to two interactive
smart boards that covered a good part of one wall. Her timeline of
mapped events projected onto one screen, its relationship lines extending between entries like coloured rhizomes. It was impressive.

She clicked on the wheelie bin entry and a point-cloud image of
the crime scene appeared in 3D night-vision green on the second
screen, a laser scan of the site generated by the FFOs — Forensic
Field Officers — who attended.

'Okay. The wheelie bin.' Boulter used a laser pointer to identify
objects on the screen as she talked. 'On Friday the second, at six-
thirty am, the bin was found here, at the verge of 23 Morrison Street
Hamilton Hill by Carlos Chavez, resident. Mr Chavez had returned
from his night shift at Henderson where he works as a welder in
a shipbuilding yard. His rubbish collection usually occurs at about
seven-thirty on a Friday and it's his habit, when he's on night shift,
to put the bin out when he gets home. He saw this bin as he drove
in and thought his wife may have already done it, which would have
been very unusual. But when he parked his car up the driveway,
here' — her laser pointed to the ghostly point-cloud image of the
rear of a vehicle in the upper right corner — 'their bin was still by
the back door. He took his bin out and then looked into this one and
saw a plastic sheet. When he lifted the top of it, he discovered the
feet of a body that had been placed head first in the bin. To avoid

them being collected, Mister Chavez then moved both his bin and this one back from the kerb, here' — she moved her pointer beam as though drawing a pathway — 'to where they are, here. His call to Fremantle Police is logged on *eye-is* at six forty-six. He remained at the front of his property with the bins until local police arrived at seven oh-eight. FOS officers' — first on scene — 'determined that they were dealing with a suspicious death. They cordoned off a ten-metre buffer, set up and manned an RVP' — rendez vous point.

Boulter paused and scanned the room. She hadn't lost anyone yet.

'Forensics have established that the bin was moved to this location with the body inside sometime between midnight and six thirty. This assumes a possible overlap of two hours in the time of transportation with the time of the murder. The bin was stolen from David Gray's in O'Connor sometime between nine am on Monday twenty-ninth of July and three-thirty in the afternoon of Thursday the first of August. A delivery driver reported it missing from his delivery. Each bin has a unique serial number, which is allocated to an address prior to delivery, as shown on this manifest.' An image of a document appeared next to the crime scene image.

'So David Gray's lose a bin,' Robinson, the team cynic, was quick to point out one early loss. His wry humour was useful for looking at the extremes of human behaviour. 'The driver dumped it somewhere on his way?'

'That's a possibility, Andy,' Boulter rejoined. 'But let's not jump the gun. The only fingerprints recovered from the bin are those of Mr Chavez, and they correspond with his descriptions of his actions. His right-hand prints are on the lid handle, his left hand on the lip at the middle front, his right hand again on both the plastic inside and the right side dragging handle which he used to move the bin.' She clicked a button on her pointer and circled each of these locations in the image as she spoke, leaving a visible notation. The image refocused on the bin, lower down and tracked around to its rear. 'There are rub marks down here' — again pointing — 'which I'll come back to in a minute. And there is dog urine splashed on this lower left corner. Mister Chavez confirms a dog walked past the bin while he was waiting for the police to arrive and lifted its leg before he could shoo it off.'

Boulter paused once again and looked around the room. 'Now, the Super wants us to wrap this thing up by Friday' — she caught McPherson's eye. 'Comments? Questions?'

Robinson jumped in again. 'Yeah, I'm hearing Billy Joel's *Innocent Man* here.' A pause as he studies the faces. 'There are holes in this that could hide an aircraft carrier. No prints. No identity for victim or perp. Makes me wonder what lies we're not hearing. This is no ordinary murder, Boss.' This last was directed at McPherson.

'Okay,' Boulter said, drawing focus back to her. 'Let's work through everything we do have and then dig around your aircraft-carrier holes. That okay with you?' A grin and a nod from Robinson. 'First, David Gray's lose a bin. Baxter, what have we got?'

'Yeah Sarge. Tom Procter, the truck driver' — referring to his notes — 'I interviewed him Thursday the eighth, here, at nine am. Had a union-supplied lawyer with him. He can't explain the loss of a bin. Says, when the truck is loaded, the manifest is checked by the company's stores clerk. His manifest accounts for thirty-six bins aboard, all destined for Armadale City depot. He didn't count them. He assumed the count to be correct. So there is a possibility the clerk made an error, either in the count or on the manifest. I talked to her on site a couple of days earlier. It's hard to see how she could have made a mistake; she checks the serial numbers in batches set aside, and then recounts them on board. It's pretty thorough, Medici would call it double entry.' He flashed a knowing look at Robinson and continued.

'But there is something interesting. Procter says he was stopped at the intersection of North Lake Road and Winterfold shortly after leaving the depot by two plain-clothes police officers in an unmarked white Toyota. He was instructed to pull into the lane that leads to McBeth Way and given a drug test. He tested positive for cannabis, and was detained in the unmarked vehicle, supervised by one officer while the other searched his truck. No infringement was issued. No incident was logged on *eye-is*.'

'So, was he stoned?' McPherson asked.

'He says he had a joint before he went to work. If that's the case he probably wasn't shit-faced. Likes to cruise, he reckoned. Apparently he had another joint stashed in the truck for later. Claims the cop who did the search took it.'

Truck driver loses a spliff, Boulter thought, and then asks, 'Did he give you a description of these cops?'

'Couple of big blokes around mid-thirties, one a little older than the other, heavier and shorter. The taller one searched the truck while the other one kept him in the back of the car, standing outside and talking on a mobile phone. They didn't question him other than to identify him and then, after administering the test, ask when he'd had a smoke. The taller of the two showed him some ID when they approached the truck, but it was pretty cursory. He couldn't recall them giving names and was pretty sketchy on their details. The car had a portable roof-top blue, in-dash comms, and system-locked doors. They both had buzz-cut hairstyles, although he thought the shorter one seemed to be balding a bit. Both had under-shoulder sidearms.'

Robinson gave a low whistle. 'An aircraft carrier's looking a mite small right now, Boss.'

Boulter glared. 'Well then, Detective, perhaps you can do some actual detecting and find out if they were real cops without firm identity, or fake cops in a real car, or fake cops in a fake car?' She took in the other faces in the room. 'Do we assume the wheelie bin was removed from the truck by the cop — fake or real — at this pull-over?'

'That's certainly one possibility,' Baxter replied. 'Of course, as

Robbo suggests, Procter could have dumped a bin and fed us this story. We'll have a better idea after boy wonder here has checked his financials and background. If anything shows up we'll pull him in for further questioning.' He looked at Parker.

'Okay, let's move on,' Boulter said, glancing at the wall clock. 'I want to briefly touch on two other things about the bin. The first is the grease found in the treads of the left wheel. FFOs have matched that to some grease on the back of a tow truck owned by the Scratch'n'Match panel shop in O'Connor' — an image of the truck appeared on screen, Boulter's laser highlighting a grubby splotch near the winch. 'They also found some plastic scrapings matching the bin extrusion on the edge of the rear platform of the truck, accounting for this tiny scrape mark down the back of the bin. So, we can say that the bin was transported, with the body in it, on the back of this tow truck. Whoever drove the truck that night is responsible for dumping the body.

'The second is the mystery. Before being used to store a murdered body and around eight litres of red paint, the bin was thoroughly cleaned with an industrial cleaner, inside and out. There are absolutely no fingerprints or other marks that would under normal circumstances be found on a new wheelie bin shipped to David Gray's, processed by their stores personnel, loaded on a truck and removed from the truck. None. On top of that, two domestic shower curtains were used to line the inside of the bin, and they too have no fingerprints.' She looked at Parker. 'Ben, you have a theory about this?'

'I think so.' Parker took the remote control from Boulter and clicked on an entry on the timeline. 'FFOs identified the solvent as a product manufactured by ICC, used in most engineering and panel-beating shops. It's a compound known as 571-B, odourless and potent, petroleum based for use in low-pressure sprayers and manually removing minute residues of grease and dirt. They use it in the paint booth to prepare a surface, and again after painting. It's a specialist chemical and has to be mixed correctly for the application. I rather feel the perpetrator in this case knows his chemicals.

'I'd like to fill in some of the missing details.' He clicked on the timeline arc labelled *paint*. 'Maybe shrink Robbo's aircraft-carrier hole a bit.'

'Senior Detective Constable Robinson to you, son,' Robinson growled.

'Whatever. Anyway, the wheelie bin was completely lined by two domestic shower curtains purchased from Bunnings or Coles — they both stock them, but there's no way of knowing which shop they came from. It contained a human body that had been completely bled, five or so litres of blood from that person, and about eight litres of red paint. Forensics ascertained the presence of blood mixed with the paint using an initial luminol sweep. The question then became how much was blood and how much was paint, and which went in first. The weight of the body was sixty-eight kilograms, the volume of blood, five point two litres, and a few mils shy of eight litres of red automotive paint was poured in after the victim had bled dry. It is our contention that the paint was used to obscure the forensic investigation, mask blood odour and possibly to give the outward appearance of a domestic clean-up. It was the paint, though, that led us to the murder scene.

'This batch of paint is for red Mini Cooper cars and was formulated by Dulux in O'Connor in late June. It had been supplied to three different panel-beating shops, including' — another image on the screen — 'Scratch'n'Match at the end of Formley Place, O'Connor. This was identified on August twelfth, and we sealed these premises as the likely murder scene. The tow truck that Sergeant Boulter referred to was also found at that site.'

Parker brought up a series of photogrammetry reconstruction images of a section of the panel beater's workshop, including a floor plan and interior layout showing car bays, hoist machinery, the paint section and the access way through wide doors in the rear of the premises.

'The chemical cleaning wasn't just applied to the bin. While the solvent carrier dissipates into the atmosphere, molecular trace elements remain. The FFOs established that this floor area in the paint booth was thoroughly cleaned, as was the under-section and tray top of the tow truck. There's a chain hoist here, and the chain was also cleaned. It appears our victim was transported here from elsewhere. FFOs found German Shepherd fibres on his clothing in places that indicate he was lying on his left side; fibres transferred from another surface, most likely car flooring. There are no traces of anything from this floor, and there are no recent traces of this breed in this site, so it's reasonable to assume that the fibre transfer occurred during transportation — although it's an assumption that needs to be tested. The absence of the fibres on any other part of his clothing would rule out him being in friendly contact with a dog. The chain-link marks on his ankle match this chain,' — another image overlay showing a tie chain hanging from the hoist shackle — 'which was looped around each ankle and then locked into this shackle, and he was hoisted up. We believe the tow truck was reversed in here' — the new image, showing an inverted, hoisted, body and the tow truck, moved through 180 degrees to show locations and relationships of objects — 'with the wheelie bin placed on its tray. He was lowered into the wheelie bin, the curtains used to limit blood spatter, and his throat was cut from behind. Once he had bled out, the paint was poured down the sides of the curtains and the body fully lowered into the bin, which was then carted away and dumped.'

'Doesn't add up,' Robinson said.

'What doesn't?' Parker asked.

'All this cleaning.'

McPherson chipped in. 'Well, Laddie, this guy obviously didn't want to leave any traces. He was thorough.'

'That's my point,' Robinson retorted. 'Everything, except for one little grease spot.' He leapt from his chair, took a red marker, circled the grease spots on the truck and wheelie bin and drew a connecting line between them.

'Your point?'

'It's a setup. This was meant to be found.' Robinson let the silence fall like leaves. 'Look, I have to say, this reads like a very thorough and professional operation, meticulously planned and executed' — he allowed the pun to register; it didn't — 'but I'm struggling to see how the perp we've got in custody fits. Like I said, I can't see this being done by one guy. Not only one guy, but a guy without identity, which means without a driving licence. Can anyone here see how a guy with this level of planning is going to put it at risk by driving without a licence?'

'Maybe he had a false,' Baxter offered.

'Then why hasn't he offered it since being taken into custody?'

Boulter mentally noted the losses adding up. She turned to McPherson. 'Sir, perhaps you would like to comment?'

McPherson was uncomfortable at being put on the spot. He narrowed his eyes and shifted his weight from one foot to the other. Here we go, Boulter thought, bullshit at F1 speed.

'I believe, Sergeant Boulter, that you are meeting with federal investigators later today?' Definitely a question best ignored, Boulter thought. McPherson continued. 'They have substantial evidence that puts Khalil in the frame and are now in a position to make it available to us. I apologise that this couldn't be done earlier, but this is a sensitive operation and involves multiple agencies and we need to be certain that everything here is done by the book. I'm certain your concerns will be addressed.'

'Still,' Robinson said, 'This guy's either got serious resources or he's a fucking superman.'

'We think his resources might be substantial and spread around,' McPherson said. 'Who owns this panel beaters, Andy?'

Robinson consulted his notes. 'The business is run by a guy called Channa Ranatunga, a Sri Lankan immigrant who came as a refugee in 2003. He's employed by the company through a local commercial law firm that acts for the owners, whose identities, they point out, they are not obliged to share with us. It's a holding company registered in the British Virgin Islands. Ranatunga receives his salary and instructions through the law firm and reports to them. The land where the business is situated is held freehold by another company, also registered in the BVI, also administered by the same law firm. The same goes for the block two along towards the intersection, which houses a small mosque.

'In Ranatunga's statement, he advises that Mahmoud Khalil is known to him, and that he sometimes comes to the panel shop to help out — usually after prayers on a Friday. It's not regular and he doesn't have keys to the premises. We've interviewed all of Ranatunga's employees, and they can all verify their whereabouts on the night in question. So, if Mahmoud is our man, where did he get his keys and how did he do it?'

Another silence, this one longer and heavier.

'Has Khalil given us anything?' Boulter asked.

Robinson again consulted his notes. 'Three things. First he says he's innocent, a friend of the victim; second he's on a bridging visa from Christmas Island in the care of a guy he says is called Yusuf; and third, that the victim has a sister who has gone missing and our guy has grave fears for her. None of these things can we confirm. There's no record of a Mahmoud Khalil receiving a bridging visa. Immigration have no record of him. His fingerprints aren't on file, his face isn't on file, his DNA isn't on file. Nor can we locate an asylum-seeker settlement agent called Yusuf. He doesn't have a last name for Yusuf, so we don't have a last name for him. He's a ghost. As for the sister — who knows?'

Boulter seized the moment. 'Okay, we'll leave it there and see what the feds have to say. Andy, see if you can get hold of the lawyer who's looking after the panel shop and get them in here. Parker, get on to forensics and dig into the wound. There must be something about the murder weapon, the angle from which the cut was applied. Something. Anything. Baxter, get that truck driver back in. I want to be sure two cops pulled him over. Find them if they exist. Also, get back out to the crime scene area and check again to see if anyone saw a tow truck that night. And Robbo, find out about that four-wheel drive that was towed around midnight will you? We're missing something here.'

Chapter Nineteen

Show Me What You're Working With

Smith and Jones were entertaining company. Boulter arrived at Balsamic & Olives a minute or two before the appointed time and mounted the steps to the main entrance. A tall gaunt-looking man with a deep olive complexion guided her to a table — the only one occupied — from which two men were rising. A man with a close-cropped haircut around a receding hairline, perhaps in his late thirties, dressed in well fitted jeans, white sneakers and a red polo shirt under a dark grey zip-up sweater, smiled in recognition. She'd never seen him before.

'Detective Sergeant Boulter,' he said, extending his hand. 'Good of you to come.'

The other person, a tall, disarmingly good-looking man — square jawed, short cropped light coloured hair, also wearing well fitted jeans and sneakers, and a smile that emphasised his eyes — extended his hand for her to shake. He appeared a few years younger than his partner.

'Smith or Jones?' she asked, taking his hand and feeling a warm, confident comfort as it enveloped hers. She allowed the grip to linger just a moment longer.

'I'm Smith, he's Jones.' He let go, as if with some regret.

'Smith and Jones. Aliases, right?'

Jones laughed. Clearly not the first time he'd heard it. 'Actually, they're our real names. I'm Ross, he's another Kelly, like you. Is it okay if we call you that? He can keep Smith.'

Boulter took the seat that Smith had pulled out, gesturing towards the room as she did. 'So, where are all the people?'

'This place is closed to the public on Mondays,' Jones replied. 'Our boss has a special relationship with the owner. It's useful for private conversations.' The thin, olive-skinned man approached the table. 'This is Milorad,' Jones continued. 'He's going to look after things for us.'

'Indeed, sir,' Milorad said, his south-eastern European accent lilting above his words. 'As you know, Mondays are only for ve'ry private affairs, hmm? So we 'ave lighter offerings than other days. The lady prefers vegetables, I think, and you sir' — directing his glance at Smith — 'I think 'ave a taste for warmer meats. We 'ave for you a special Spanish flavour, hmm?' And he proceeded to unveil what was about to be served.

Boulter opted for water, Smith made his the soda variety with a splash of Angostura, which arrived with a twist of lime. Jones took an Alhamra Mezquita. 'A fine Catalonian beer,' Milorad said, complimenting him on his choice.

A waiter arrived with a collection of appetisers, including diced bread with grapes and chopped winter melon, bell pepper *excalivada* and a chef's special of *garbanzo* beans.

'Malaga brought 'ere to you, to excite your palate,' Milorad purred, as he placed Boulter's napkin across her thighs. 'To prepare for Ramon's famous *Couseila*, a ve'ry aromatic dish of couscous paella with dried rosebuds and white and purple grapes flown in fresh from Cap Bon, and *deglet nour* dates from Tunisia. You will enjoy, hmm? Buen provecho.'

'This is very flash, boys,' Boulter said, watching the waiter's back disappear towards the kitchen, and reaching for a stuffed capsicum. 'But why all the cloak and dagger? And where the hell did they get that guy from?'

'Hong Kong, I believe,' Smith replied. 'Word is, he knows every taste there is to know and precisely what happens when they are combined. But we're here, Detective Sergeant, because the discussion we're about to have must be kept between us. This room is more secure than your office or ours. It's swept daily for bugs. If a conversation were taking place at that table over there' — pointing — 'you wouldn't hear it here.'

Boulter smiled. 'Cone of silence, huh?'

'Something like that. A bit more technologically advanced.'

'Okay, I'll buy,' Boulter said, bringing a frown to her brow and fixing a cool stare on Smith. 'What are you selling?'

Jones began, leaving Smith watching Boulter. 'It's a privilege to meet you, Kelly,' he said, with a little more heart than she imagined he felt. 'We don't get much opportunity to meet officers like you. We've heard great things about you, right Smith?'

'Great things,' Smith confirmed.

This wasn't the conversation Boulter had been expecting. When she reflected on it afterwards, she struggled to recall all that they talked about. They touched on mutual friends and colleagues. The challenges of covert operations, how blame gets reapportioned when things go wrong. Smith seemed to know people Boulter knows, but perhaps he knew them better than they knew him. He'd spoken to those who could vouch for her integrity as a police officer who could be trusted. He knew of her problem of promotion denied, or deferred, as he claimed it was put to him.

'Some among your establishment don't appreciate officers who do great things,' Jones said, waving for another Alhamra Mezquita. 'We have the same problem in our organisation. It gets to a point where you don't know who to trust. We think we can trust you.'

'It seems as though you've landed an unsolvable case,' Smith added. And then, with a knowing grin, 'Although that's not something altogether unfamiliar.'

'Our pitch, if you like' — Jones reclaimed the narrative — 'is to help you regain that lost ground by giving you what's needed to land a result. As you might appreciate, we also need a result. Different business, same people.'

'Sounds familiar,' Boulter said. Smith and Jones both gave knowing laughs. 'But I don't get it. I've got a murder case. Where do you guys fit?'

'Your perp,' Smith said. 'Mahmoud Khalil—'

'Alleged.'

'Right. Although once we've shown you ours I think you'll find you've got the right one. Then, of course, you show us what you're working with—'

Boulter held a hand up. 'Show you what I'm working with? What, you want to look under my dress? Fuck you.'

Jones adopted a soothing, gentler tone. 'Kelly, I realise this is all coming a bit out of left field, but if you let us get to it, I'm sure you'll see how this pans out for all of us. We all know that you've got something hidden in there.' He points to her head. 'No point hiding it because we'll get to it sooner or later.'

Déjà vu rose from the pit of Boulter's stomach. She felt she was in a room with a pair of Toby Keith fans whose bullshit idea of being cowboys made them men. She was stuck between a fiddle player and a chicken picker like a washboard in a jailhouse laundry.

Jones ceded the floor to Smith to paint the picture, to spell it out like he was taking the next solo. He sat back, clasping his hands before him like a preacher between moments of transporting morsels from plate to mouth, his voice adjusted for their interpersonal distance, paced evenly, giving pauses where pauses were required, punctuated by the distant clinking of Jones's cutlery. Smith had the preacher's way and Boulter was ensnared within its cadence. He painted a picture of an impending crisis, starting with the ghosts of the Tampa and rising to today's heights of people smuggling. Your man is evidence of its new dimension.

'He is Hazari from Afghanistan,' he went on, in the same endearing tone, 'one of those Tampa ghosts, a child thrown overboard, rescued and brought safely to shore, fed and sheltered on Christmas Island by the generosity of the Australian people, and in 2011 among the first to be granted a bridging visa into the community. His visa was sponsored by an agency for refugees and among the seventeen others in his group to be offered bridging visas were brother and sister, Ishmail and Falullah Salim. We believe Ishmail is your wheelie bin victim.'

Isha, Boulter thought, Mahmoud called him Isha, said he was his friend, said he was innocent, that he did not kill his friend, he does not know who killed him. He has no papers, he says Yusuf keeps them. What will Smith and Jones make of Yusuf?

'We've had an interest in Mahmoud Khalil for some time. We think he has unsavoury links. He prays in a mosque in O'Connor and spends some time in a panel-beating shop a couple of doors along run by Channa Ranatunga, a Bangladeshi who came here as a refugee from Sri Lanka. Ranatunga has dubious links with Islamist militant groups stretching from Bangladesh through Pakistan and Afghanistan. We have people inside watching, and Khalil came to our attention. A forensic examination of where he lives turned up several items of interest — some to us and some to you. What we are about to give you proves that Mahmoud Khalil murdered your wheelie bin victim — a gruesome souvenir photo of the crime, clothes and shoes with the victim's blood on them, and the knife used to cut his throat. Of course there were additional items of interest to our other investigations. Our boss thought it best for your boss to arrest Khalil on suspicion of murder, that way no suspicion is thrown onto ongoing covert work. And because Khalil has no identity documents, you can hold him without charge. The evidence box is in our car.

We'll sign it over to you when you leave.'

'So, I guess we're counting on you, Kelly.' Jones picked up the pitch. 'We need to protect our covert ops, but get this guy put away for his crime. It has to be done reasonably quietly. You see?'

'I think so,' Boulter said, feeling that she'd been fed, but the most tasty morsel withheld. Still no mention of Yusuf.

Jones leaned his right forearm on the table and titled towards her. 'Has Khalil mentioned anyone else?'

Ah. Casting the line. Leaving the fly floating. Dominant male. Boulter decided to shift the conversation.

'It's all very difficult, Ross. You see our man — who you say is Mahmoud Khalil — has no identity papers. We can't confirm who he is. If, as you say' — nodding toward Smith — 'he holds a bridging visa then there would be immigration papers, his fingerprints and DNA samples would be on the national databases. They're not. This guy we've arrested doesn't exist, and neither does the victim. Any defence lawyer is going to shoot that down with a bloody big cannon. If we're going to prosecute this guy, we have to be able to prove who he is, and what his relationship to his victim is. I presume you have that proof?'

A look passed between the two men. 'I'm sure we can produce the visa with photo ID,' Jones said.

'What do you know about our vic, then?' Boulter pressed. 'Can you lay your hands on papers to confirm his identity too?'

'That might be a little more difficult. I'm sure Khalil destroyed anything that identified Salim. We'll have something. But you need to hand over the sister to us.'

'I don't know anything of a sister.'

Smith resumed in a non-challenging tone. 'Surely Mahmoud has mentioned that he was in love with the sister?' First name now, she notes. 'He fought with Ishmail over her. She knows this, and she's on the loose. You see, Kelly, we know you know about the girl. We know you've been in contact with those hiding her, we know you know where she's hidden. She's a crucial link in our investigation, but out there, well, she could put good men and women in danger, send the whole thing down the river. Best if she were left to us. I'm sure you understand.'

'I understand, but I don't know the girl or her whereabouts.'

'You've been undercover, Kelly?' Jones again. 'Of course you have. Last year, right? Or was it the year before? Kylie something... Baker. Yeah that's right, Kylie Baker? The job Bob Prichard got gunned down on, right? A cockup I heard. Sad when a good cop gets shot up by the bad guys. Still, it happens.'

'Well, the thing is, we have to catch the bad guys. The problem is, there's too many of these boats. This government's opened the gates and we're getting swarms, more than we can handle. The boats have to be stopped. That's why we've got the Channa Ranatungas and the Mahmoud Khalils. These guys don't have our national interest at heart. The girl's an illegal, we can't leave her out there — she's gotta be brought back in.'

'Wish I could help you boys, but I know nothing about the girl.'

Smith screwed up his face. Boulter was surprised that even with such contortion, it was still very attractive. 'Yeah Kelly, I don't think you're telling us everything there,' he said.

Bingo! Ground of contention, boys. Let's see who gets out unscathed. 'I'm sorry to disappoint boys, but I think you're dancing in the shadows here.'

Jones looked genuinely perplexed. 'Dancing in the shadows? Kelly, we've given you all of ours. It's your turn.'

Boulter was not quite as contrite as they appeared to have hoped. 'Don't think so, Ross. As I see it, I've got the verses, probably the choruses and the bridge too, but I don't have the hook, do I?'

'The hook?'

'I believe his name is Yusuf.'

Boulter might have reasonably expected the conversation to be abruptly halted at this point, but Jones, with a little more sharpness than he might have intended, simply said, 'We need Yusuf to stay put.'

Perhaps Smith felt the edge in Jones's voice, and perhaps he felt the need to reset the tone, to put it right again.

'What Ross means is that Yusuf is an important thread in our investigation. We've got big fish sniffing at the line, people-smuggling is doing ripe business here and if we inadvertently uproot Yusuf, it could spoil the whole thing. A lot of work has gone into this. Years in fact. We've got assets in play all over the shop, walking the ground up there in Indon and Malaysia, expensive assets in dangerous places moving among the movers, shaking among the shakers, getting in place to shut the traffickers down. If we shake this tree too soon, bad fruit's gonna fall.'

This time, Boulter's need to know was not as easily assuaged as they perhaps thought it would be.

'Forgive me,' she began, 'but I don't really call all the shots on this one. You will need to give me a little more because I'm going to have to go back to my Super. As you know he's the one who signed the warrant application. I don't see him taking kindly to a push that sends him down the void. Could be shit at the other end. Mahmoud Khalil, as you can imagine, protests his innocence and insists we talk with Yusuf. It would certainly be good to get this fellow Yusuf's version of events.'

'I doubt Yusuf has a version of events,' Smith said, with his little smile. 'Yusuf simply provides bridging visas. But your boss, McPherson, he's happy with this version, happy to proceed on the basis of what we've told you and the evidence we have for you. He's confident the prosecutors will have no problem with it, after all you've got a murder weapon, blood and clothing to match, and a pretty damning photograph. Your part is to give us the girl.'

Smith's inflection left this as a question. Boulter left it hanging unanswered for so long Smith might have wondered whether she grasped it. The problem was not so much as whether she grasped it, but how far over the fire she might leave Art Lazaar dangling. He knew where the girl was.

'So, let me get this clear,' she said, caution sounding loud in her inner ear, 'I get this incontrovertible evidence against Mahmoud Khalil, that he did in fact commit this murder. Even though we don't know how he did it, we can prove that he did it.' Jones nodded. 'We don't get to confirm any of it with this Yusuf character, but you will provide us with the missing identity information that we might otherwise have got from him.' Another nod. 'And in exchange for this, I give you the victim's missing sister.'

'That's about it,' Jones confirmed.

As she left, Boulter was not at odds with herself, although she was tempted to ask whether Smith and Jones had veered towards Kardinya in their investigative travels. Smith retrieved the evidence box she signed for from the boot of a white Toyota Aurion and the haircuts and build were close enough to the truck driver's descriptions.

'Office car?' she asked taking the box under her wing.

'It's what we get,' Jones offered. 'Fortunately, he drives.'

The cry of pain she felt driving away mixed with a shout of pleasure. There was something worthwhile about the thought of sticking it to Art Lazaar, although she believed she had limited the potential of damage only to his character and not to threaten the lives of others who had placed their welfare under his care. He needed needling. Since his re-emergence in this case, she felt the weight of his moral force pushing her in directions she had not wanted to go, yet his sleight of hand seemed to always be the upper one. Well not this time. This time he would have to justify his morality. The games between him and the feds should make for interesting spectator sport.

It had been a long lunch and was close to five when she threaded up the stairs of the dingy Fremantle detectives building. McPherson must have been watching the CCTV from his desktop. He stepped out and halted her.

'I need you in my office.'

A bit grumpy, Boulter thought, shifting the weight of the box to her other arm. 'Sure Boss, just let me log this in and I'll be right with you.'

'With that form.'

'Form?'

'The one from the Audit Office.'

'Sorry Boss, I don't know what you're talking about.'

McPherson's face coloured and his lips drew thin. 'This morning, before the briefing, I gave you a form from the Audit Office with explicit instructions that I have it before close of business today. I can't keep saving your pretty little arse, Boulter. Get it, fill it in, and get in my office in the next five minutes.'

Her apology was lost as she hurried away, returning a few minutes later to McPherson's office, only then unfolding the paper and looking closely at it.

She sat at the side table in his office, pen poised in hand. He sat on the edge of his desk, arms folded, scowling down at her.

'You have to give a written explanation for why you still have an active legend that was retired from duty over a year ago. Covert Ops Management have rescinded this legend only to discover that you are still holding photographic identity documents, bank accounts and God knows what else. The Audit Office want me to tell them why.'

Boulter zoned out as McPherson ranted about the Public Officer's Act, a misuse of government property, and potential grounds for dismissal and the enormous costs involved. She scribbled a few lines, scrawled her signature and handed him the paper. He glanced at it and set it aside on his desk.

'So, quid pro quo, sir? You cover my arse on this, I'll cover yours on our wheelie bin case.'

'How exactly does my arse need to be covered?'

'You were the one who applied for a warrant to arrest without probable cause or any evidence to hand. You took the word of Max Glendinning. Sir.'

'That's Superintendent Glendinning, Boulter. A highly decorated officer, now serving with the AFP. Show some respect.'

'Okay, you took the word of *Superintendent* Glendinning. All I can tell you is I've just come from a meeting where there was more bullshit flying around than you'd find at a Kimberley cattle muster. I don't care how much evidence they bring along against that poor kid, I'm beginning to seriously think he didn't do it. But, for the sake of expediency, I'll go along with it. Apparently I have clothes with the victim's blood, the murder weapon and an incriminating photograph. They're getting back to me with identity docs. Imagine that? We can't find one skerrick of information about this guy, or the victim, and then along comes a couple of cowboys from God only knows what federal agency and *voila!* everything we need. I'll log the evidence and send it up to forensics, and then prepare the charges. Should have a wrap by Friday. Back scratching, sir.'

She turned to leave the room, but before she could pull the door open, McPherson stopped her.

'One more thing. Someone's waiting for you in interview room two. I don't like this one bit, but I have my orders. You are to share everything you know on the case. Everything, clear?'

'Sure Boss.'

Boulter left the room and decided to pop her head round the door of the interview room to let her guest know she would be a few minutes. She opened the door, looked in, and stood momentarily frozen as she took in the face studying her.

'Oh, it's you,' she said, and turned and closed the door behind her.

Chapter Twenty

Stuck in the Middle With You

When I'm stuck, I'm not free, and I have to credit Stealers Wheel with the concept, because they got it bang on. Rafferty took on Dylan and that makes me feel as though I'm in good company. To try to settle the demons in moments like these, I turn to my Lamy fountain pen, and go with its flow, its ink like blue mercury, losing myself in a notebook of unlined pages, a hundred or so words of my quick scrawl and a sense of freedom rises. I begin by noting down a single observation in just seven words: a complete thought, a full sentence captured quickly, with a definite end point.

`I'm sat at a table, alone, erect.`

The middle word begins the next observation: again, just seven words.

`A chair beneath my arse, cold, hard.`

And then another line, again, starting with the middle word.

`My arse itches from crusty cold sweat.`

`From cheek to cheek I rock, relieved.`

`Cheek of these people, left me here.`

As my output speeds up, the observations become more random, but always triggered by what I sense from the place, tapping into feelings, sounds, images, tastes and smells as well as visceral responses. A conversation with myself in rapid seven-word bursts.

```
People without soul, without a bare backbone.
Without: where they see through the glass.
See me waiting, impatience in my eyes.
Impatience, when they are interviewing in here.
Are they good cop, bad cop routine?
Cop this, and one lash for truth.
One way glass, they see me through.
They see what I see, only me.
I smell aftershave through these wall cracks.
Through a nightmare of pounding, interview me.
Of course, I'm a guest, not interviewed.
A crack, the door opens, her face.
Door slams, her face drained, she leaves.
Face it, this is not the time.
Is not the time, the time again?
Time fell apart when she saw me.
When I heard Oh, it's you! Click!
```

I work quickly, not taking the pen from the page, and not stopping until the page is full. When it is, I start playing with what is on it, seeking out two or three-word combinations that strike me as unusual. Unusual in their sounds, their linkages, how they combine, the images they evoke. I read backwards from the end, and on the adjacent page, note down any combinations I deem worthy of attention. Those of special significance find their way into my phrase book, a collection I call upon when a cold, crusty itch needs to be scratched. Often the answer is found in those pages.

In the time between Boulter closing the door on me and her returning to the room, I close my notebook, pocket my pen, and smile at her by way of greeting.

'Boulter.'

'Lazaar.'

'Busy day?'

'Interesting,' she says. She brings a laptop with her and takes the remote from a holder on the side of the screen and clicks it.

'Yours?' she asks, returning to the seat opposite me.

'I've had better.'

'I'm sure.' There is something cagey about her tone. I wonder how long this serve and volley act will last. She studies my face. No emotion.

'I've been instructed to share what facts I know about our wheelie bin murder,' she says, bringing up what appears to be a comprehensive timeline onto the screen. 'I have no idea on what authority McPherson has instructed this. I think it's a big risk to an ongoing investigation and, frankly, I think you should be behind bars.'

'You said that a week ago when you brought your thug down to my office. I don't know what it is you think I've got.'

'Yeah you do – Calvin Bishop. Now, I want to eat, go home and get some rest, so this is what I know.'

Over the following few minutes, I sit thoroughly engaged by the narrative. An incomplete picture of how events of that night might have unfolded begins to form.

'Who have you arrested for this?'

'That I can't tell you. All I can say is we've got a good case for this crime. But, I want to know what you and your mate Bishop have got to do with it.' Her stare is accusatory. I feel a dire need to steer her away from this line of inquiry. Bare-faced lying seems to be the only way forward.

'Come on Boulter, let it go. I told you, the last time I saw Cal Bishop was ten years ago. And you know that my only interest in this is finding the killers, because there's a young woman out there whose life is in danger, who you should be protecting. Tell me who you've got locked up.'

Boulter is an expert interrogator, she knows how to catch the winds of diversion and tack straight back to the point at hand. She's hiding something, and I'm certain that that something will turn out to be important.

'You realise this is a multi-agency inquiry, Lazaar? We've got a murder victim with no identity and a perp who is an illegal, so the feds, Immigration and Border Control are involved. Your best course would be to give the girl up to Immigration.'

'She's an asylum seeker, Kelly. You know that's not illegal. But threatening someone harm — that's definitely against the law. So, your suspect is a refugee?'

'He's an illegal.' Clearly she isn't budging on that.

'You've got evidence?'

'Boxes of it.'

I laugh. 'Boxes? I don't think so. If he's come here seeking asylum, I doubt he's got boxes of anything. How did you get on to him?'

Boulter falters. I've struck a nerve. For all her bluster, she thinks the source is suspect. When she eventually speaks, her tone is lower, more reserved.

'First of all, I've got nothing to suggest this perp is an asylum seeker. So, as far as I'm concerned, he's an illegal who has committed murder. We've got information and concrete evidence that puts this guy squarely in the frame. That evidence has gone to forensics. I don't have full confirmation of his identity yet — I'm told I will have that tomorrow. Until then, I can't tell you anything more about him.'

'I thought McPherson's instructions were pretty clear,' I say, trying to suppress my natural tendency to be patronising.

Her response is quick. Obviously she's thought about it. 'They were. I don't actually *know* who I have in custody. You'll have to wait. Is there anything else?'

Plenty. But not here, where we may be under observation

from behind the glass or recorded. I need a way to get her to meet elsewhere. I play my reserve card.

'I'm curious about your boy, Kelly.'

'My boy?'

'Yeah, Lucas, isn't it?'

Her face reddens. 'What about him?'

'That's who you're meeting tonight, right?' The confusion on her face is clear; I begin gesturing with my hand, in a 'come on' manner, and continue talking, nodding. 'I'm sure you mentioned it ... that little Thai place ... near Canning Bridge, yeah? ... what time?'

'Eight.' One thing that makes Kelly Boulter an exceptional covert officer is her ability to read others and think quickly on her feet.

'Well,' I say, gathering up my notebook, 'I'd better let you get there.'

As I drive, I find myself in need of something soothing. I opt for David Sanborn's classic Double Vision album with Bob James and let my mind wander through the patchwork of memories that were the day. Like Sanborn's floating melodies, synaptic sparks strike in all directions but unlike his, mine mostly fail to connect, severed by an escalating frustration in my quest to discover who the police have in custody for the murder of Ishmail Salim.

My search started early that morning with a visit to Ree Porter at the *Herald*. He is usually well informed about all matters Fremantle, including the police activities — perhaps, especially them. I suspect he gets most of that sort of information through a cosy relationship with Karl Baxter, a senior detective far too long in the same nick at the same pay grade. A lowlife, in my opinion: shop anyone for the backhand of a grub. But, if he is Porter's source, in this case, he must have had nothing to trade.

Although Porter has no idea who was being held, he does have ideas about the upcoming election, and before I manage to excuse myself with all manner of indicators that I have to get to work, he fills me in on his worries that LNP policies on border protection might strike sympathetic chords among voters. He is pessimistic about the outcome. I wonder what those chords might sound like: minor, augmented, sharpened fifth. I suggest the only answer is to keep 'em out, a statement only a moment after emitting it I have to qualify.

'Sorry, I meant keeping the LNP out, not asylum seekers.'

It's a busy morning of lectures and tutorials, into which I fit a quick update about the lie of the academic turf with Donna Gardner. As far as she knows, plans are surging ahead for the reordering of schools and the hiving off of my discipline to the cultural capitalists. A student fails to show for a scheduled meeting, without notice or apology. I spend a few minutes worrying that he is okay but soon take advantage of the time it frees up to cast a few phone calls at shady contacts hoping for further information about the suspected killer. By lunchtime, I am of the opinion that this is either a very high profile suspect, or the whole deal is some sort of elaborate stitch-up. The problem for me is Falullah's safety: she is due to move into the student village this week. If they have the right person in custody, she has little to worry about. But if it isn't the real culprit, her situation is more dangerous than ever.

By two o'clock, I feel I have no choice but to make the call I'd been hoping I wouldn't have to. There are always consequences, and they are devilishly difficult to predict. But so puzzled am I by the secrecy surrounding this arrest and so afraid for Falullah's safety that I'm convinced a hand needs forcing. As a general rule, the police broadcast their successes but they are keeping this one tighter than a clam and for the life of me I cannot work out why. When I put this to McPherson, he says it is the sensitive nature of the investigation that prevents him from making details public.

'All I can say,' he says, 'is that we have a suspect in custody, and enquiries are ongoing.'

It is a meeting McPherson does not enjoy. His instructions arrive via secure communications and he understands they are inviolable. They come from the highest office. They are secret. They cause intense discomfort.

'I've instructions,' he says, the Scots roll of his 'r' like a boulder thundering down a mountain, 'that you are to be given information. Boulter is leading the investigation. She'll be back presently; she'll fi' yeh in on what she knows. From me, personally, y' get bugger-all.'

A line of hairy caterpillars has formed a bridge above his red-rimmed eyes, ready to flay me with daggers. He shows me into an interview room where I feel so exposed I reach for the sanctity of my notebook.

I pull into a full parking lot at Thai Corner and wait for Boulter to arrive.

The owner seats us at the back, next to a rowdy table of blokes who appear to be enjoying a last supper before embarking on another two-week stint on a rig seven hundred kilometres west of Barrow Island. Conversation of the kind I have in mind is impossible. Perhaps it's for the best. Her manner is icy. The food is good, and eventually the oil riggers are washed away on boisterous parting slaps and jibes about how wives and girlfriends will be looked after in their absence. A reasonable silence descends as I sit, comfortably replete, contemplating dessert.

She looks hard at me. 'What do you know about my son?'

'This has nothing to do with your son,' I say. 'I told you there was much more at stake here than a simple murder.'

'Perhaps. But answer my question.'

'Look, all I know is that most parents would do anything to help a child of theirs in trouble. Your boy was in trouble, you did what you could. More, perhaps. It's really not that much of a worry.'

'He grew up without me.' Her voice is now distant, regretful.

'I'm sure that wasn't your fault.'

Boulter sits forward, the dark chiselled slits of her eyes bore right through me. 'You've got no idea Lazaar. How dare you? You come into my place of work, demand I hand over sensitive information, threaten me. And then tell me it's not much of a worry. How fucken' dare you?'

I too sit forward, hoping my outward expression is soft, appealing. I cup my hands before me, the supplicant seeking a final forgiveness. 'I'm not threatening you, Kelly. I had to get us out of your office because I don't know who might have been watching or listening.'

'You're doing it again, Lazaar — compromising an investigation because you have some paranoid righteous bullshit idea that a conspiracy is afoot.' She lifts a hand and points at me. 'I have a murder, a suspect, and enough evidence to put him away. It's a good case. I get a conviction. If there was anything else, I would know. You need to get out of my way.'

'What moral code has bent so far that you would ignore what's going on here?'

'Look, whatever it is, if it is in any way real, it's way above my station and way above my calling to deal with. I have a bust and I have a ticket back to Midland. That's all I want.'

'Do you think it will be that easy?'

'I don't know what you mean.'

I am playing on a hunch that Boulter is not only a good cop, but one who would like to correct the mistakes of the past and let the waters flow unhindered. Time for some bridge building.

'They have you over a barrel, Kelly,' I say, choosing my tone carefully to suit the words that are about to follow. 'Someone is sitting on unprosecuted crimes involving your son, Lucas.' She makes a start, but I lift my hand to hold back her reaction. 'I don't know who it is, it could be McPherson, or someone more senior, but while they're holding those cards, you're going wherever they want you to go. I wouldn't be surprised if Glendinning has something to do with it. Whoever is beholden to him may be the one holding the cards.'

'Jesus.' Tears well behind her eyes. 'So that's how it was done.'

'I'm sorry.'

'I got a *please explain* from Audit Branch today. This explains it.'

Actually, it doesn't, I think. But I decide that that particular truth is best kept where it is. 'We can get you out of this, Kelly. With careful, little steps. We need to find our allies, don't you agree?'

She stares into the distance, eyes moist, a wistful little smile forming. It isn't at global warming levels yet, but the ice is definitely melting.

Chapter Twenty-One

My Old School

Wednesday 28 August — 10 days before the election

I know people who believe teaching is the easy gig you get into when you retire from your real job, or a career pursued by those who can't get into law or medicine. In both cases those people are wrong. There are fewer occupations that are as poorly supported, poorly paid and lonely. Most teachers are honourable, people who care deeply about developing minds, who take time out of their own precious share to ease the burden of a student worried about exams, or console a colleague troubled by the onset of impostor syndrome.

Our school is no different from others in the university or in other universities. We are troubled by the same budget cuts, the same withdrawals of support staff, the same demands that we meet KPIs dreamed up by some consultant who has never taught anything, nor set foot in a university since they earned their undergraduate degree in accounting or business administration. They make us do our own photocopying, attend meetings that have no bearing on students, and suffer the rush from classes of diminishing sizes to the deadlines of grant applications with their ever-increasing form-filling drudgery. I don't know of any other profession that could be so cruel as to force most of its workforce to apply for their own jobs on an annual basis. It can't ever go back to how it was before tensions between academic staff and management were close to boiling point.

Whenever I run into our school manager, Sarah Jollie, I think about that. As I walk out of a tutorial room just before lunch, she stands at the threshold with an arched look of disapproval etched across her brow. 'Two detectives are waiting with a warrant to search your office,' she says.

'What are they expecting to find?' I ask her.

'I didn't ask.'

'Where are they?' My tone is, perhaps, a little too tart. 'I have a lot to do.'

'They're in the small conference room.' Sarah turns to go. A step later, she turns back. 'The Dean expects to see you immediately you're free.'

Of course she does. Police officers turning up to talk to a member of staff is definitely not good optics, as they say in media school.

I enter the conference room expecting to see Boulter and her oversized sidekick. Instead, two men are waiting. They have been served tea and biscuits and are quietly talking when I enter. The older one, judging by appearance, stands. He is bordering on portly, thinning a little on top, but still clearly quite light on his feet. The second man, taller, broader, blonde-haired and blue-eyed, with the kind of smile that issues warnings of charisma, remains in his seat and smiles at me. I place them both in their late thirties.

'I'm Art Lazaar,' I say, 'You fellas are looking for me, I'm told.'

The man standing takes a step forward and extends his hand. 'I'm Jones.' We shake, brief and uncontested. 'This is my partner, Smith.' The man sitting gives a short wave by way of greeting and smiles.

'Right,' I chorus, 'Smith and Jones.'

'That's our names.' Jones is making it clear that I am not the first to make the observation. I wait.

'We're not really looking for *you*, Doctor Lazaar,' Smith says, as he crunches through a dark chocolate Tim Tam. A spray of crumbs showers the table surface. 'We have reason to believe you know where we might find the person we are looking for.'

'Reason to believe,' I say, taking the seat at the head of the table, Karen Carpenter's lovely voice floating mystically above my thoughts. Jones, momentarily nonplussed it seems, looks at me, then his colleague, and then resumes his seat.

Jones wades in. 'We can't be too specific. We're in the middle of a sensitive investigation. I think it best if we take a look round your office, your laptop and your phone. If we have questions after that, then we might all head off into West Perth for an extended chat. How's that sound?'

My insides are churning. I assume that West Perth is a reference to AFP headquarters. That is to say, it is not East Perth, where the WA police is headquartered. I pour myself a glass of water and take a sip, trying to weigh the options before I speak. I give them a jowly, thoughtful nod. 'Well, I am pretty much free. I do have to catch up with my Dean, that's the only pressing matter. I take it you have a warrant that specifies what you're looking for.'

A certain look passes between them. Smith removes a sheet of paper from his zipper satchel and unfolds it in front of him. He makes no effort to share it with me.

'I don't suppose you could each show me some identification that confirms your bona fides,' I say, extracting a pen and notebook, leaning forward, expectantly, on my elbows, holding my pen in both hands as though it has the power to strike down anything before it.

Smith smiles, full teeth, and points at my pen. 'Gonna take notes?'

'A poet is always ready with a pen, Mister Smith.'

'Agent Smith,' he corrects me.

'Really? Talent agent, booking agent, travel agent?'

'He's an agent of the AFP,' Jones intercepts. 'You call him Agent Smith, and you call me Agent Jones.'

'In that case,' I say, pushing my chair back, 'you'd better give me evidence that confirms that, and you'd better present me with a written warrant specifying precisely what it is you are looking for in your intended search of my office and effects.'

Jones raises his hand to show me his warrant card. I reach toward him, indicating that he should pass it to me for inspection.

He smiles and shakes his head. 'Uh-uh. Can't leave my hands I'm afraid. Regulations.' Smith nods, also smiling.

'In that case,' I say, standing, moving to the door and cracking it open, 'you'd best be on your way.' I poke my head through the door and call, 'Sarah, can you get security up here please?'

Smith and Jones are no longer smiling. Jones comes forward and stands a couple of arms lengths distant. Smith lifts himself easily out of his chair, pushes it in and stands behind it.

'This is an official warrant card of the AFP,' Jones snarls into my face, holding a wallet up above his shoulder. I can only see it at a distance; the insignia of the Australian Federal Police is visible, but it is too far away to identify a name, photograph or number. 'It's the only authority I need to arrest you or make a search of your property if I suspect you have links to certain crimes involving people trafficking.'

'Be that as it may, Agent Jones,' my words struggling to sound resolute, 'I can't see the details of your card from this distance, much less record them so I can check that you are in fact who you say you are. As it stands, it would appear you are here on false pretences. Without a proper warrant, you won't be getting access to my rooms and personal effects, and if you wish to arrest me, you will have to demonstrate to the university's security officers that you are exactly who you say you are, with the authority you say you have.'

I stand back from the door. Jones returns his wallet to his pocket, nods across at Smith who makes a show of revealing a concealed firearm beneath his left arm as he pulls his jacket around and buttons it. He walks around the table, stops in front of me and looks at me, cold, smiling.

'Not today, Doctor Lazaar. Lucky for you we are needed elsewhere shortly. But keep an eye out. We'll meet again.'

Donna Gardner is standing at the door flanked by two uniformed security officers as Smith and Jones leave the room. I stand with her in the doorway, watching as they fade into the hallway art. She ushers me back in, follows, shuts the door and sits in the chair I'd recently vacated, indicating that I too should take a seat. I choose one on the window side of the table.

'You realise, Lazaar, that you have just threatened two officers of the Australian Federal Police.' I feel sure there is the hint of glee somewhere in her voice.

'What on earth makes you say that, Donna?'

'They told Sarah they had a warrant to search your office. Why? What are they looking for?'

I meet her eyes, and pause, basking in her rescue. 'It's hard to explain, Donna, but rest assured it has nothing to do with my investigations into the value of my discipline.'

'That assurance makes me more afraid. What did they want?'

'I don't know,' I say, unsure of how much to tell her, 'I doubt very much that they had a warrant. If so, they refused to show it. I'm not even sure they are AFP agents, as they like to call themselves. As to what they wanted — they said they weren't looking for me, but looking for *someone*. They didn't get around to saying who, or how searching my office could help them.'

'I see. You know I will have to bring this to the attention of the VC?'

'Up to you Donna.'

I get out of my seat and leave the room without looking back.

Chapter Twenty-Two

What a Fool Believes

Friday 30 August — 8 days before the election

I am alone in the back of a black BMW as it whisks along Leach Highway, a low murmur rising from below and a fading breath of wind filling the vacuum behind its remarkable aerodynamic form. At the wheel is a dour faced woman. I watch how she sits, erect in her seat, watchful pearl grey eyes taking in the movement of the world as it approaches, passes and recedes at precisely the speed limit of the highway. I get the feeling she misses nothing and will not, when it comes to her place on the road, put a foot wrong. A bluetooth device extends from her ear, her hair cut so that it folds neatly behind to accommodate this necessity of the job. While she drives, she directs a conversation into it: short, brittle sounds with the cut of a northern European accent extending above the aural splendour of the vehicle's sound system.

I have been summoned.

A phone call from Lipschitz's assistant late yesterday instructs me to join him for lunch today. The whole thing strikes me as absurd. Lippers doesn't usually lunch with lower forms of the academy such as me. He reserves his time for those of influence and worth. When I get to the appointed place at the front of the university's main entrance, at the appointed time, he isn't there.

This woman is.

She introduces herself as Lipschitz's driver and guides me to the rear of the vehicle, opens the door and gets me tucked up inside, where for just a moment, I luxuriate in the soft leather and firm lumbar support, and the sweet ambiance of newness and meticulous care. There are few luxuries quite like it.

'We are to go ahead. Lipschitz will join you there,' she says, closing the door on me with just the right amount of *thunk!* and cutting short any opportunity for me to enquire after the location of 'there'.

She sits behind the wheel and asks what I'd like to listen to. I'm feeling the need for some lightness and suggest anything country. She finds Lee Roy Parnell, and, as the car leaves the campus car park, its sound system envelopes me with *On the Road*, the first four bars of solo drums setting up for Lee Roy's classic guitar entry crying a plaintive twist that sucks me right into a story of not knowing where things are headed. I can't help but wonder about the choice, because I feel quite certain she knows precisely where we are heading. Another thing I know for certain, Lipschitz is a man for whom every second matters, a man who knows precisely what it is he's searching for. Again, I get the feeling I've been exposed, and I am drawn to a memory of our first meeting.

Not long after my appointment I am at a Vice Chancellor's Awards night at the Esplanade Hotel in Fremantle — all part of my new assignment to keep an eye out — and, although the chance meeting is unlikely to be an event he recalls, it is cemented in my memory. We are shoulder to shoulder at the urinal and exchange the kind of pleasantries men exchange in those intimate moments. Am I enjoying the evening? Have you got a child collecting an award? Happy with the food? To which I respond yes, no, yes, and launch my own inane line of inquiry with 'You're the VC, right?' He grins and nods as he shakes.

He commands extraordinary presence. His blue suit, mineral in tone, with its delicate shadow stripe lifted by the soft glow of the downlights draws me to the light blue of his eyes. The fit is perfect. Beneath it, a blue spruce shirt, and a skilfully-knotted tie in dusty lilac with a mustard gold stripe dances off the top edge of his belt. His appearance is simultaneously vigorous and chic, with no small hint of the classic man. He packages and zips, washes and studies his hair for a moment in the mirror. Adjusts the smile, gives me a look, nods, and glides from the room.

Few men are made like Lipschitz. He makes you feel known and recognised while in his presence yet you know he has no idea who you are. Nor does he care.

My ruminations on Lipschitz last until we cross Stirling Bridge. The river is bloated with winter rains, choppy and driven like black thoughts. The poet in me is composing, sifting the remnants of memory into something else, something materialising as character, something I can deal with when we reach the end of this journey, unease rising like bile.

The river throws *fishy* at me as I jerk my gaze from it and struggle to place the objects of my thoughts into something that might make sense. Basho's words — *Let not a hair's breadth separate your mind from what you write* — haunt me, remind me that, in the end, the eternal struggle is not with others, but with one's own capacity to rise above the mundane.

'We write,' I say aloud, 'because we resist.'

The driver looks back at me in the rear view mirror. Her bright eyes unsmiling, she dutifully asks what I'd said.

'Nothing,' I reply.

I am met at the front door of Balsamic & Olives by a tall, slender man with a dark complexion. Jet black hair, full and slicked across his forehead in a wave of provincial valour, frames a practised smile. Deep crow's feet that lead to a focus point at the centre of his eyes suggest years of slog.

'Doctor Lazaar.' His greeting positions me as some soul long absent from his village and now returned with the elixir of fortune. I bet he does that with everyone and yet I feel welcome as I follow him to a low table in the lobby. 'You have a few minutes to wait, sir. Can I get you an apéritif?'

I struggle to place the accent. Baltic, I finally decide, but with other languages acquired since. 'Lemon, lime and bitters,' I reply, taking a seat by the window. The deep water belt at the centre of the river appears to have darkened since I crossed the bridge: if that is at all possible. Angry little fountains splash against the bridge pylons leaving swirls of white on the surface just long enough to be swept away before another splash creates a new pattern. I turn and follow the maître d' with my gaze, noting the ease with which he instructs a young waiter and then mounts the steps heading towards what I imagine to be an inner dining area, answering a call on his mobile phone as he goes.

So this is Balsamic & Olives.

I look around, admiring representations of the far corners of the world in the fine art lining the walls. The lighting, subtle and moody, murmur haven of the rich and powerful. Plush seats in muted urban tints speak to the virginal white of the tablecloths, and the reflected pin lights of the silverware draw my eye to the meticulous detail of the settings.

I can see why Lipschitz picked this place. It oozes power. Lipschitz likes people to see his power. To feel it. That's what it was that night way back then, in the men's room — power, not presence. He needs to know that I know where the power is. Why?

My drink arrives. I scoop it from its coaster, rattle the ice with the stirrer — an olive twig, no less — and stand to gaze out the window as a sudden squall squeezes its way out of the south-western sky. The light falls as mountains of green and black thunderheads paste Fremantle into an apparition and swallow the cranes over the harbour. In seconds the chemical grey murk engulfs the limestone cliff across the water and the old harbourmaster's control tower that sits on top. A sky tsunami rolls across the river, venting a blast of rain and hail against the window with such ferocity that I reel back involuntarily, almost falling into the arms of one of the richest people in the state.

'Doctor Lazaar?'

I'm not sure if it is a question of recognition or surprise. I look stupidly at the outstretched hand before recovering something of a sensible demeanour and grasp it to shake.

'Roger Lamord,' he says. His grip firm, his hand warm and dry to the touch. 'Are you okay?'

'Yes,' I reply, pausing to reflect on what had just happened. 'The weather caught me by surprise.'

If anything, the wind has intensified and the rain drives from the sky in horizontal tracer streams. A boat tears from its moorings downriver and pitches and bucks its way into the jetty before us. The wind snatches its listing hulk and tosses it across the boardwalk leaving it high, but not dry, on the footpath. I've never seen anything like it.

Lamord smiles. 'Yes, it can do that here sometimes. Lipschitz has been held up — he won't be joining us after all.'

'Us?' I feel completely on my back foot.

'Yes. Actually, it was me who wanted to have lunch with you.' He pauses and looks back into the dining area. 'Come, let's go up — leave your drink, Milorad will see to it.'

When we are sat, I think I might try to recover some of the initiative. I admit to feeling a little flighty, unsure if it is the suddenness of the storm, or the fact that I am alone with a man I have always considered a sociopath with a dangerous combination of money and power. He is unnaturally smooth-shaven and his fine gold spectacles almost lack lustre next to his skin. I wonder whether money alone gets teeth so even and polished.

'Mister Lamord, why would you want to have lunch with me?'

The smile widens, but it doesn't reach his eyes. 'Roger, please. Can I call you Art?'

'That's my name,' I say, and a vision of Smith and Jones from the day before pops into my head.

'Wally Lipschitz tells me you have a talent for finding missing things. How did he put it? Yes, that you investigate lost theories.'

'Lippers told you that?' I am fast losing any grip I might have had on initiative.

'He did. In fact, he said you were quite good at it.'

Drinks arrive before I can answer, along with a consommé, its aroma strong and unusual. I proffer a smile and hold my counsel.

'You see,' Lamord says, taking up his napkin and spoon, advancing on his soup with reserved relish, 'a colleague of mine has had something taken. He'd like it restored.'

'A colleague?' The taste is strong, fiery. It strikes the back of the palate and remains long after the swallow.

He smiles. I'm not sure if it was at my reaction to the food, or to carry the conversation forward. 'In my position, I curry a lot of favours? People owe me. I owe them. I'm sure you're familiar with the currency.'

I nod and take another draught of the soup. This time the taste is a little less of a shock. It contains something I feel needs to be made more definite. I take another spoonful, sure that I will identify the mystery flavour, but the closer I get, the further away its label drifts. It makes me think of the wisps of story that advance from the fog of the mind but never quite materialise.

'Are you enjoying the soup?'

'Very much. I can't quite place the flavour.'

Roger Lamord tells me the story of how he came to realise his dream of building a restaurant that serves the finest cuisines from all over the world. Flights arrive every day carrying fresh ingredients from wherever specialities of the day were originally mastered. Culina mundi, while perfectly describing the scope of the menu, simply does not meet the poetry of the experience. I am supping on a soup of cassava spiced with guasca and finely chopped coca leaf, all of which, he informs me, was freshly harvested not more than two days ago in the jungles of Llanos and Amazonas. Cassava is among the seven deadliest foods in the world — up there with fugu. Had I been to Colombia, he asks. No, I had not. He likes the Colombians, he says. They *survive*. The Amazonas region is home to the most exotic and the most dangerous foods, and potent drinks. A simple mistake in preparing the soup can result in a painful death. By the time my empty bowl is whisked away, my face is flushed and my head lighter than a fistful of fairy floss.

A silence falls between us, our table like a chess board waiting on a contest. A plate is placed before me. I study it. The main feature appears to be the carcasses of two small frogs, served on steaming tubers with pink surfaces and yellow centres, and a bed of green leaves bathed in a tangy sauce. I remove a frog leg and place it in my mouth. It has a creamy surface texture with delicate bones that crunch as I bite into it and draw the succulent meat away. The flavours are extraordinary.

Our conversation veers into political waters. Lamord takes me on a journey of his vision of a world embracing the glorious benefits of the free market. He points to my plate.

'Like it?' He cannot restrain his delight. 'You wouldn't get that without successful enterprise creating new things, fresh innovation. That's how we take this country into the twenty-first century. Reduced regulation, freedom of speech — a strong economy promoting our competitive position in the world. Successful enterprise brings stability, strong leadership.'

Having disposed of one of the little frogs, I wipe my lips and laugh.

'If I may, Roger, while delicious, this meal doesn't appear to be novel. A recipe pilfered from some exotic culture that doesn't have the means to resist isn't innovation. What's new is that you've brought it here and elevated its value well beyond the peasantry where it originates. You can call that innovation if you like, but it's hardly new.'

Lamord leans forward. 'The soup you had earlier' — I nod — 'a speciality by the Colombian natives. The little burn at the back of the palate comes from fresh coca leaves. These juvenile bullfrogs secrete a poison so potent, the natives use it to tip their hunting arrows. If the chef is not careful in skinning them, you could die. Hell, he could die. And the eyes from that tuber contain a potent neurotoxin. You're eating that today because you're my guest. And because my substantial business interests enable it. Because I have planes ferrying ingredients to us, right here, fresh, every day.'

I shake my head, dismissive. My face is warm, my heart racing. Bugger it, in for a penny, in for a pound. 'Like most entrepreneurs, you profit most from the tried and true. That's why you're called conservatives. You thrive where you can take something that's already proved, like power grids or student loans. If it weren't for governments raising taxes to bankroll ideas over the years, we'd still be in the dark ages. Pinching stuff isn't innovation, Roger, it's appropriation.'

Lamord dismisses my response. 'People like you don't get it. That's why you'll never amount to anything. Look, government has no business running organisations that can function more efficiently as business.'

I laugh. 'More efficiently? Let's look at what happens when public organisations get privatised. They get gutted, the money that was being put to public good, employing people, delivering real services, ends up in the hands of shareholders, individuals, where it does no more than increase the wealth of people like you, Roger. How many of your businesses have reaped great benefit from exactly that? You feed prisoners — privatised; asylum seekers — privatised; clean government offices — privatised. Tell me, are you paying everyone employed in those businesses proper and correct wages? My bet is that's where more efficiency comes from.'

I return to my plate to mop up the remains of the sauce, sip my lemon, lime and bitters, and allow my eyes to meet his. His face hardens. I relax my tone and shift the focus of the conversation.

'Those holes in the ground, those farmlands, those logged forests are put there by the taxes paid by our forefathers — maybe not yours but certainly mine. Our royalties are traded out for false promises of downstream processing by a mining industry that sucks on the public teat, returns fuck-all in taxes, employs bugger-all people, and expatriates our money to offshore havens and foreign homelands, where — guess what? — it still pays bugger-all tax. The banks you use to launder your money, the roads you drive your trucks on to deliver your food to the mining companies, where you top up your tanks tax-free were built by our taxes, by the community. So don't give me that bullshit about free enterprise being the creator of innovation.'

Lamord stares at me. I feel suddenly small. 'People want jobs, Lazaar. People want our young people to have jobs, not waste their time at universities on educations that don't lead to anything. They want jobs in mining, construction, food, agribusiness. Jobs that earn good incomes, jobs that build a country.' He pauses, shakes his head, and lets out a short brittle chuckle that sounds like a cockatoo squawk. 'Creative writing. What's the point of that? Universities need to leave arts to the artists and focus on things that matter in the real world. It's high time their leeching off the public purse came to an end. It's a bad business model, a swamp that should be drained.'

I look around the room, making a point of stopping my gaze occasionally, resting on an exquisite piece of art. 'The real world?

Like your art collection?'

He thought I was complimenting him on his taste. 'Yes. Great works from all over the world. Worth around two and half billion now.' His smugness rubbed like chili in my eyes.

'Curate it yourself?'

'No, I have a curator on staff. She does a good job. We lend pieces to museums and galleries.'

I sip my drink, nod my approval. 'Educated in a university? A fine arts degree? And who tots up the two and half billion for you? An accountant? Perhaps you have lawyers drawing up contracts of purchase, or leases? Do you go to the theatre? Oh, wait, you're on the board of the Perth Theatre Trust.'

Lamord sets his knife and fork down and removes his napkin. Our plates are whisked away and coffee arrives. 'Fascinating as this has been, Art, I'd like to know how you go about finding these lost theories your reputation boasts of.'

'I'm sure you know how, Roger. You seem to have found a few things yourself, and you've certainly got some lost theories there — enough, I imagine, to understand the methods.'

He laughs. 'Oh really? What have I found?'

'Several billion dollars, for one thing. You've found ways to set up a foundation or two to avoid paying taxes, ways to get around paying workers proper wages, maybe even ways to avoid their protection, keep them safe — keep them alive. Truth is, I can't help you.'

'But you don't know what my colleague wants found.'

'Your colleague?' I try my hardest to mimic an incredulous look. 'Even if I could help, what you need to find, deep down, can't be found.'

Lamord pauses, sits back in his seat and furrows his brow. 'Do you know a journalist by the name of Calvin Bishop?'

My coffee halts midway between the table and my mouth. 'Knew him. I worked with him in Kalgoorlie many years ago. But he's been dead for ten years.'

Lamord leans forward and spreads both hands out on the table, doing his best to look down on my eyes. 'What kind of fool do you think I am?' He fans his hands across the table in front of him: a smoothing action. 'Three weeks ago Bishop caused an explosion in Fremantle that killed a man who worked for me. He hid something from a colleague. You know what — or rather, who — and you need to work your magic, and effect her return.'

I do my best to impersonate confused. 'I have no idea what you're talking about. Cal Bishop died ten years ago. Perhaps your man ... Dosek, right?' — his eyes flicker — 'was chasing a ghost.'

'It was no ghost.'

'Okay, then. Can I tell you what I think?' A nod. 'A young homeless man died in that explosion, Roger. Your man had done a deal with this homeless kid, a deal one or both intended to renege on. Dosek was sent after the kid and it was, in fact, he who caused the explosion. At least, as far as I understand, that's the official version.'

The colour drains from Lamord's face. 'Bullshit! You might have a gift for shifting facts around, Lazaar, but I know Bishop was there. That's a fact even you can't fuck with.'

I smile. 'Whatever you think happened in that tunnel, the official version will be that the explosion happened because of a drug deal that went wrong between your man and the homeless kid. He was cooking meth and it went off.' I pause and soften my tone. 'Of course Dosek did have a history of depression and amphetamine use and that will be a substantial part of the story. Shit, even you admitted as much with the opening of your new foundation, which, by the way, I think is admirable. Far too many vets are denied proper support, especially mental health care. All that aside, while your noble gesture might be the only thing that can connect you with Dosek, we know — you and I — that there's much more.'

We lock eyes across the narrow space of the table. 'There are other things I know, Roger. shall I tell you?'

'I'm listening.'

'Your colleague — Yusuf?' A brief light of recognition flares in his eyes. 'Real name, Tuah Johari, brother-in-law of the Malaysian Prime Minister's wife. Enjoys diplomatic recognition in Australia and the title of Tan Sri at home, where he gets called a big shot. Rich. Powerful. Connected. A bit like you, Roger. Yusuf runs sham immigration schemes across the region, he's been doing it for years. He's a trafficker with a penchant for enslaving people and selling their labour.

'A fortnight before the explosion, a young man was murdered and dumped in a wheelie bin in Hamilton Hill. Last week, the police arrested another young man as a suspect for that murder. Both men had connections to Yusuf. The one they've arrested didn't commit that murder — couldn't have done it — yet the Fremantle detectives seem to think it's a slam dunk. They have evidence: the murder weapon, blood, an incriminating photograph. Trouble is, this was a professional job; efficient, cold, calculated. Word is the victim was about to blow the lid on Yusuf's operation so he had to be stopped and someone else has to be put in the frame.

'The problem I have, Roger, and this is the real worry, I can't for the life of me understand why you would be mixed up with the likes of Yusuf. Unless, of course, he's a source of cheap labour. Or dodgy money.'

Lamord laughs. 'Sounds like a hell of a book Lazaar. A work of fiction of course.'

I laugh along with him, then look at my watch as a precursor to a parting gesture. 'True, my profession does allow me some latitudes with the facts, Roger. Perhaps your maître d' would call me a taxi back to the university.'

'Of course.' He signals a waiter, issues an instruction. We sit in silence for a few minutes, and I gaze out the window. The storm has subsided, although it's still dark and rain falls steadily. A minute later, the waiter returns and whispers in Lamord's ear.

'There's a car waiting downstairs,' he says. 'Take the lift to the lower basement level. It'll pick you up by the lift.'

We rise from our seats together, and he extends his hand. I take it and his grip firms up on contact. 'You have twenty-four hours, Doctor Lazaar. The package and Bishop. After that, your meals may not be so pleasant.'

Chapter Twenty-Three
Black Water

The lift dings its arrival. I step out into a gloomy underground car park and turn left towards an approaching car.

'Lazaar.'

The call comes from behind and I wheel around. The blow to my kidney has such force that I crumple, gasping for breath, fighting against rising bile as I border on unconsciousness. Pin lights dazzle before my eyes. Rough hands force me face down, wrench my arms behind my back, loop and tighten bindings around my wrists. The hood thrust over my face stinks of vomit. I kick, but another blow in the small of my back sends a knife of pain through my spine, paralysing my legs. I feel myself hauled from the ground, dumped into the back of a vehicle and pressure applied to my neck. I slide into darkness.

I hold and hold, and my lungs heave as I fight against the involuntary actions of breathing. The surface is near, just above and I strike out with my legs, but it does no good. I am anchored below the surface. Black water keeps falling. Pressure from within increases as I fight back the urge to breathe in.

A momentary vision of the seven-year-old me pelting down the gravel hill on my twenty-six inch bike flashes into my mind, the snake sliding across my path, too slow to avoid the inevitable. I run over it and it gets caught up in the spokes of my rear wheel. I ditch the bike, narrowly avoid the needle-fine fangs as they snap at my bare legs, covered in gravel rash. I fall headlong into a twelve-year-old me rooted to the rocks at the Cape Leeuwin lighthouse, a wild ocean foaming spume behind me as a car veers from above, crashing through the car park barrier, thundering straight at me, and my quick-thinking dad throwing me aside as the front wheel crushes his foot into the rocks. Another lash for the surface. Again, I am restrained. Again, I fight the urge to breathe. The crushing force from within my lungs burns as a swift out-of-control slide becomes a roll and tumble, turning slow motion as the vehicle's steering wheel is wrenched from my eighteen-year-old hands, my head banging with a metallic thud against the side bulkhead and the huge Hammond organ in the back slides towards me, pushing into the twenty-seven-year-old me, drunk, sliding down a snow covered mountain towards a car park, unable to avoid the child in a toboggan dragged by his parents up the hill. One more push toward the surface. A desperate attempt. Then a breakthrough.

A light so bright the glare burns my eyes. I squeeze them tight and dare take a breath. My lungs heave. I pant. Water droplets spray into my airway, producing a coughing fit, and another bout of panting and panic. I open my eyes but immediately squeeze them shut against the light. As I do so, my head is wrenched back, compressing the vertebrae in my neck to crushing point. Some device anchors my head in this position, my legs trapped beneath me, the stretch between the two painful and uncomfortable, the rasp of my breath loud in my ears.

And then, a voice.

'Open your eyes, Doctor Lazaar.'

It is a gentle-sounding voice. Old. A nasal Italian lilt makes it strangely comforting. I try to comply, but the searing pain of the light is too much. A hollow whack and a shattering pain erupts from my side.

'He said open your eyes.' This voice is not kind. It has a thick Italian bearing to it. Mechanical. Thuggish.

I open my eyes to slits, trying to comply with the instruction, while reducing the pain of the glare.

'It seems, Doctor Lazaar,' — the kind voice again — 'that you are in possession of certain knowledge.'

I try a grin, although I'm certain no humour is visible. 'I'm in possession of quite a lot of knowledge, actually,' I manage.

'Oh aye? Smartarse.' This voice is behind me. It is different. It has a Celtic lilt. 'What he means is quite specific knowledge, Doctor Lazaar. Where is Calvin Bishop?'

'He's dead. Died ten years ag—'

Another hollow whack sounds just before the pain strikes. The blow lands immediately below my right ribs, but the pain shoots round my gut and lodges in my bowels. It's all I can do to prevent an involuntary evacuation.

'Wrong answer, Doctor Lazaar.' The high-pitched Italian again.

My voice is feeble and my eyes are drowning in tears. 'I haven't seen him because he's de—'

This blow is from the other direction and digs a pit in my solar plexus so deep I think my spine has torn. An undertow of bile floods my mouth, but I can't turn my head, or pitch forward to get rid of it so, again, I hold my breath. This time I can no longer hold back. The soft spluttering motion spreads through my trousers in putrid liquid form.

'Oh Jay-sus!' the Irish voice cries. 'What the hell is that?'

A blow rains down on my right hand and the sound of bones crunching reaches my ears. Strange though, there is no pain.

'All right, Doctor Lazaar. Ye'll know the answer to this one.' The

Irish voice, now very close to my left ear. 'The girl. Where is the girl?'

'Wha ... irl?'

'See now, we know yeh know.' A faint click and then the sound of my voice. *Come on Boulter, let it go. I told you, the last time I saw Cal Bishop was ten years ago. But there's a young woman out there whose life is in danger, who you should be protecting.*

Amid the blur of lingering unconsciousness and the waves of pain wracking my body, I have to ask myself who I am in the room with, and how they had come by this conversation. I can't place it, but obviously it's a conversation with Boulter. Has she sold me out?

'I don't know where she is,' I say slowly, trying to form words and avoid drowning in my own vomit. 'The police—'

The next blow lands just below my heart. I have time enough to register its impact, but not enough for any pain.

Chapter Twenty-Four
Playing to Win

Sunday 1 September — 6 days before the election

The western face of the hills across the river from Roger Lamord's Swan Valley mansion sat deep in morning shadow as the sun's early rays split the trees on the ridge into ghostly silhouettes like back-lit ramparts. The morning air on his rear porch felt crisp and moist on his cheeks as remnants of an overnight dew floated in a spectral mist above the river, glistening on the new buds bursting on vines that ran in parallel rows down the slope. The sky above rendered blue and cloudless. A perfect morning for the opening of spring.

Lamord's acreage spread on both sides of his house down a gentle slope to Swan Street, continuing in two lots to the river, and then across the river right through to Great Northern Highway. Forty-four hectares in total, with just under thirty in vines. His porch offered a view of practically all of it. On the other side of the river, in the centre of the panorama, sat the old Lucchessi homestead surrounded by newly tended vines, an image of perennial decay amidst new growth, kept as a reminder of Alfonso's great generosity toward a young Roger on the run from a brutal school, and also as a symbol of the finality of the family's financial destruction at his whim. It served as the epitome of his power, his tenacity, patience, and utter contempt for those who wronged him.

The weekend papers sat on a small table, *The Telegraph* on top with its full-page portrait of LOTO and a great tick alongside indicating the preferred choice of the free press in next Saturday's poll. A great picture, a great message. Only five per cent of voters had yet to make a choice of where their vote would go. The fact that seventy-one per cent of that five per cent were women mattered not at all. A woman had all but destroyed our functioning democracy, and that would be put right one week from now in a trouncing the left had never before experienced. The party of waste and open doors would feel the wrath of the people.

He had just hung up from a call with Bob Conroy, the Liberal Party national director, an arrogant, lop-sided apparatchik who claimed ownership of everything that passed through the party lines. Including it seems, his own media analyst.

'What's the name of that media analyst you got working with you?' The undertone suggested he knew the answer. His way of making sure people answered to him.

'Samantha Codlin, Bob.'

'Yes, Samantha, right. A mate of runs a think tank in the UK and he's looking for someone with her sort of skills. Okay if I put her name forward?'

Couldn't stop you if I tried, you smug prick. 'Of course, Bob. She's done a fantastic job. But there's a whole team over here working on this, and that needs proper recognition.'

'Noah will get a cabinet spot. Maybe junior to start with—'

'He's a very experienced member, Bob.'

'Yes, but only in a West Australian context, Roger. Leadership's a bigger game. You understand?'

Oh yes, I understand. But not for long, my friend. Old money eventually becomes tired money. 'Yes, of course Bob. And Superintendent Glendinning?'

'Oh absolutely, Roger. Border protection will be headed up by a military figure. We all think that's necessary, given the circumstances, but Max will come in at a very senior level. He's got a great track record and knows the field better than most. But let's get next weekend over first, shall we? We still have to win.'

'The only way we play, Bob.' Lamord had made Little River Band's song his anthem, and he was damned if the East was to get all the glory. I'll make my move when you bastards least expect it, he thought. You've got no idea of how little you know.

'Excellent, Roger. Keep me posted.'

The silence left a rancid taste in Lamord's mouth and, were it not for the ringing of the gate alarm, he would have beelined for the bathroom and a mouthful of Listerine.

The driveway to the house led from West Swan Road and past a lake he'd created by damming a section of Henley Brook. It was lined with maple trees, their fallen leaves rotting around the roots. Perfectly manicured grass rolled up the slopes into garden beds about to burst in springtime renewal. Renewal. That's exactly what this day is about. He clicked an app on his phone and Max Glendinning's face through his car window appeared. He hit the open button. The double gates began separating, swinging silently and smoothly open, inward, a welcoming gesture.

It wasn't Glendinning's first breakfast visit to the vineyard. He was dressed in jeans and a black linen shirt over which a loose-fitting, fig-leaf green, all-weather jacket hung open. He was fit and moved easily from his car towards his host, an action that gave Lamord a momentary pang of envy. They went through the house to the rear porch, where the breakfast table was set on a heavy jarrah sideboard, attended by a portly Italian woman of indeterminate age who muttered in her mother tongue as she poured juices and coffee, signalling that the two men should take their seats.

'Damn, I love this view,' Glendinning said. 'It's like being in another country.'

Lamord looked at his guest, smiled. He pointed. 'That section is a new planting of Merlot, but just down the bottom there we have a section of Tinta del Pais — there's a patch of soil there closer to the water table — it's a grape that loves a damp root and a full rising sun. It's perfect. Comes off the harvest about two weeks earlier than the other black fruit, full of sugar and an aftertaste that lingers like a woman in your beard.' He smiled and poured a sparkling rosé for each of them. 'I think I'll call it Le Tempérament.'

They laughed and toasted the morning and the anticipation of the following weekend's celebrations. He hit play on his music player and John Farnham's voice surrounded them, reminding both men of the stakes in the game when you miss the moment. Hot pastries arrived and Glendinning, singing badly off key, attacked the condiments with the relish of a stockbroker at a merger. As the song faded, Lamord grew serious. A man whose mind was made up.

'Sean Dower is a liability.' Glendinning looked up, attentive. Lamord continued, 'He's out of control. Reckless. Making mistakes.'

And just like that, the meeting was all business.

'How, exactly?'

'There've been a number of things, but this time...' His gesture was a wiping motion, clearing waste.

'What's going on with him?'

'Can't really say. Dosek's death affected him badly. Whatever it is, we have to deal with it. Things are too close — we can't afford any more cock-ups.'

'The girl?'

Lamord shrugged.

After a moment's thought Glendinning continued. 'I thought you were sorting that out. Did you get anything from Lazaar?'

Lamord shook his head. 'Wanker. Full of shit. When he realised what he was eating, I thought he was about to cave' — he gave a short laugh — 'his face was like chalk. But it turned out he knows things.'

'Like what?'

'Yusuf for starters — his name, his origins, his connections. And then he said the official line on the explosion that killed Dosek was that it was an accidental death and most likely due to some drug deal gone wrong.'

'I heard about that.'

'Well perhaps you can explain to me, Max, exactly how that can be.'

'I told you Roger, this guy moves like there are no walls.'

'Yes, well, thanks to Sean Dower and a couple of Enzo's thugs, his movements might have come to an abrupt end.'

Glendinning managed to say, 'Jesus! What's happened?'

Chapter Twenty-Five

Can't Stop The Feeling

It had been nine minutes past five on Saturday morning when Boulter closed the door on her Lockhart Street home. She timed every morning run. The previous night's storm had dispatched a branch from one of those gum trees favoured by turn-of-the-century property developers for their quick growth and dropped it across her front boundary. It took part of a native hedge with it and blocked half the driveway. Even in the half dark she could see it would need professional removal. But as she went to walk around, a lump lying next to it in the shadows of the streetlights caught her eye. She played the torchlight from her mobile phone on the shape and saw Art Lazaar's battered and unconscious form, his face glistening with a strange, silvery purple from rain-soaked, drying blood in the dappled glow of street lamps.

Boulter reacted quickly and professionally. Within twenty minutes a team from Kensington Station and an ambulance were both on the scene. The paramedics performed a quick but thorough examination and left within minutes for the emergency ward, leaving Boulter to provide as many details as she could to the Kensington police. She knew they would log the details on the central records system as a possible assault and dump. She held back details on anything that would reveal her personal relationship with the victim.

As soon as the local police had left the scene, Boulter called McPherson. He insisted she let the locals handle the matter, have her day off and meet him the following day — Sunday afternoon — to ward off any negative impacts of an Ethics and Standards investigation. It was standard protocol: all events in which a police officer has some direct involvement are investigated for Ethics and Standards clearance. She had skyped McPherson from her laptop, using his personal mobile number, keeping the conversation to bare essentials. The last thing she said was that when she left the office Friday evening, she'd left a mess in the interview room and it might be an idea to get the cleaners in. By the time she was seated in McPherson's office Sunday afternoon, the entire two floors had been swept by the tech team and a haul of listening devices and miniature cameras found.

McPherson gestured toward the printed stack of images left behind by the techs. 'What made you suspect this?'

'Well, you know how it goes, sir — just can't stop the feeling. Lazaar was paranoid about hidden devices when he was here. And whoever dumped him at my place is sending me a message. It's creepy, like whoever it is can get close. Really close. When was the last tech sweep?'

'It's done quarterly — not that long ago — July.'

'Nothing found?'

'Nothing. To my knowledge this is the first time ever.'

'How many?'

'Three devices in my office, two in yours, three in each of the interview rooms and four in the situation room. More downstairs.'

Boulter picked up a printout and studied it. 'This is a door handle casing.'

'Yep. Door handles, light switches, desk caddies... This shit is super-tech, lassie. These little cameras and microphones are sensory activated, they use bugger-all power, batteries last forever' — shuffling through the paper — 'this little beauty is a 4G wi-fi router mounted in an exterior camera housing. All these devices feed this and off it goes into the ether, encrypted, rerouted, impossible to trace.'

'Is it someone on the inside?'

'You tell me. I have to go to cybercrimes. My guess is they'll take it to the feds or ASIO.'

'Can we keep it in-house?'

'Jesus Boulter, what are ye' suggestin'?'

'I'm suggesting we sit on it and work our cases. Don't let anyone else know, not even others in here. Can you ask the techs not to report it?'

'Christ! Division'll have my nuts just for asking.'

'All right, how long do you think you can sit on it? Can it wait until I get the forensics back on Lazaar?'

McPherson shifted in his seat and reached into his bottom drawer for a bottle and two glasses. 'What forensics would they be?' He slurped two generous shots. 'I thought I was pretty clear — you were supposed to have yesterday off. You can't work this. Ethics will have a field day with it.'

Boulter took a lengthy sip at the liquor and let its heat flood her mouth.

'You were perfectly clear. But we don't know what we're dealing with. I went to the hospital, recovered his clothes, took some swabs from his injuries and beneath his nails, and got them into the lab. I'm afraid I used your name and probably one or two of your favours. I'm hoping to get results tomorrow.'

McPherson drained his glass, topped it up and said, 'Okay, would you like to walk me through the whole thing?'

Boulter handed over two typed sheets of paper, stapled together. 'The chronology is all in here, sir.'

'All the same, Boulter, I want to hear it.'

Over the course of the next hour, Boulter narrated the events of her actions following the discovery of the unconscious Lazaar in her front yard the previous morning. When McPherson was satisfied that her actions would stand the scrutiny of Ethics and Standards, the meeting came to an end.

As she left the office, the sun had sunk behind the city buildings throwing long shadows across the street to the car park. A voice called to her from a doorway.

'Detective.'

Boulter turned towards the voice and found Spider standing in darkness.

'Spider, what is it?'

'I need to talk to you.'

'Would you like to come over to my office.'

'No. Not there. Your car?'

Boulter led the boy to her car. Something had spooked him. 'What's up?'

'Them men that night of the explosion, in the black four-wheel drive...' Spider faltered into silence as he drew a scrap of paper from a pocket.

'What about them?' Boulter prompted.

'They're looking for us, you know, us bruvvers, 'cos of what we might of seen that night.'

'What you might have seen?'

'Yeah, like their faces and some girl, but I dunno anythink about that.'

'Did you?'

'What?'

'See their faces?'

'Not really ... well yeah, there were, like, two uvver guys in the car — could of bin free — I saw the driver 'cos he got out to watch Tor go in. Had really hard eyes, like steel. I seen 'im again last night wiv a dog lookin' for our cribs, me an' my bruvvers, like. Man, I'm shit scared, these are fucken' heavy people.' He thrust the piece of paper at Boulter. 'This is the number plate, black Range Rover.'

Boulter took the paper and read the letters scrawled in no better than an infant's hand. SECS06.

'Thanks for this Spider, it's really helpful. What sort of dog?'

'It's a fucken German Shepherd, a big fucker.'

'Have you seen them today?'

'Nah. I been hidin' here till I saw you. I got a safe spot though — they'll never find me.'

'Okay. Would you prefer if I took you somewhere safe for tonight?'

Spider grinned. 'What a jail cell? Nah, I'll be fine.'

'It wasn't exactly what I had in mind, but if you're sure.' Boulter handed Spider a twenty dollar note. 'Look after yourself. I'm going back into the office to run this plate.'

'Yeah, but that's not all.'

'What?'

'There's some Italian guys lookin' for Hunter. They ain't with the uvvers, these are gangsters.'

Boulter looked away, past the markets towards the oval. 'Yes, well, we're all looking for Hunter, Spider.'

The vehicle was one of a fleet registered to a security company called SECSUR, leased from Barbagello Motors about nine months earlier. Boulter called the company's head office in Burswood only to get a recorded message about office hours being 8 am to 6 pm Monday to Friday. No after-hours number. She ran a corporate check on the company through ASIC and Police databases and read through the company website for any useful information. SECSUR was one of the sprawling SANCO group of companies. It held contracts with the federal and several state governments to provide security services to prisons and detention centres. It was frequently called upon to provide security for international officials visiting the country, government ministers and other specialist travel requirements by important government and corporate luminaries. The managing director was listed as Sean Dower. Boulter left notes on her desktop in preparation for a follow up the next morning. She left a written instruction on Robinson's desk to obtain a complete corporate workup on the group first thing.

She went home via the hospital and was told that Lazaar was conscious and no longer in intensive care, but it was the doctor she'd come to see. He was a young African man, tall and graceful in his movements, with a wide smile that revealed white, even teeth. Concern lines showed on his forehead as he examined the details on the screen in front of him.

'The injuries are consistent with a severe beating,' he said. 'Three cracked ribs, two broken fingers, a severely bruised kneecap, some injury to his spleen and a whole company of cuts and bruises to his face and upper torso.' He was thoughtful for a moment as he re-read the notes. 'It seems that he was tied to a chair with his arms pulled back behind him.' He tapped an image on the screen with a perfectly manicured fingernail. 'This, though, this points to something much more serious.'

Boulter looked at the notes. Her years in the navy medical corps paid off. 'Injury to the upper spine and soft tissue at the front of the neck. Is this a whiplash?'

'Not quite. It appears that Doctor Lazaar had his head pulled back to a point where these upper vertebrae were severely compressed, and the front tissue torn. That's considerable force. The initial examination showed an abrasion across his forehead — something like a carpet burn. I think a strap of some synthetic material was used to keep his head in that position.'

'Jesus!' The doctor gave Boulter a hard look of disapproval. 'Waterboarding?' She had come across similar abrasions before. An image floated on the edge of her consciousness.

His eyes darkened and his voice dropped in pitch. 'I'm afraid so. This method opens the throat completely and restricts movement to allow any clearing of water. It's remarkable he didn't drown.'

'If you don't mind me asking, Doctor, have you seen this before?'

'In my country, in the Sudan, this method of tying the head back is a favourite torture practice of special forces units. It is meticulous and planned. They took their time.'

Boulter headed home. Twenty minutes later she sat on a stool at her kitchen bench, her mood sombre. Joni Mitchell's *Big Yellow Taxi* on the stereo reminded her of just what people can take away. She drained a glass of red wine and refilled it. She had no easy explanation for what she'd learnt at the hospital. Nor for what she deduced from it. What had Lazaar stumbled upon?

198

Chapter Twenty-Six

I Can See Clearly

Monday 2 September — 5 days before the election

Boulter headed into crisp morning air, stretching each stride a little more than the one before as she wound up to optimum pace. The river was still, a fog rose around small craft moored along the shoreline, their reflections mirrored like acrylic ghosts in the glassy surface. As she pounded the footpath along Bateman's Bay, a small flock of pelicans emerged from the rushes, flapping their enormous wings as they pushed out into the river. Miniature waves slurped up against the resting hulls.

Boulter's rhythm set her mind to work like the gears of a clock, ticking over with each footstep, winding the complexities of her cases into a tight coil and then releasing the energy in a smooth fluid motion. She worked each problem with artistic relish, anticipating the pleasure of deduction. She posed imaginary possibilities that the evidence might support, parking viable solutions in a crevice of her mind for later retrieval, while discarding those without potential into the neurostatic mix for another day. By the time she reached home, she had shaved fifty-four seconds off her personal best, and a plan for the day was forming like white, wispy clouds in a clear sky.

She showered before working over a breakfast of cereal with yogurt, Arabic black coffee and a commercially packaged combination fruit juice, scribbling on loose leaves of photocopy paper with a 2B pencil, and Jimmy Cliff playing on her stereo in the background, his words finding sympathy with the day outside. Several sheets later, her bowl pushed aside, and her coffee cup drained, she reviewed her summary. *Chase up the forensics, a phone call, emails, then a trip to SECSUR in time for the opening of their office, seize the vehicle; check on Lazaar and follow up the wheelie bin victim's pathology.* At the bottom of the page, two words *THE GIRL*?

The police forensics team uses several science labs. Active investigations are managed through the Forensics Centre at Midland, usually under a triage practice to deal with demand and urgency. It was nigh-on impossible to game the triage system, and little could be achieved by trying. In a general investigation, forensics reports were usually loaded onto the IIS, flagging the investigating officers who could then download the reports.

For the examination of Lazaar's clothing, she bypassed the Forensics Centre and went directly to the man who ran the forensics sciences program at Curtin University, Professor Iain Methuen, another Scot and, coincidentally or not, a close friend of McPherson. She traded on this friendship, an action likely to darken the spreading blots in her copybook.

For the evidence she'd received from Smith and Jones, Boulter had taken the step to request a limited distribution of the findings, which meant the reports would be made available only to her and McPherson, as her immediate superior. When she logged on with her laptop, she learned that some reports were available, but there was a concern with the knife which was still being investigated. She raised her question about the wheelie bin victim and flagged it for the urgent attention of the pathologists and then downloaded the reports on the blood from the sneakers, the digital camera and the data associated with the image. These were all pretty damning for Mahmoud Khalil: it was the victim's blood, it appeared consistent with spatter patterns from similar crimes and Khalil's DNA was inside the sneakers and a match for the grease spot found on the back of the tow truck. Khalil's fingerprints were the only ones found on the camera, a good forefinger print taken from the shutter button along with both thumbs on the rear casing. This was reported as consistent with someone aiming the camera and taking pictures. The EXIF data gave the time as 12:31:12 on the morning of Friday, 2nd August for the first image, with three subsequent images within the minute following.

She wondered what the remaining question over the knife could be, and whether that would show further damning findings or turn up something that put the case in jeopardy.

Her arrival at SECSUR was on the dot of eight, where she was informed by the pretty young woman at the reception desk that Sean Dower had left early that morning for Christmas Island. She asked after the flight details, only to be informed that Mr Dower was a pilot and flew one of the company planes. He was expected in Derby around midday and would then fly on to Christmas Island the following day. She would later learn that the company provided security services for the Curtin Detention Centre at Derby and Christmas Island. After that, she hit a brick wall.

Her inquiry as to the whereabouts and driver of a vehicle registered to the firm produced a burly young man in a perfectly fitted pinstripe suit, with a complexion as smooth as Teflon. He informed her that the information she sought, for security reasons, could not be divulged.

'Many of our clients,' he told her, 'are government ministers and high ranking officials. I'm afraid we can't give out information about our operations. You could come back with a court order, but I have to warn you that may not be enough. The Official Secrets Act has jurisdiction.' As he spoke, the young man shepherded her towards the door and wished her a good day.

From her car, Boulter called Command Central and issued an alert for the vehicle. Both the driver and the vehicle were to be detained on sight as part of an ongoing inquiry into a death and possible abduction.

There were several messages on her phone. She ignored the first, from Art Lazaar. A detective from Kensington asked if she could call in to the station sometime this morning for a chat, and McPherson demanded a meeting at eleven.

Somehow, she thought, her day's bright sunshine was clouding over faster than a bathroom window on a cold day.

Chapter Twenty-Seven

The Rhythm of the Saints

Tuesday 3 September — 4 days before the election

Time itself languishes in hospital.

The mood of a hospital ward, at least from the patient's perspective, grows toward tedium in notches of inquiry into pain levels and bowel movements. A young doctor who, judging by appearance and accent, had recently emigrated from northern Africa shows as much interest in potential gaps in my general health as he does in my immediate predicament. I take it as a sign that my predicament is not nearly as dire as my internal monitoring suggests.

'Oh not at all,' he says, 'your situation was quite critical for some hours' — critical here being a medical term as distinct from a literary one — 'but your high blood pressure, cholesterol and slightly erratic heartbeat are matters of concern as well.'

I get the impression that Dr Mboko has designs of jumping into surgical solutions while I am at my most vulnerable. He chooses to refrain from engaging in banter about either how he came to be a doctor, or my desire to be free from the restraint imposed by powerful painkillers and the tubular connections that feed them directly into my blood stream. Your body needs time to heal is his refrain, and I wonder how familiar he is with Midnight Oil.

I flick through television channels, looking for anything other than politicians exhorting Australians to betray their basic humanity and invest their vote in building an impenetrable sea wall against the northern hordes. Ninety new refugees have arrived in the time I had spent unconscious, and three more boats were intercepted this very morning.

'Our Safe Borders operation will stop this flood permanently,' LOTO insists, while TAPM is equally sure that his party's policy of new detention camps on foreign lands would keep them out in a more humanitarian way.

My annoyance with the language these party machines use to peddle their ideology, in particular the repetitive rhetoric and the alarmist ramping that is clearly having a divisive effect on the voting population, grows with each utterance. News and current affairs commentators, rather than take a critical ear to it — we've heard these lies before — appear reluctant to call them out.

I switch the television off and turn my thoughts towards my own investigation. It takes less than a minute for me to decide on a quick and quiet phone call. I ask for a short visit.

Nick Fairgough has been in my room for about half an hour. He is dressed in jeans, a polo shirt and casual jacket: his preferred dress mode when he can avoid wearing a uniform. He hasn't brought flowers, nor does he appear particularly sympathetic to my circumstances, but I do manage a smile or two among the grimaces over how they came about. Things grow a little more serious on the subject of Wallace Lipschitz. I hit him with the question straight out of the blue.

'What have you got on him?'

I am dealing with a master of the long game. He knows the rules;

knows how to play; and the sidestep is his signature. 'I'm sorry ... Lipschitz?'

'Yeah, Nick. Wally Lipschitz. What have you got on him?'

'Why would I have anything on him?'

'Because you're the police commissioner, and he's a university vice chancellor playing in the mud with some pretty dirty people. You know why I work there.' He shifts on his feet. Not a big move, but a move that's been with him since I can remember. There's something he doesn't want to say. Well, too bad, boyo, you're gonna tell. 'In case you hadn't noticed, Nick, I was beaten to within an inch of my life last Friday.'

'Yeah, Art, I get that. But I don't know...' The head shake is another of his giveaways. Great negotiator, lousy poker player.

'Bullshit. You know something. If it wasn't for Lipschitz and his hundred-and-twenty thousand dollar car, it wouldn't have happened. Roger Lamord calls him up and gets him to deliver me. He calls him by his first name, too — he's the first person I've ever heard do that — so, they're either in bed together fucking each other and figuring out how they can fuck me, or they're in bed together fucking a whole load of others, probably you included. There's something tying this whole thing together and my gut tells me Lamord's got more than a little to do with it. Lipschitz just might be how I can get to him. What have you got?'

'Are you saying Roger Lamord is responsible?'

'I don't know Nick. That's the worry. I had lunch with the man, dead set wanker if you ask me, but fucking excellent food. It was a setup. Lipschitz was supposed to join us, but that was never the intention. After lunch, Lamord sends me downstairs where he says a car is waiting to take me back to campus. Fucking car was waiting all right. So was a thump in the head, followed by a whole chorus review of professional torture by a mob of sick fucks with fists like rock breakers and a water torture manual.'

'Maybe it had nothing to do with Lamord.'

I close my eyes and wait while a shot of morphine dissolves a lingering headache. I sigh, exasperated. 'They knew I was there. Who else knew? Lamord, Lipschitz, whomever his driver was talking to in Croatian or something ... I don't know, but they're in this thing. Just give me something, anything.'

'It's not going to help you.'

I slam my fist down on the bed. My heart monitor reacts with a series of irregular beeping noises. A nurse appears at the door, I wave her off. 'Nick, I don't care what you think. I need leverage and I know you've got it.'

His face clouds over in a carefully prepared, solemn look. 'I think it might be best to put your theories on ice for a while. That gadget over there is suggesting that you're anything but well, and these are sensitive issues; potentially explosive.'

They are his best chosen words yet, only it is me who is potentially explosive. 'What are you talking about? You want me to lie down and play nice until what? Until the police wrap this up? Your police? The Kensington cops? That's not going to happen Nick. The rot in your department is like gangrene. Christ! Kelly Boulter is working this case in secret because she can't trust the people in her own office, in her own team. She doesn't trust me either, but at least she knows what she gets. We need leverage, just give me what you've got.'

'This conversation can't go anywhere,' he stipulates. I agree.

'The Fraud Squad have just made a recommendation to the Crime and Corruption Commission to investigate a range of activities at your university. It's a rocky course, though. The triple-C instructs the university to undertake an internal investigation first—' I guffaw. Nick glowers and continues. 'Then, if the university uncovers anything untoward, it goes back to the triple-C and they will proceed with corruption charges. It's likely to take years.'

I have my own ideas. 'Buying a BMW saloon on the campus credit card? Flogging off a parcel of land to some dodgy consultants proposing a film studio? He wants me to work there, did you know?'

Nick grins. 'Facetious bastard. But yes, credit card use, excessive balloon payments to retiring personnel who land lucrative consulting roles, allocating land parcels to certain interests, a couple possibly including your other mate, some pretty dodgy overseas travel — I don't know many details. I'll be taking it to the minister later in the month.'

'That might be tricky.'

'Depends a bit on how far up the chain it runs.'

I am thoughtful for a moment, then say, 'If Lamord is involved, you can safely assume the higher you climb the more slippery it's gonna be.'

'Maybe, but I—' He doesn't get to finish because Kelly Boulter walks in.

It takes a moment for her to recognise who is in the room with me. They'd never met, but she knows who he is. More surprisingly, he knows who she is. He spends a few minutes complimenting her, drawing on specific examples of her work as a detective. It is one of the qualities that makes Nick Fairgough the man he is. He takes a moment to wish me well and excuses himself on the grounds of pressing business. And fires a parting comment: 'Whatever you need, Art. Just keep the rhyme simple.'

Boulter stands at the foot of my bed for some moments in silence. Recovering from her stupor, I imagine.

'So that's how you do it,' she says, her voice low.

'Come again?'

'How you get involved, how you get away with things: it comes from Commissioner Fairgough — right from the top.' She emits a short, brittle laugh. 'You're fucken unbelievable, Lazaar.'

I demur. 'No, Kelly, that's not it at all. Nick and I have been friends for thirty-five years, we're mates.'

'Right, which is why he said, "whatever you need, Art." Don't bullshit me Lazaar—'

'He's a mate, he cares, which is more than you seem to—'

'I saved your fucking life Lazaar. I'm beginning to regret it. I should have listened to McPherson and just left the investigation to Kensington Station. They should have a result in a year or two.'

'Kelly, whether you like it or not, this is also about you. Someone is sending a message for you to leave well enough alone. Are you just going to fold?'

'I'm beyond caring about you Lazaar. I'll do what McPherson wants — make the case against Mahmoud Khalil and be done with it. The evidence is there, it's a solid case.'

'Only it's not, is it? A solid case? You'd be perverting the course of justice, in which case you'll just be another one of them, and, trust me, they'll keep you wherever the bloody well they like.' There's a look on her face that gives me a moment's pause. 'Something tells me you've got contradictory evidence,' I say. 'Does McPherson know?'

Before she can answer, her phone rings. I only get one side of the conversation, and that is at best semi-audible.

'Robinson? Derby Police, yes … Jesus! When? Are there any details? Okay. Well that's good news, at least … Tonkin Highway? Sorry, who was the passenger? And what? to the airport? okay … Yes take the vehicle to Maylands … every square inch. Any word of Singh? No, well keep digging … Belmont, right? Okay, meet me there at one-thirty. Okay three o'clock then. And get a warrant for his address.' She disconnects and I look expectantly at her.

'What?' she demands. I hold my hands up. 'No, Lazaar, you don't get to share in this.' She hesitates, as though contemplating whether to follow through with a next action. And then says, 'There is one thing though. I told Kensington I'd follow up on this.' She pulls a printed image from a folder and hands it to me.

I am staring at a grainy image of two big men manhandling a smaller man like a sack of flour into the back of a black four-wheel drive. One of the men is significantly larger than the other, his profile offering a caricature nose that draws focus away from every other feature. The sack of flour is me. I look expectantly at Boulter.

'So much for your theories, Lazaar. This wasn't Roger Lamord's doing. Lamord's maître d' called Lipschitz's driver to collect you. This image was taken from her car's dash cam as she turned toward the lifts to get you.' She pauses while I intensify my study of the image. 'This is the clearest image from the camera', she says, pointing at the vehicle. 'The number plate is obscured, but I think I know it.' She points at Big Nose. 'How about this guy — you ever see him before?'

'Can't say I have. Who is he?'

'Don't know yet. Thought you might have a theory.' This last word is loaded with ice. 'After all that's what you do isn't it, make up theories?' She reaches for the print. I keep hold of it. 'Fine, suit yourself. But just so you're clear, that ape there is not the cause of your situation Lazaar. You are. Sticking your nose in where it doesn't belong. I should have arrested you days ago. If I had I wouldn't be wasting my time with all this shit!'

At that, she turns on her heel and sweeps from the room, leaving me in stunned silence.

Chapter Twenty-Eight

Third World Man

Sam Codlin called Lamord just as he was concluding a meeting. He excused himself from the boardroom, leaving his guests to depart under the guidance of his assistants and went through to his office, closing the doors behind him.

'I'd like a few minutes, Roger,' Codlin said. 'Is it okay if I come up?'

'Of course.'

Lamord was sitting behind his desk when she entered. The desktop was clear, and he positioned himself central and upright as she settled into a chair opposite and placed a folder and notepad before her.

'What's up?' he asked.

'Sean's plane has gone missing,' she said, a perfect balance of sympathy and concern in her voice.

'Missing?'

'He was in Derby overnight, he left at six this morning. The last radio contact was at seven-eighteen. He was expected at Christmas Island at eight forty-five. There's been no contact and it's now nearly eleven. There's no sign of the jet, we have to assume it went down about a thousand kilometres out from Derby. I'm so sorry, Roger.'

Lamord sat in silence. At length, in a faraway voice, he said, 'Can you organise a presser, Sam? Something sensitive, just an announcement ... maybe talk to someone at Seven, they've probably got some art they can use. This is terrible news. Terrible.'

Sam Codlin waited while Lamord turned in his seat and stared across the water. The midmorning sun was bright, pitching the water a deep blue with a crystal shimmer and a clear view to Rottnest, the island appearing high on a low tide.

'He was a good soldier, a good man,' she heard him say. 'Hardly what you would call a third world man, but he made it safe for the little guys.' Then he swung round and faced her again. 'There's a Steely Dan song he loved by that name. Add it to the press package.' He waited while she made her notes. 'Anything else?'

'Yes, more bad news I'm afraid. Joe Swaddick has been arrested.'

'What?'

'I don't have any details. He hasn't been informed of any charges, apparently he's being held at Belmont Police Station awaiting questioning. I can tell you, although I haven't been informed, that Detective Sergeant Boulter put out a call to locate and detain his vehicle. I assume he was detained along with it.'

'Was there anyone else in the vehicle?'

'He was taking Yusuf to the airport. The police officers who impounded the vehicle arranged a taxi for him. His flight leaves in a few minutes.'

'Okay, leave it with me. That it?'

'More or less. I'm pretty confident of a win on Saturday, so I hope you're okay with me moving to the UK.' She left an opening, but he didn't bite. She pressed on. 'I do have some concerns about how we shut down the offshore business model — especially in the likelihood that we've lost Sean.'

Lamord shrugged, rolled his chair back, stood and faced the

window with his arms folded. Eventually he turned his head and shoulders and peered at her.

'Not our concern, Sam. Our concern is only to win.'

Chapter Twenty-Nine

Ship of Fools

Boulter was late getting to McPherson's office and he was quick to point it out.

'Lateness seems to be a thing with you recently.'

'I got distracted. There was busker down the street and I stopped to listen to him. Are you familiar with a Bob Seger song called *Ship of Fools?*'

McPherson shook his head. 'It's a song about a guy who joins a voyage — an outsider — and he finds that his shipmates don't share, they keep secrets. The ship goes down with all hands lost. Except the outsider. Only he survived.'

'What's your point, Boulter?'

'I don't know about you, sir, but it seems to me that we may be sailing a similar vessel, and I don't intend going down with the ship. If you get my drift.'

'Are you implying I'm a fool?'

'Only if you don't listen, sir.'

'Listen to who, Sergeant? Lazaar?'

'I think it's more about listening to what's going on than anyone in particular.'

'You're talking in riddles, lass! Anyhow, the DPP is still waiting on instructions to prosecute Mahmoud Khalil.'

'A case in point, Boss. We can't.'

'What do you mean?'

'The "evidence"' — air quotes for emphasis — 'is tainted.'

McPherson's brow lowered and his eyebrows linked together. 'In what way, exactly is it tainted, Detective? I thought you brought back a whole box of it from the feds.'

'I did. The other reason I'm late for this meeting is because I needed to check that the chain of custody of that box, as you call it, hasn't been compromised.'

'Compromised?'

'Yes. As in fiddled with.'

'And?'

'It hasn't.'

'Are you saying there were problems with the evidence that was handed to you?'

Boulter nodded. 'That's what it amounts to.' She handed over two sheets of paper and on a third, scribbled, *Better not talk about it in here?* and placed it on top of the other two.

McPherson looked at her and then scanned each of the pages beneath the note. Without looking up, he said, 'What do you suggest? We can't let him go.'

'Why not?'

'Because he's an illegal.'

Boulter found two more documents and held them in front of her. Mahmoud Khalil's identity and bridging visa. 'I received these the day after I got the box. They appear to be genuine.'

McPherson stood and walked around his desk. He stuffed the pieces of paper in a small leather carry bag and retrieved his coat from the rack by the door. 'Feel like getting off the ship?' he asked.

———

They occupied a corner courtyard table in a small coffee house along High Street. The morning was bright and sunny, but the air a crisp August cool, chilled by a gentle icy breeze wafting in from the east.

'So what's wrong with the evidence?' McPherson eyed Boulter over his cup, his eyebrows once again mimicking hairy caterpillars.

'First, the red paint on the shoes doesn't match the paint found in the wheelie bin. The blood matches, the paint doesn't.'

McPherson's brow furrowed even further. 'Someone added paint to the crime scene because of the paint on the shoes?'

'I'd say that's about the size of it. My guess is that the perpetrators in this case intended to frame Khalil — or at least be prepared to. They had the shoes and wanted to make sure all the pieces fitted.'

'Maybe Khalil thought he could fool us by including the paint, perhaps to mask the blood on his shoes. That alone doesn't exonerate him.'

'Yeah, look Boss, I know it would be nice and neat, but I really don't think Khalil did this. The paint on the shoes is older than the blood. We wouldn't know this had I not asked for further analysis on the shoes.'

'I didn't see that information on *eye-is*.'

'I deliberately kept it off the system until I could talk to you. It's that first page you're holding.' She braced for the admonishment, but McPherson was reading. He looked up and waited for her to continue.

'Khalil has denied any involvement in this, and let's face it, that's what you'd expect from any perp, but I needed to be sure our case didn't have any holes, so I thought some aspects needed re-examining.'

'Why the shoes?'

'It seemed too convenient.'

'Okay. But why not log it in the forensics file?'

'The same reason we're out here discussing this, sir, and not in the office. I'd rather not tip our hand at this stage.'

'Tip to whom?'

'That's the magic question, isn't it, Superintendent? You acted on a tip-off, which, in my opinion, was highly suspect.' She waited. 'Some might think I'm taking a risk even discussing it with you.'

'Is that what you think?'

'I'm discussing it with you, aren't I?'

He nodded and turned to the second report. 'I take it this one's not on *eye-is* either?'

McPherson put the second report down before him and stared across the table at Boulter.

'I asked the pathologist for more detail on the knife,' she explained. 'The knife supposedly recovered from Khalil's home was not the weapon used to cut the victim's throat.'

'But it had the victim's blood on it, and Khalil's fingerprints.' McPherson pointed to a detail on the page. '"The knife is not sharp enough to make a cut like this." Could it have been blunted after?'

'Not without some evidence. The knife that was used in this attack was so sharp that hardly any pressure was required to separate the tissue surrounding the arteries and windpipe. But there would be tearing on either side of the wound if it had been the one we have in evidence. You can also see that trace evidence was left in the wound.'

McPherson screwed his face up. 'Are we sure about this?'

'Trace DNA can be isolated at several levels these days, and it can be recovered from very small transfers. If I touch something, then you touch it, then someone else touches the same thing, the DNA from the oils on our skin can reliably be recovered; each of us can be identified. What's more, a non-porous surface like a knife blade can transfer as much as ninety-five per cent of DNA. And when the biological material is saliva, DNA recovery can be higher than other sources such as skin oils, semen, and even blood.'

'DNA from saliva in the wound, apparently transferred from the knife? What the fuck would the killer's saliva be doing on his knife?'

'It's not just the saliva, sir. Look at note five there: it says traces of saliva mixed with a very fine machine oil. This guy sharpens his knife. He uses spit on an oilstone. Now tell me, sir, what kind of murderer is that meticulous with his tools?'

McPherson was thoughtful. 'We could still present a case against Khalil, and then it's done.'

'Well, sir, if you want an expedient result you might try it. But my signature won't be going on it. I support the notion put forward by Robinson the other day — that it's highly unlikely one man could have done this. We have found no evidence of collaborators. And, circumstantially, I can't see Mahmoud Khalil for this either; this forensic report supports that position. This was an execution by persons who knew the ground.'

'I don't know, lass. As evidence goes, this looks pretty flimsy. If you want a fast ticket back to Midland, it would be best to sign it off and leave this new stuff off *eye-is...*'

Boulter's patience was wearing thin. It's one thing to walk away from an investigation, but another to push for a just result. McPherson was clearly not going to allow that to happen easily. She wanted to know if he could be trusted. Maybe he's simply testing me.

'You know Khalil has a lawyer, sir?' she said.

'Who?'

'Ron Cando.'

'How the fuck can he afford that?'

'Compliments of Art Lazaar, I believe.'

'Jesus! Boulter. I'll have that cunt for interfering in police business if it's the last thing I do.'

'Might be a bit of a challenge after what I learned this morning, Superintendent.'

'I want to formally interview him under caution,' Boulter announced, making a careful note of the time.

'Interview who, exactly?' McPherson asked.

'Lazaar, of course.'

'Oh.' McPherson seemed momentarily nonplussed. 'Why's that? I thought we were talking about the limestone cave-in and this person of interest who's done a disappearing act. What's Lazaar's connection to that?'

'This is all about a girl.'

McPherson let out a small laugh, as if to dismiss the idea altogether. '*Ooh, Wakka Do, Wakka Day ...* I thought he was gay.'

Boulter started. 'Wakka what?'

'Oh nothing, just a song. Go on.'

'We got this wrong right from the start—'

'We? Who's the "we" in this, Boulter?' Clearly he wasn't shouldering the responsibility.

'All of us, sir. There are some things I still haven't told you.' She fished around in a folder and drew out two plainly typed pages and an 8x10 photograph.

'These are reports of forensic examinations I had Iain Methuen do — I probably traded a few favours you've yet to earn...' She handed the pages to him.

'The first is a comparison of some dog hairs found on the wheelie bin victim's clothes with ones found on Lazaar's after his beating. In each case, they were found on the shoulder and hip sections of their clothes, suggesting the transfer happened when they were lying on one side.' She pointed to the picture. 'You can see from that image that Lazaar is being hoisted, apparently unconscious, into the back of a vehicle. The hairs came from the same dog and I'm willing to bet my transfer back to Midland on this vehicle being where the dog hairs came from.'

McPherson studied the report. 'Okay, Iain's top notch so there's no reason to doubt his findings. This other one?'

'There was a graze on the wheelie bin victim's forehead. It puzzled me, so I asked the pathologist to have another look at it and then got Methuen to compare their report with Lazaar's medical report. He concluded that the same kind of nylon webbing was used on both victims to pull their heads back — Lazaar's while he was waterboarded, and the wheelie bin victim's while his throat was sliced. Khalil was in gaol when Lazaar was bashed.'

McPherson was thoughtful. 'What did you mean when you said it was all about a girl?'

'You first. What did you mean?'

McPherson smiled. 'It's a Gilbert O'Sullivan song from way back, about a girl called Rita. It's Lazaar I thought was gay. Now your turn.'

'I'll tell him you think that. Look, the reason he contacted me in the first place was to arrange protection for a girl he says is the wheelie bin victim's sister. He reckoned she was also at risk of being murdered. I dismissed the whole thing, but after this morning, I think Lazaar knows more than he's letting on. I didn't tell you earlier, but the feds I met, those two who gave me the box of evidence, also demanded I tell them the whereabouts of the girl. Of course, I had no idea and told them so but now I realise that everyone is looking for the girl.'

She watched McPherson as he sat quietly, mulling things over in his head. At length he said, 'When will you interview him?'

'Tomorrow morning, at the hospital.'

Chapter Thirty

That's Freedom

Wednesday 4 September — 3 days before the election

I get a call from Detective Robinson at about 9:30 asking if Boulter is with me. I ask why he thinks she would be, given my frustrated attempts to get her to talk to me since yesterday, and her lack of response to my calls.

'She told Superintendent McPherson that she was going to interview you this morning. I thought she might be there.'

'Interview me?' my tone is deliberately equivocal.

'I'm sorry Doctor Lazaar, I don't know the details.'

'Bit of a worry if you don't know where she is, then.'

'I'm sure there's a simple explanation.' He hangs up before I can dig any further.

I dislike the feeling crawling around in my belly. If there's one thing that can be said about Kelly Boulter, she is utterly dependable; she doesn't go off docket. I sit my head back on the pillow, close my eyes, and reflect on the events of yesterday after Boulter's stormy exit.

First, the report that Sean Dower had disappeared somewhere in the Indian Ocean, between Derby and Christmas Island. Boulter had been wanting to talk to him.

Channel Seven ran the item on its midday bulletin as breaking news, the unmistakable Rhodes piano of Donald Fagen's entry statement from *Third World Man* accompanying it. Interesting choice.

Chief Executive Officer of major security company's plane goes missing on flight from Derby in WA's north-west en route to Christmas Island. Sean Dower, Managing Director of national security firm SECSUR, was on a routine visit to Curtin and Christmas Island detention centres where his company supplies security services for the government. His plane left Derby shortly before six o'clock this morning and was expected in Christmas Island before nine am. All radio contact with the flight ceased about an hour after take-off. Mister Dower is an experienced pilot who frequently flies to remote operations. He was alone on the company jet and there are fears for his survival.

And then fireworks explode in the corner of my eye. An image of a group of men appears on screen and focuses into a mid-shot of Dower. The shot from Channel Seven archives appears to be taken from an event at The Vines golf course. What piques my interest is the company he is in.

The television in my room is one of those modern ones that can replay and capture recent broadcast segments. I think the rental company was trying them out to see if they could up their returns from private rooms. I guess I was a lucky guinea pig. I navigate the remote to review the previous minute to see the group in more detail. It is an interesting tableau to say the least. In clear view are Roger Lamord and the Malaysian Prime Minister at a golf tee. Dower's image is highlighted in the foreground of the shot, standing behind the tee in the company of a man I have seen before. He was driving a black Mercedes away from the Railway Hotel a couple of years ago. My guess is that this is Yusuf, or Tuah Johari, brother-in-law to the Malaysian PM's wife. Framing the left-hand side of the image is an arm wearing a distinctive watch, a single shoulder with a lapel badge I would recognise anywhere, and part of the face of Wallace Lipschitz.

While she was in my room, Boulter took a call from Detective Robinson — I gleaned that much from the half of the conversation I'd overheard — along with the arrangement to meet at Belmont at three o'clock. A car impounded and someone or something at Belmont. Whose address did she ask a warrant for?

I then move onto wondering whether the events that Donna Gardner called about just as I'd finished my lunch yesterday might have something to do with it. Her call is hushed and anxious.

'Those two federal police officers who were here the other day returned this morning with a warrant. They searched your room and left with several boxes, your desktop computer and a laptop.'

'What? And you let them in?' The boredom of hospital automatically amplifies the querulousness of my tone.

'I had no choice, Art. They were accompanied by a campus security officer, and the VC instructed them to comply with the warrant.'

I'll bet he did. 'Was anyone present during the search looking after my interests?'

'I was there for most of it. I felt a bit violated to be honest.'

I take that to be a good sign. 'Did they say what they were looking for?'

'It was all a bit vague. They said something about you having evidence connected to someone they wanted to talk to. Something to do with fraud and corruption. They didn't elaborate.' The line goes quiet and I sense there's more.

'What, Donna?' I prompt.

'The VC has asked that you take extended leave.' This time the silence is thunderous.

'Has he indeed?' is all I can muster by way of response. At that moment, a sudden thought is leaden in my belly. 'I'm going to have to call you back, Donna. I'll need to contact my union rep and talk to a lawyer.'

'Of course, Art. But I will need to make arrangements.'

I no sooner hang up than I dial Lavender Jensen. She answers on the second ring. There is no time to explain. 'Lavender, grab the package and head south. Now.'

I hang up before she can respond. We'd discussed it. She knows what to do. Her father lives on a property in deep forest near Denmark on the southern coast. It is far away and isolated, as safe a place as any for Falullah.

Next, I call WiFi. He assures me that there is no need to worry about the raid. If Smith and Jones happened to collect the USB with the files Hunter had supplied me from the secret compartment in my top drawer, they will be in for a surprise. He has loaded it with a malware code which boots as soon as the USB is plugged into a computer. Unless it meets a handshake code on the host computer, the virus immediately locks the computer into which it is installed, infects its network with a paralysing code, and a false message and link to a ransom agent in Russia. The laptop removed from my room is my campus-issued one; the notebook from Hunter is still with WiFi.

I let a call from Eli Mendopulos go to voicemail. He leaves a message asking me to reschedule last night's missed appointment. Instead, I again study the image of my abduction that Boulter had left.

The guy doing the heavy lifting is a big man with a face like a sack of busted arseholes, his head oversized and gnarled. By far the most prominent feature is the nose: a caricature in itself that even the most gifted caricaturist could not exaggerate. In searching for this man, all one has do is ask about the burly Italian with the nose

— anyone having ever seen him will know him. As I try to focus my mind on how I might find him, loose threads bombard me. Among the chaos, one thing stands clear: I can find neither Boulter nor my assailant from inside a hospital.

While I wait on a schedule of drugs and a discharge form, I make plans, arriving at a decision that the time has come to free myself from the shackles, deflect the wind and shed some light in the dark. Time to put some poetic licence into play.

WiFi meets me at the front of the hospital. I limp to his waiting car where he hands me a new mobile phone, the notebook computer I'd left with him, and a USB with the full Channel 7 clip I'd seen on television the day before. I want the footage as evidence of the connection between Lipschitz and Yusuf, although I have no idea if it will ultimately hold any leverage.

'All of your accounts at work have been suspended,' WiFi is saying as he inserts his ignition key, 'including your security access to buildings, your office and classrooms.'

'Jesus!'

'I mean, if they're open, they're open. You can still walk in. But security has been alerted and, unless you're carrying a pass issued that day by the chancellery, they have instructions to escort you from the grounds.'

'And do you know what it is I'm supposed to have done?'

'Nothing's been announced. There's been a bit of email traffic between the VC and the Deputy Provost discussing what they should say. She's leaning toward some kind of sexual harassment. She's sounded Donna Gardner out on the possibility and believes she knows someone willing to support the claim.'

'What does *he* say?'

'He agrees, only...'

'Yes?'

'He'd like to be sure he can get rid of you and has suggested some form of improper academic behaviour — something that falls under fraud and corruption.'

The same words Donna Gardner used. I am thoughtful while he heads for the car park where I left my car the previous Friday. 'Not fucking around, are they? When was the last email?'

'About nine this morning.'

Right before the Smith and Jones raid on my office. Utter bastards. The whole fucking lot of them. 'And the phone?' I ask, holding it up.

'Same as the last one, but with a new number. Anyone trying to contact you with your old number will be routed to a voicemail. The link is in the phone.'

'Thanks,' I say as we reach my car. I climb down, suppressing the pain, thank him again and close the door.

Chapter Thirty-One

Move Along Train

Although the sun is shining and the sky has wide patches of denim blue, the trees I pass along South Street as I head to Fremantle are dripping from an early morning shower, and their leafy crowns toss about in a stiff westerly as if swatting flies. The feeling is like floating above the road as I find some truth in Greg Quill's soothing lyric and think that, in the end, we are all looking for the *Gypsy Queen* in some fog of our mind that pulls us in directions we are not entirely at ease to follow. My struggle to find the connections between recent events is frequently interrupted by the intrusion of the oversized snozz of my Italian abuser and Sean Dower's voice. I'm not sure they are even connected to reality, and I don't quite know what might be memory and what might be painkiller. If Boulter is right, and Lamord and Lipschitz didn't set up the mugging, why do I hear Sean Dower's voice? And why is it connected to Big Nose? And why is Dower now dead?

I enter my room. It appears untouched except for housekeeping's daily visits.

My first call is to Nick Fairgough. I catch him between meetings and explain quickly what I need. It takes about fifteen minutes before I get a return call from a Commander Novice. He is all business.

'The person detained at Belmont was Joseph Swaddick,' he is saying as I scribble. 'Detective Sergeant Boulter had issued a detain request for a VOI and its driver as a POI. The vehicle was stopped on Tonkin Highway by two officers from Belmont station. It was taken to Maylands for forensic examination. The commissioner has requested an urgent process. There was a passenger in the vehicle. The arresting officer's report identifies him as Tan Sri Tuah Johari, a diplomat from Malaysia who was being driven to the airport. The officers called a taxi and he left on a flight for Kuala Lumpur shortly before midday.'

My involuntary expletive interrupts the commander's flow, but I urge him to continue.

'Detective Sergeant Boulter arrived at Belmont station at three o'clock only to learn that Swaddick was removed from the station by two AFP officers at about one-thirty pm. The custody documents were signed by an agent Smith, citing federal jurisdiction over a driver of a foreign diplomat.' I laugh, a kind of fucking-knew-it grunt. Novice continues. 'She left a few minutes later and hasn't been heard from since. Calls to her mobile have gone unanswered. Its tracker is inactive, so it appears to be switched off or destroyed.

'You asked about the Parry Street explosion...' There is a pause while Novice turns a page. 'Her *eye-is* notes indicate that early in the piece she talked to a street kid called Spider who she later notes as the one who identified the vehicle she impounded. This kid says there were two groups searching for someone called Hunter. One group was in this vehicle, the other group unknown, except...' The pause makes me feel Novice has noticed something. 'There is a flag on this as late as yesterday morning with an image of a guy with probably the ugliest nose I have ever seen. Does that make any sense to you?'

'Is this guy identified?'

'No. Do you know who he is?'

'It's one of the guys who mugged me. I'm the sack of potatoes in the picture ... if you're seeing the whole image.'

'I've just got the head shot. Anyway, this kid Spider might be one lead to follow up, but there's no information on how to contact him. The commissioner has authorised three plain-clothes special officers to work with you. You don't need to know their names. They will meet you in the atrium of your hotel at four o'clock today. The commissioner wishes you all the best on this but asked me to remind you that it is deniable.'

Apart from tracking down Spider, one other possible lead did present itself to me. I wonder if any of the kitchen staff saw something on Friday or might recognise Big Nose. I check with Kensington Police. The detective working on my case tells me they found no-one to identify him. They had asked at Balsamic & Olives, he says. Nothing. They'd canvassed Fremantle detectives. Nothing. They circulated the image on IIS to all other stations. Nothing. How could that be? How could a thug so big, so ugly, not be recognised? It could only be that he was brought in for a specific job by someone. Who? Lamord? And then the penny dropped. The one person with a special interest in Hunter — especially once his cover was blown.

The pieces in my mind implode like a jigsaw interlock. *Click!* Enzo Gordioni.

Four o'clock is still some distance away. I call the lobby and secure a private meeting room for the hour to five, then sit staring at the phone. There are two calls that have to be made, the only decision is the order in which to make them.

First, Donna Gardner.

'Art, I've been waiting for your call back.'

'I'm sure you have. They're setting me up, you know that, right?'

'You know I can't comment. I'm your line manager and right

now I'm looking at a report from a PID' — public interest disclosure — 'officer that names you as someone who has acted improperly. My duty is to inform you of a mandatory suspension from duties and that you must register at the chancellery if you come on site. Any breach will be considered an offence under the act.' Her officious tone rankles.

'This is bullshit, Donna. What am I supposed to have done?'

'A copy of the PID report has been mailed out to you.'

'I'm not at home, Donna. Tell me.'

'It alleges you traded sexual favours for grades. That brings the integrity of the university into disrepute.' A cold, articulated summary. No feelings. No judgement.

An edge creeps into my voice.

'First he has me fucking mugged and now trumped up charges.' My brain is momentarily numb. This is a squeeze, a turning of the screw. Lipschitz is doing Lamord's bidding. Elise Jarman, the Deputy Provost doing his. And Donna Gardner doing hers. 'Donna, I need you to get a meeting with Lipschitz tomorrow afternoon.'

'I'm not sure he'll want to see you.'

'I'm bloody sure he won't. Don't mention me. Cook up something — school business, private, urgent, his office. Let me know the time, I'll step in, you step out.'

'I don't know, Art—'

'Donna, whose fucking side are you on here? You know this is bullshit. Lipschitz knows it's bullshit; Elise Jarman certainly knows it's bullshit because she's the one cooking the charges. For *him!* This whole thing is fucking corrupt. Why would you support it?'

A different silence clings to the connection. A silence of veering, like there is a trackmaster lurking down the line, waiting to switch tracks, to derail and redirect. A creepy feeling strikes the nerve at the end of my tailbone, like the rub of synthetic upholstery on my bare back and the haunting sounds of Levon Helm singing *Move Along Train* coinciding. It's a coincidence that is not meant to be, a signal that all is not well in the world and there will be ghosts to face, the shapes of which I have yet to determine. I just know they are there.

Her voice returns. It is soft, a whisper. 'I'll do what I can.'

And the line is dead.

I wait. I pace. I challenge my mind to be in the right place. This next call depends upon stoicism, unbridled reserve, dignity of the right, integrity of lost causes. It's all about loss. And finding again. I use the number he gave me. He answers on the second ring.

'Roger Lamord.'

'Roger,' I say with far greater enthusiasm than I ever imagined I could have. 'Art Lazaar here. I'm calling to enquire as to whether your friend had any success in recovering what it was that was lost. You see, I've been a little indisposed...' I had often wondered whether these rich arseholes actually spoke with this kind of affected air.

'Yes I heard about that.' His tone is matter-of-fact. Businesslike. 'You do understand that I had nothing to do with it?'

'Of course. It was all recorded on a camera. Fortunately. Although, I'm not sure you get off scot free.' Tread lightly. I'm self-counselling now. Small steps. No need to eat the world.

'I'm sure I don't understand. What is it you want, Lazaar? I'm busy.'

'Far be it for me to waste your time. I've lost something, Roger. I'm wondering if you know the whereabouts.'

'I thought lost-and-found was your art.'

'In a manner of speaking. But this may be something more up your alley. A police officer has gone missing, last seen seeking an audience with someone connected to you. I'd like to find her.'

'There are a lot of people connected to me. I don't know anything about a missing police officer.'

'Oh, don't misunderstand me, I'm quite sure you don't. Joseph Swaddick. Does that name mean anything to you?' Fishing, my grandfather used say, was about the right hook, the right bait and watertime — he always said it as one word. Watertime is the ebb and flow. *The waves set you free.* Ella Fitzgerald was a favourite of his.

'Can't say it does.'

'Well, let's just say...' I pause, as though it is a moment before closing a deal 'that Swaddick is employed by one of your companies—'

'A lot of people employed by my companies—'

'One or two fewer in recent days ... but if I can continue, I was going to say by one of your companies which has recently lost its managing director under what could only be described as tragic and mysterious circumstances—'

'Best to contact the human resources department in the company for an answer to your question. In the meantime, my friend is still waiting for the return of their loss.'

'Hasn't that friend already left the country, Roger?' Then I think, perhaps, he talks about a different friend. I continue with an emphasis that indicates a level of certainty I cannot prove, 'I'm curious, how did Enzo Gordioni know I was dining in your restaurant last Friday?'

'I'm sure I couldn't say. Now if you're done?'

Chapter Thirty-Two

I Hung My Head

Come four o'clock and I'm ensconced with my three plain-clothes special officers in a small meeting room on the mezzanine floor of the Esplanade Hotel, an elegant colonial affair that stands on the first site used for housing convicts transported to Fremantle. After it was decided that the Swan River Colony would not be a place for convicts, labour supply became a critical issue and the decision was reversed. Convicts were sent to shore up immigration numbers and supply labour at the governor's pleasure. Through the window, past the Moreton Bay figs of Esplanade Park and the fishing boat harbour beyond, I watch the sun splitting banks of metal grey clouds into streaks of light bouncing off dark shadows on the water.

My PCSOs comprise two male and one female who go by the names Peter, George, and Jo, respectively. These are monikers that serve for quick, direct communications over the next few days and to provide a shared capacity to forget we ever met should we run across each other any time in the future. Our primary mission is to find Kelly Boulter, although I have some secondaries to add. I've thrown the names Swaddick and Big Nose with Smith and Jones into the mix.

'So exactly how many baddies are we looking for?' Peter has the kind of drawl most often associated with a youth spent in the country.

I try, unsuccessfully, to match the measure. 'Hard to say, Pete. Kelly was working in muddy waters. Her key case is a murder for which her nick has a guy in custody they'd like it to be. But she was having doubts. Things didn't add up. It's possible she found evidence that makes their choice implausible. But there's also the Parry Street explosion. Two people died, one's missing, and there seems to be a link to the murder. Still a bit of a theory, though, until something shows up to confirm. Then there's my mugging — officially out of her hands but if I know Boulter, she would want to clock the guy who did it. She was chasing down some evidence that links that to our murder.'

My pause gives George an opportunity to wedge in. His voice is nasal with the hangover of a central London accent.

'So, just the five, then? The murderer, who you reckon is not the guy in custody; the guy driving the car seen at the Parry Street explosion, who was arrested and has now gone missing courtesy of these two feds, and the guy who decked you in the car park of that fancy restaurant, yeah? Although the same badun could have a hand in more than one, couldn't he? Which one's grabbed our missing detective?'

Peter again: 'Thoughts on where we start?'

Jo sits quietly, listening while swiping through her iPad, jotting a note or two on an open notebook before her. I marvel at this quiet multitasking.

'Commander Novice suggested a chat with this street kid, Spider,' she says, before looking up at me. 'We'll leave that to you.' I nod. She continues. 'I'm going to have a chat to McPherson, and Boulter's team, at the local nick. I want to know more about her meeting with the Super yesterday; like, why did they leave the building? And why wasn't the warrant that Sergeant Boulter asked for actioned? Why didn't this other detective meet her at Belmont? Peter, see if you can track down these AFP plods and find out their story — I'm as interested in their raid on Art's office as I am in their sudden appearance at Belmont. George, the car, eh? Keep in touch.'

Peter and George leave. The door closes behind them with a click. Jo hasn't moved. Not a finger. Not until she had my full attention and she'd read beneath my eyes.

'I'm not convinced you've told me everything. Things you've left out, or maybe skewed. Why did Tweedle Dee and Tweedle Dum raid your office? Why did they take advantage of your lying in a hospital bed? Why were you lying in a hospital bed? How does that connect to Kelly Boulter's disappearance? These things are done at someone's bidding, Art. Do you know the someone?'

'I have my suspicions. I think it's more than one, and on the surface for different motives, but odd things tie them together.' I open the file showing the footage that Channel 7 used for its news report on the disappearance of Sean Dower, and put it in front of her. 'What do you make of this?'

She looks, clicks, rewinds, looks, pauses, studies. 'Do you know these people?'

I point. 'Roger Lamord. I had lunch with him last Friday at his fancy restaurant. He wasn't responsible for my mugging — at least, not directly.' Point again. 'Wallace Lipschitz, Vice Chancellor of my university, whose driver took me to that lunch, and whose dashboard camera caught a few moments of my abduction.' Another point. 'Sean Dower, whose plane ended up in the middle of the Indian Ocean yesterday morning, with him in it, we presume. The one about to tee off is the Prime Minister of Malaysia, with whom I believe Lipschitz and Lamord were cooking up some deal for a campus in Malaysia, special opportunities for Malaysian students here and God knows what else. The one at the back, on the other side of Dower is, I suspect, the brother-in-law of the Malaysian PM's wife, Tuah Johari, also known, I believe, as Yusuf. The bodyguards, I don't know, although I suspect one of them is Joseph Swaddick.'

'So what links them?'

'Money for sure … at least where Lamord, Lipschitz and the Malaysian PM are concerned. Maybe politics, I don't know. I think this Tuah Johari is an important link, but he's done a bunk, so we may never know.'

'Two other names have come up: Enzo Gordioni and Calvin Bishop.' Her look has *your turn* etched across her forehead.

'Boulter claims a picture taken at an ATM the night before the Parry Street explosion is Cal Bishop. He died ten years ago. But my guess is that somehow Gordioni has been informed of this picture and that it's Bishop. For Gordioni, that's a ghost come back to haunt him. I think he was behind my mugging with some twisted idea that I can lead him to Bishop.'

'How would this supposition of Boulter's have leaked to Gordioni?'

'Fucked if I know, Jo. Find that out and we might find Kelly.'

She leaves and closes the door. My mind is spinning, looking back at some lost moment when I hung my head in regret of unnecessary death. The weight of secrets is heavy and I wonder if the minute I tell all, will it be over? Or not? How many ghosts am I yet to meet?

Suddenly, I wonder how the election is shaping up. Last I saw, the boats are still coming, Pacific islands will be flooded under TAPM's scheme. LOTO is still vowing loudly in tweet after tweet that he will turn 'em back. The ghosts of the Tampa are haunting the land.

I find Spider a little before midnight, after walking and rewalking the streets of Fremantle, poking my head round dark corners and into hidey holes only the homeless know about, shelling out over a hundred bucks to would-be informers, all capable of peddling a story with a politician's skill, but only one of whom with a clue about the kid's whereabouts. Desperation has no place for distinguishing between truth and lies. What chances their bullshit will be called to account? What chance I'll ever see them again? What's a $20 scam when you've got nothing? The guy standing next to Spider got $30, but at least he told the truth.

'What do y' want wiv me?' Spider demands. 'If y' need gear, I ain't got'ny.'

'No,' I say, 'it's not about gear. I'm wondering if you've seen a friend of mine, a police officer, she's gone missing.'

The kid standing nearby, the one who scored the $30, pipes up, hand over his loins in a lewd gesture: 'I seen 'er man, an' she don' wanna see you.' And he bursts into an uncontrollable giggle.

I beckon Spider to move away, where we can talk a bit more privately. 'You know Detective Kelly Boulter?'

'Yeah. Nice lady.'

'When did you see her last?'

'Yesterday.'

'What time yesterday?'

'Why y' wanna know, man?'

'She's gone missing.'

'Maybe she wanted to.'

'Spider, what do you know?'

'I don' know nufink.'

'Listen, you like Kelly Boulter, right? Help me here. Why did she see you yesterday?'

A long moment passes. I feel his eyes on me. Then he says, 'You know Hunter, right? Well she arks me to spread the word that I seen Hunter since the explosion, an' I know where to fin' him.'

'You've seen Hunter?'

'No I 'aven't seen him. She jus' arks me to tell people I 'ad — an' I know where to fin' him.'

'Why did she want you to do that if it's not true? For all we know, Hunter is dead.'

'Nah, man. He ain't dead. He jus' don't look like 'e used to.'

'So you have seen him?'

'Nah, 'aven't seen 'im. Guys been lookin' for him, but. First it was them guys at the explosion — soldier lookin' guys wiv dogs goin' roun' bustin' everyone on the street to tell 'em where to find him. They don' know shit these guys — you don' find Hunter, 'e finds you. But I fink she was lookin' for one of them. Then there's these Italian guys, fucken' thugs. They jus' fuckin' animals, man. An' guess what? So after I spread the word, the Italians were back las' night. The soldier guy was with one of them, but not in 'is car. No dogs neiver.'

I fish out a picture of Big Nose from my pocket and hold it under the light from a nearby streetlamp. 'This guy one of them?'

Spider squints, turns his head sideways, then to the other side as if he could get a clearer view. 'Yeah, 'e wus there. 'e was the one wiv the soldier guy. That's a fucken' ugly honk but, ay?' And he laughs.

'Did you tell any of them where to find Hunter?'

'Nah. Not me. But some of my bruvvers did.' He glances in the direction of other members of his gang.

I fish a crisp fifty dollar note out of my pocket and hold it. 'And where did they tell them to look?'

Spider eyes the money and reaches for it. 'There's a crib in bush under the railway bridge on Tydeman Road. Tol' 'em they would fin' 'im there.'

'Thanks Spider.' I release the note.

'I hope she orright, man. She a good lady.' And he melts into the dark in company of his gang.

237

Chapter Thirty-Three

The River of Dreams

Thursday 5 September — 2 days before the election

'Let's just see if we can get this straight.' It's breakfast, and Jo is talking while crunching muesli. 'Sergeant Boulter gets this homeless kid to spread the word around the street, and within hours there are people with violent intent looking for this guy who's supposed to have been involved in the Parry Street explosion because they need him ... for what?'

'There's two camps,' I say, pointing at the 10x8 of my mugging. 'This guy, Big Nose, I suspect is working for Enzo Gordioni. They want Hunter because they think he's someone else—'

'And is he?'

'No. And the other guy, the one the kid describes as a soldier, I'm certain is Joseph Swaddick. He'd been ordered to find Hunter by Sean Dower. But Dower's dead, so he must be getting his orders from somewhere else. Whoever it is must believe Hunter knows something about the murder Boulter is investigating — something I suspect puts them in the frame.'

'And does he?'

'Can't say.'

'So where is this Hunter guy?' Peter asks, his drawl flying low. 'Did he cause the explosion and disappear?' He makes a conjuring motion with his hands.

'He's been missing since the explosion,' I hear myself say, 'but that doesn't mean he's not dead under the rubble. They still haven't cleared it all.' Was I defending him? Clearing him of all blame? Wondering about my own culpability in it all? Perhaps the tables are turning. I lose myself in the depths of my coffee cup and wonder just how much I might miss it when it's gone.

The three of them discuss the impounded vehicle, which has been detailed and yielded little except a few dog hairs in the cracks behind the seats. Forensics have drawn a preliminary match to two other sets of hairs submitted earlier by Boulter. Of Smith and Jones, nothing can be found. These two agents of the AFP, as they like to call themselves, are not in the personnel records of the agency. The vehicle they used to collect Swaddick from the Belmont lockup is a nondescript white Toyota Aurion with plates that have no record at the Department of Transport. It seems no-one at Belmont thought to verify the order to remove the suspect. At that point I drift off into wondering how much I might miss the university's property that was removed from my office.

According to Robinson, Boulter's request for a warrant to search Swaddick's house was actioned, but McPherson claimed never to have seen it for authorisation and execution. The system had clearly been at fault. Robinson didn't meet Boulter at Belmont to question Swaddick because he had been dispatched urgently to another job. McPherson's diary entry shows that it was Boulter who requested they remove their meeting from the office to a coffee shop. The best lead to Boulter's whereabouts, Jo informs us, is the information I got from Spider. She decides that we concentrate on the railway bridge at Tydeman Road.

I park in the Railway Hotel car park. It seems most logical because the railway bridge crosses Tydeman Road right next to it, where the rail lines separate into three. Two main lines run straight across to handle commuter trains between Perth and Fremantle. The one that veers wraps round the back of the hotel, a track running into a borderland of freight yards with banks of containers and razor-topped security fences. The Doobie Brothers had it right, as far as I could see — it takes everything with it. I climb a short rise at the rear of the hotel into vacant land. My footfalls crunch on cans and bottles and food wrappers and condoms, the detritus of revelry scattered among remnants of broken tarmac that suggests an industrial past which won't be coming back. Nestled into an embankment with a four-metre high, heavily graffitied concrete wall fencing off the railway line are several outbuildings separate from the main hotel complex. They are behind a locked gate and spike-topped fencing. Two German Shepherds prowling the yard make it known that I'm not welcome.

George has taken a small triangle of bush between the hotel and the railway line, Jo a section, also bush, on the other side of the bridge, and Peter is scouring the area on the river side of Tydeman Road. I make my way up the rise and come to a dilapidated fence that borders the railway reserve.

Finding an opening, I push through and follow the concrete wall until it ends about fifty metres along and becomes a fence of steel posts and chain-link wire, long fallen into disrepair, with sections of the wire cut away and poles bent as though standing against a terrible wind. Beyond the fence is an embankment with the railway line disappearing up around a corner. I push through a break in the wire, climb the embankment and cross the track to the other side. The fence on this side is far taller: a modern, well maintained chain-link and steel affair with razor wire spiralling its full length. It protects a freight hardstand, populated with islands of shipping containers stacked four high in parts, clearly organised in some fashion understandable only to the world of the forwarders.

Several containers, which appear to be long settled in situ, are arranged parallel to the fence. Two, next to each other, are directly in front of me, the first a rust-stained and grubby white, and the one behind it, a dirty red, both are faded and weathered by salt and age, long decommissioned from the ocean. At the end, there's a space wide enough for a vehicle, and then another two containers, much newer looking, stacked together, and farther along, another. In the gap there is a car. I stop and study it for a moment, and then a realisation dawns.

I am staring at the headlights and grille of Kelly Boulter's car.

I break into a run, heading along the fence, hoping a gate to the yard is at the end. But it isn't. The fence turns without a gate, isolating it from a large warehouse complex, and disappears into the distance.

'Jo, I've located Kelly's car,' I rasp into my communicator, 'in a yard on the other side of the railway line behind the hotel. I can't get to it from here, I'm at Barker Street cul-de-sac. I think the only access must be from the other end at Irene Street. I'm heading that way.'

It was easily five hundred metres from me to the entrance, first along the industrial cargoland that is Bracks Street and then down the spit of Irene Street, and then another four hundred and fifty metres back to the southern fence where the car is inside. It is a sizeable yard.

Jo, with George and Peter, in her rugged Toyota SUV, picks me up about halfway along Bracks Street and she guns the vehicle round into Irene and through an entrance at the end of the street next to the Perth–Fremantle railway line, the second of two entrances separated by a row of trees and low scrub serving to divide truck traffic in from out.

About two hundred and fifty metres in is a complex of portable offices, with a few cars parked nearby and what appears to be a weighbridge and control station at the rear. Stacks of containers line the yard along the railway line perimeter, another stacked row extends from near the office buildings. A lift truck is working, shifting a load to a truck dolly. Jo pulls up in front of the office.

Peter and George disembark and are met on the verandah by a rotund and balding weaselly faced man who, by virtue of his mannerisms, I take to be the manager of the yard. Peter shows the man his warrant card, and points to where we want to go. The man pulls a phone from his pocket and goes to make a call, but George takes his phone and indicates he should join us in the SUV.

We pull up by the aged red and white containers in front of Boulter's car. George checks the car while we head for the nearest container, the red one. The yard manager claims not to have keys for the locks. George appears from behind our SUV with a set of hydraulic bolt cutters and makes short work of the lock. The inside is stacked with what appear to be mostly washing machines and refrigerators with Chinese origins on the packaging. George repeats his trick with the lock on the rusty white container next to the fence, which turns out to be about half full of agricultural machinery. Thinking that containers no longer fit for transport stacked with newly packed goods is suspicious, Peter stays with the first container to have a closer look. The rest of us move onto the ones on the other side of Boulter's car.

I lead the way to the container nearest the fence, noticing the door is not closed. I swing it back and peer into the gloom. As the scene before me registers, my breathing freezes and my heart palpitates. Slumped in a chair along one side is the form of Kelly Boulter, a dark sticky pool spread on the floor beneath her. Deeper into the container, the shape of another form lies on the floor.

Before Jo could stop me I am at Boulter's side, fouling what is obviously a crime scene, but desperate to find signs of life.

'There's a pulse,' I hear myself call in a pitiful voice. 'Faint, but there.' I place my cheek in front of her nose, hoping to feel breath.

Jo is at my side, pulling me back, conscious of the conflicting needs to preserve life and to secure a scene of crime. I hear George calling Peter, and in the next breath, asking for an ambulance. Within seconds Jo is on the phone, urgently requesting scene of crime officers and forensics field officers. She catches a look from Peter and relays a message that a police officer has been seriously wounded, another man is dead, and the site may contain contraband.

George has marshalled all personnel on site in the lunchroom. Peter is at the gate barring entry and egress to all except police and emergency. Jo talks softly on the phone to someone in the command chain while I wait in a state of suspended disbelief, numb, angry, despondent, pacing, crying, blaming myself for every evil visited upon humanity on this earth for all time. Someone has to shoulder the blame and right at this moment, the only person I can find is me. So, without *John the Revelator* at hand, I will have to do.

An ambulance pulls up, two paramedics climb down, pulling a stretcher out of the rear of the vehicle which they park at the entrance to the container. Jo guides them through the section of the crime scene I have already fouled, suggesting they try to stay within the same space. They are carrying tool boxes and begin their ministrations in quiet, cool earnest. It takes them only a few minutes and they zip off, siren *dyoo-dyooing* as it dopplers down the yard and then a few moments later as it loops back along Tydeman. I still hear it as it crosses Stirling Bridge all the way to High Street in a mad dash for the Fremantle emergency ward.

In an attempt to distract the numbness in my head, I busy myself helping Jo string police tape around the site. I hardly notice the arrival of a SOCO team and a pair of FFOs: even though I watch them don the vinyl coveralls, gloves, boot covers, hair nets and face masks, it barely registers. My mind is still regurgitating the horror I had seen, and the dreadful sense of the impending loss of someone I care about. If I'm honest with myself, and that's becoming more and more difficult as the days wear on, I have never been a spiritual man in the God-fearing sense, but I do, like Billy Joel, wonder what happens next. My whole being feels lost in the swirls and floods and rapids and tranquil waters of *The River of Dreams*. I'm not sure I will ever be on solid ground again.

In the distance, I see a black four-wheel drive, Lexus or BMW, pull up in front of the office buildings. The driver gets out and opens the rear door. The lanky, silver haired figure of Enzo Gordioni striding for the front door is unmistakable. As is the bulky bodyguard by his side, although I can't distinguish his nose at this range. A moment of revulsion drives the bile in my stomach upward as my phone rings.

'Hello?'

'Lazaar, are you okay?' It's Nick Fairgough.

'Yeah, sorry Nick, something caught in my throat.'

'Listen, I've had a call from my minister, seems Enzo Gordioni's a bit upset about my people closing his freight yard. That where you are?'

'I'm at the crime scene. An ambulance has just left with Boulter — she's alive, but that's all I know. Was stabbed through the thigh and suffered a nasty cut below her rib cage, lost a lot of blood. I think it's touch and go. Gordioni has just arrived at the office. Jo's instructed George to detain him there and wait for Novice to arrive. There's another body here, but I don't know anything about that yet — SOCOs and FFOs are in there at the moment. I can't leave just yet because I fucked up the crime scene, so I have to be eliminated. Jesus! That didn't come out right, did it?'

'Okay Art, sit somewhere and take it easy. Chances are you're in shock. I need to go and talk to the minister.'

'Nick.'

'Yeah?'

'There's something else ... there are two shipping containers here, both rust buckets that haven't seen an ocean for yonks, chock-a-block full of apparently new appliances and agricultural equipment.

Peter had a quick deco and found more than a fistful of MDMA. And the container I found Kelly in...'

'Yeah?'

'It's where I was waterboarded.'

Chapter Thirty-Four

Everything You Did

Friday 6 September — 1 day before the election

My recollection of events following the discovery of Boulter and, as it turns out, the body of Joseph Swaddick is no more than a blur. Donna Gardner calls at some point. I dismiss it. This morning, I notice a text message from her informing me that she rescheduled the meeting with Lipschitz for eleven-thirty. I recall wandering the streets late into the night and bumping into a gang of street kids. They took me under their care, and I have no idea what pain-numbing medications I must have taken. Spider was especially concerned about Boulter, that I remember.

I burst into Lipschitz's office at eleven thirty-five. From outside, I'd watched Gardner enter a minute or two earlier. My entrance catches the great man completely by surprise, I see it on his face. Gardner sits aghast, most likely because of the state of my appearance.

'Thank you, Donna,' I say, indicating the door in the manner of a trial lawyer making a public gallery point to a jury.

She leaves and Lipschitz makes a remarkable recovery. 'What are you doing, Lazaar?' He reaches for his desk phone, I assume to call security.

'It's all right, Vice Chancellor, I've signed in. The front desk knows I'm here.' The phone goes down. 'We have things to talk about so I'm taking Donna's meeting.' I am feeling a desperate urge to push on. 'I have no doubt that you will want to hear what I have to say, and that you will not want any other audience.'

My point made, I pause for breath, pull a chair round so that we face off across the desk. I point to a set of polished and spotless golf clubs sitting in the corner of his office.

'How's your golf?'

'I'm just learning.' A glossy 10x8 appears in my hand and I put it in front of Lipschitz and wait. He looks up, the hands of a supplicant. 'What is this, Lazaar?'

'You learning, I imagine. I'm just not sure what the lessons were, or from whom they came.' I wait just long enough for him to draw a breath and ready his retort. I jump in. 'Actually, this is you instructing Elise Jarman to withdraw the ridiculous charges she's cooked up against me. This is you admitting to her that you made a mistake. This is you preparing yourself for the shitstorm that's about to rain down on you. This is you getting the chance to exit gracefully and step down before that choice is taken from you.'

He laughs. A bold, contemptuous laugh that accompanies flinging the photograph back at me. 'You're out of your mind,' he says.

'Perhaps,' I say. 'And perhaps with good reason. In the past week, I've been beaten nearly half to death, with some not so small thanks to you—'

'No, no, no, Lazaar'— a refuting finger goes up — 'I had nothing to do with that.'

'Nothing? You invited me to a lunch at which you had no intention of showing up, and without telling me I would be in the company of a sociopath of the highest order. Your driver took me there. Your mate, this mate'— finger jabbing at the figure of Lamord in the photograph — 'calls in a car to bring me back here, only I get

abducted, waterboarded, beaten and then thrown out in the street —
presumably with the intent that I might die of exposure.' I hold up a
hand for his silence.

'What's more,' my tone approaching fever pitch, 'my good friend,
Detective Kelly Boulter, is now in intensive care with knife wounds,
massive blood loss, and less than fifty per cent chance of survival.'
And then, I thump the table and squeeze my vocal chords tighter
than a Simpson wringer and spit the words out, 'Now. You. Tell me.
Everything. You did.'

'Everything *I* did? What about your fraudulent and offensive
behaviour towards a student?'

'Oh, fuck you! There was no fraud, there was no sexual
harassment, and you know it. I've got the emails — you had Elise
Jarman cook that up at your mate's behest. This fucking mate.' Again
my finger jabs the photograph.

In reply, the contemptuous laugh. 'It's time for you to leave,
Lazaar.'

'In a moment, Vice Chancellor. But before I do, tell me who are
all of these people in this picture with you?'

'I don't know all of them.'

'Really? I'm surprised. First your mate, Roger Lamord. Seemed
to think I know someone who has something that he said a friend
wanted returned, and you sicced him on to me. Which friend do you
imagine that might be, Wally? He's the only one I've ever heard call
you that, you know. Which friend?'

'Well it's not me.'

'Okay, what about this guy?' I point.

Lipschitz laughs. 'That's the Malaysian Prime Minister.'

'Ah, so you do know him. Have you wondered where the money
might be coming from for this flash university he wants to build with
you and your mate Roger? I bet he's shown an interest in your film
studio plans too.'

'We have discussed possible opportunities, both in Malaysia and for Malaysian students here.'

'Okay, not him then. What about this guy?' I point to Sean Dower. Then I go on, before Lipschitz can answer. 'No, he's dead. Did you hear? You knew him of course, Sean Dower. Managing Director of SECSUR — a stupid name for a security business which belongs to Lamord — only he crossed the line, so he had to go. He was there, you know, when I was being waterboarded, I heard his voice. But he's dead now. Plane crash Tuesday morning, so we don't need to worry about him.' I point to the Asian man standing next to Dower. 'What about him? He's the one isn't he? I'll bet he's the "friend".'

'I don't know him.'

'But you played golf with him. Looks like you were partnered with him here. I bet he wasn't just learning, eh? Oh no, he's a player, isn't he? You know him, What's his name?'

'He was here with the Malaysian PM. He's a diplomat. Tuah Johari, I think.'

'Yep. That's him. He's the "friend", but he's gone now, did you know? Scuttled back to KL Wednesday afternoon. He doesn't only have the one name. Did you know that?'

'Can't say I did.'

'I bet you did, Wally. You see, I think you met with him on several occasions, possibly at one or two of Lamord's soirées out at that fancy mansion on West Swan Road. He brought girls, didn't he? Asian girls, Middle Eastern Girls? His other name, Wally?' No answer. 'Yusuf, Wally. This is Yusuf.'

'Look, Lazaar, this is all very interesting, but I've got a lot to do.'

'Indeed you do, Vice Chancellor. For one thing, you need to call Elise Jarman and deal with these bullshit charges against me. But in just a minute, okay, because before I leave, you need to understand just how all of this affects you, right?'

'Make it quick.'

'See these two guys at the back here? Do you know them?'

'They're security guys, I think. Dower provides services to

visiting dignitaries.'

'Provided, Wally. Provided. Dower's past tense now. But you are so right. They're both dead now too.' At that, there seems to be a definite fading of Lippers' normal ruddiness. Perhaps he was doing a little mental maths. 'This one died a few weeks ago in an explosion at Parry Street in Fremantle. Both of them were there that night. That's been verified, witnesses, you see. A homeless man was there too, still missing, possibly buried under the rubble. This one' — I point at Swaddick — 'was shot dead Wednesday night, found in the same place as Detective Sergeant Boulter. It's not been established who shot him, or the weapon used.' A little pause, just to make sure that what I'm saying is finding its mark. 'It's possible Sergeant Boulter shot him in defence of her own life, after she'd been stabbed twice. But the pathologists need to confirm that.

'Now, just thinking back over this, and the diminishing remains of this picture, it does seem possible that your very good mate is cleaning house. Why do you imagine he would be doing that?'

Lipschitz doesn't answer but turns his gaze to look out the window over the car park. I continue my onslaught.

'I have a sworn statement from a witness who can identify your friend Yusuf as a human trafficker and slaver. This witness can connect you to these people. These men' — again pointing at the two at the back — 'committed murder. Kelly Boulter was about to arrest this one for it' — finger on Swaddick — 'but he has, as I said, met his end, and she has been seriously wounded attempting to bring him to justice. The way I see it, there are only two people left in this photograph, and you're one of them.'

I take a marker from the desk and draw crosses through all except Lamord and Lipschitz, place the photograph back in front of him, and say, more of a suggestion, really: 'A bit of a worry, don't you think?' I turn on my heel and leave the room.

Chapter Thirty-Five
Black Sky

The kitchens at Balsamic & Olives are a combination of technological marvel and interior design brilliance that occupy the floor below the restaurant's first-floor dining room. There are two large kitchens separated by a wall housing the ventilation and hydraulic systems and terminating at a long serving counter shared by both. Each with islands of gleaming stainless steel cooking stations and prep centres running the length. A bank of coolrooms with discrete climate controls lines the far end. There are separate cleaning stations and crockery stores in alcoves along opposite walls, and a passage that runs behind the coolrooms provides staff access to the car park at one end and the refuse management area at the other. Small dining rooms and lounges, specifically to accommodate staff and drivers while their employers are dining in the restaurant upstairs, line the opposite side of the passage. Both kitchens are designed to ensure produce fitting to a chef's art can be set apart, while simultaneously affording optimum efficiency in preparation, and clear separation between the culinary and the servir d'art.

Master Chef Mashimoto and his team had chosen kitchen two,

partly because the bench height had been set 50mm lower than kitchen one, affording him, on account of his short stature, better control over his knives, and partly because the management of the waste product from his preparations requires meticulous care, and kitchen two better suits his refuse requirements. He did not want to be responsible for death because of mishandling, such incompetence would not be acceptable, and death can come from what is discarded much more easily than from the edible.

Mashimoto had been brought in from Kyoto to prepare two celebration banquets, the first tonight and the second tomorrow. He had begun work early in the day. His Number One assistant unpacked his knives, honed them to a razor edge, and replaced the stone in its safe box. This role is trusted only to Number One assistant. Number Two assistant inspected the liver, intestine and ovaries as they were extracted to ensure no traces were left behind. He sealed them in a plastic drum marked with hazard labels and placed them in the hazardous section of the waste disposal area. Mashimoto worked with great care, nothing left unattended, nothing left to chance, for a reputation is built on the finer aspects of the craft. And his reputation was the highest in the world.

It is customary at Balsamic & Olives for the doorway from the car park to the kitchens to be manned by a liveried doorman. The refuse area is secured by locked gates to which only the trucks and maintenance staff have keys. As Angelo Tassione entered, the doorman, an older, angular man with a warm, welcoming smile and a sense of purpose greeted him.

'Good evening sir. I trust Mister Gordioni is well and looking forward to his evening.' He gestured outdoors. 'I noticed a black sky forming on the ridge, sir; much better to be inside on a night such as this. If you will follow me, sir. Mister Gordioni requested a private room for you. Just down the end here, sir.' Of course, no such request was made, but the Italian with the big nose could not know that. He would assume that such a request is made to protect his privacy, and the safety of his master.

The man with the big nose responded with a smile. The doorman, in a limp that favoured his left leg but seemed in no way to impair his progress, led him to a small lounge at the end of the corridor on the left, handed him a menu and a refreshing citrus juice and closed the door, leaving him watching a large screen CCTV displaying notable guests arriving and settling for the occasion about to begin in the opulent privacy of the second floor dining room. The staff of VIP guests cannot be served alcohol, but their meal is complimentary. Twenty minutes later, the doorman reappeared with Angelo Tassione's meal.

He closed the door as he left and went out to the refuse area, using a key to unlock the gate to the access lane and locking the gate behind him when he left.

Meanwhile, as Chef Mashimoto was putting his final touches to the fugu sashimi in kitchen two, Enzo Gordioni's eighty-fifth birthday was getting under way on the second floor. It was a gathering to behold: money and influence rubbing shoulders with diamonds of opulence and pearls of wisdom, each guest personally welcomed by Roger Lamord, the affable host to his good friend's celebration. For Lamord, it was the rehearsal for the greater celebration to follow the next evening. Some of those here tonight would be back again tomorrow, joined by other luminaries of industry and power. And Mashimoto would work his magic again.

At precisely 9 pm a contingent of officers from Australian Customs descended on Balsamic & Olives and took Enzo Gordioni, several members of his family, and associates into custody on charges relating to the importation of drugs. Diners and guests sat dumbfounded, chopsticks with selections of fugu sliced by the world's greatest chef of his art were poised halfway between plates and mouths as gasps and murmurs swept the room. Roger Lamord, with the support of political figures and notable lawyers also present, remonstrated with the officer in charge, only to be shown a warrant for arrests and asked to remain in their seats. Mobile phones appeared in hands all around the room, some recording the events as they unfolded, others making calls to discuss them with persons unseen. It was all a bit chaotic and guests were visibly unsure about how they should behave. After all, a good many of them considered themselves to be above laws that affect ordinary people.

One of the officers was overheard speaking in Enzo's ear. 'The price you pay when you walk on the ledge.'

The events played out in living colour on the CCTV in the small dining room at the end of the corridor behind the kitchens, and Angelo Tassione would have seen it all were he not nose down in a pool of his own vomit. While death from fugu poisoning is slow and agonising, vomiting is a prompt second stage, quickly followed by paralysis. Angelo Tassione did not die for some time, but paralysis meant he was unable to raise the alarm. And the events unfolding on the second floor ensured he was not missed, nor sought after.

Chapter Thirty-Six

Go Rest High On That Mountain

Saturday 7 September — Election day

Out of the slung mud of election campaigning; out of swarms of fake news and even faker images; out of the loosely packed mistruths of mainstream journalism, shock-jock solecisms and social-media rants by influencers vested in the coal and dirt-shifting industries that drive the intense lobby groups of conservative capitalists emerged a new chapter that would, in time, be recognised as one of the bleakest in Australia's lived future.

'I can tell you this is a new day, a new government,' declares TAPM-elect at around 7:30 pm, further adding that the party now relegated to the opposition had scored its lowest ever primary vote in a hundred years. It was a sweet victory. In the days that follow, the news is awash with a government getting straight down to the business of removing taxes on carbon, delivering welfare cuts to force welchers into the job market, and forming the new pseudo-military Australian Border Force that would turn the boats back, stop the illegal invasion of asylum seekers, and define the new Australia.

It was to the ranks of the latter that Max Glendinning was

catapulted as Deputy Director Operations: a debt paid, and the removal of one last security risk for Roger Lamord. With Noah Carter tapped for a cabinet post, and Codlin whisked off to a new political mess in the UK, Lamord had a successful campaign behind him and a clean slate ahead.

The charges against Enzo Gordioni grew in sizeable chunks over the weeks that followed, ensnaring a broadening network of family and associates in a spread of drugs, money-laundering, and intimidation offences. The release of documents and papers previously held under escrow by a team of lawyers prepared by Calvin Bishop and an unidentified associate reporting content sourced from confidential informants over a number of years contributed to an expansion of the investigation beyond Australian Customs to include the Serious Crimes Divisions of Fraud, Vice and Drugs, and the Australian Taxation Office. The irony of his removal from the chambers of power, which symbolised much of his life, to a much smaller chamber at Grevillia, a private prison operated by Lamord's SANCO group of companies, was, according to some in the know, not lost on Enzo. In time, assets thought to have been purchased or partly funded by his illegal activities would be seized and sold under the Proceeds of Crimes Act, slotting a reasonable return to the taxpayer.

The coroner declared the demise of Gordioni's bodyguard, Angelo Tassione, to be death by misadventure, finding no explicable reason why a man who ate a gourmet burger and chips prepared in the kitchen of Balsamic & Olives as his last meal came to have a minute trace of tetrodotoxin in his system, a substance which under any logical explanation could only have come from the preparation of fugu sashimi. Yet, as Mashimoto would testify, all precautions had been taken and to his knowledge only he and assistant Number Two handled the material and did so in the prescribed manner. The unfortunate events did not tarnish his reputation in any way.

The knife found near Detective Sergeant Kelly Boulter was a

military issued Italian-made tactical combat knife with a 184mm stainless cobalt steel blade, one of a variety of instruments favoured by certain members of the SASR as a close combat weapon. Its edge had been honed with precision to a razor angle. The forensics examination concluded that the knife belonged to Joseph Swaddick, a conclusion drawn from the scabbard found on Swaddick's belt, DNA traces of his saliva mixed with machine oil on the blade, and his fingerprints on the hasp.

Boulter's stab wounds, a deep penetrating wound in the upper thigh and a severe slice to her left side fortunately deflected by a Kevlar vest, were both found to be made by the knife. The forensic pathologists matched the cutting profile on Boulter's wounds to the wound that sliced Ishmail Salim's throat, drawing the further conclusion that Joseph Swaddick had been responsible for that murder. This was further supported by dog hairs found on Salim's clothes matching those found in Swaddick's vehicle.

In light of that evidence, the case was closed and Mahmoud Khalil freed.

Of Swaddick's death, little could be firmly determined other than the fact it was Boulter's service Glock that delivered the fatal shot. Boulter herself, when she could finally be questioned on the matter, had no recollection of pulling the trigger. Her fingerprints were the only ones found on the weapon, but its location on the floor between the two bodies could not rule out the presence of a third party. No question mark hung over Detective Kelly Boulter's actions in the death of Joseph Swaddick.

She was, however, reprimanded for acting alone contrary to service protocols, which was cause for a further deferment of promotion. When the doctors eventually proclaimed she was fit for duty, she did not return to Midland, but was given a posting to the Police Academy in Joondalup to teach a course in forensics awareness and scene of crime management to pre-service officers. Superintendent McPherson gave testimony at her hearing to the effect that the detective was wanting in her capacity to act as a member of a team and described her as an 'opportunist who had a tendency to pursue theories instead of following the evidence to hand'. He blamed a culture of outsourcing aspects of vital investigations to undisciplined amateurs and suggested that a full review of how investigations are handled should be undertaken. His retirement by the end of that month drew no attention.

On his release, Mahmoud Khalil led police and immigration officials to two compounds where asylum seekers who had been granted bridging visas under the previous government were housed. The man Mahmoud knew as Yusuf, who took care of the refugees, was nowhere to be found. It unfolded to authorities that Yusuf had arranged work for them, with wages annexed to cover their care and housing, but no records of such payments were found. When authorities arrived, the residents were malnourished and had received no care for several days. None could produce any identity documents or copies of their bridging visas releasing them into community detention.

Even more troubling to the authorities was that no record of these visas, nor of these two addresses supposedly registered for community detention, nor the names Yusuf (other names unknown) or Mr Singh appeared anywhere in the system. Under the new government, claims to the bridging visas were dismissed and the refugees transferred to asylum-seeker facilities for processing. The local press made a gourmet banquet of the very idea of slavery being present in wholesome Perth in this day and age, extending the outrage to the incompetence of previous governments in dealing with asylum seekers, even to the extent of encouraging slavery.

Falullah Salim commenced study in her newly assumed identity which, with support of senior police management, was conferred under the terms of a witness protection order. In a private ceremony, she was able to bury her brother and spent her grief surrounded by the three people who knew the truth.

Universities across the nation were in turmoil. New funding cuts were imminent while a performance-based model was devised, and this had a follow-on effect at a local level resulting in reduced course numbers and added academic loads. Both Vice Chancellor Lipschitz and Deputy Provost Jarman were stood down from their respective university positions with an impending internal enquiry into supposed abuses of power, which would ultimately be returned to the CCC to pursue any charges that might arise. Public opinion swung wildly as to whether any of this mattered.

With Enzo Gordioni in custody, and his reign of control over most things Fremantle at an end, and the release of years of hard work in secret by journalist Calvin Bishop, Hunter was free to return to his life before exile. But he chose, instead, to remain on the streets, in his street identity. He never discussed the reasons behind this decision, although those few who cared speculated that after ten years, he had become a different person.

One summer Monday, later that year, Lavender Jensen and Falullah Salim sought him out at his favourite spot opposite the post office. With them was a third young woman, about the same age. With tears in his eyes, Hunter led them to a lock-up in the old wool stores building, where he opened a safe locker and removed nine birthday gifts.

Lars-Erik Nordstrom Trio's *Poetic Licence* is playing in the background on my home stereo and his haunting piano is filling me with a morbid regret. My voice is thick and my words slur as I hold the phone a couple of centimetres from my ear. 'I just called to offer my congratulations,' I say, fearful that the voice of Roger Lamord on the other end will attach itself to my inner brain and inject me with poison.

'It's very kind of you to call, Lazaar. Thank you.' He is jubilant, I can hear his joy plain as day, even though it is close to midnight. 'It is certainly a good win.'

A good win? My addled brain struggles to make sense of his words. What the fuck constitutes a good win nowadays? My brain says it was a devastating loss. I'm the guy so far down I can't get up. Winning doesn't compute. My world was dissolving like the GFC melting down the money, one brick falling after another. This was no single loss, I'm feeling, as it takes my heart with it, and its poison violates every part of my being.

The writing on the wall for Labor was clear by lunch time and my slide into a bottomless quiet despair was the kind only a malted whisky had any chance of halting. I'm more than halfway down and it hasn't done its trick so far, so I push on towards the bottom, trying to fathom the depths to which my stomach has retched.

I came home the previous evening to a house that was dreadfully lonely. The image that remains with me on entering is littered remnants of abandonment. Where my mother's house had a plaque that read, 'Shelter here all who step across this threshold', the plaque in my mind's eye carried Dante's words: 'Abandon hope all ye who enter'.

When I cast my eye round, I'm faced with the scattered remains of some fruitless search by persons unknown for the secrets I am guarding. It wasn't in me to return the house to order. In the circumstances, it seems necessary that it remain as it is, a sign of how my life appears to me in that moment, wherever along the temporal horizon that moment occurs.

My thoughts shout at me in random sketches. At some dark hour I must have figured that direct congress with the enemy was all that was left.

'I hear not everything has been a winner for you,' my voice submits a limp attempt to get under his skin, or, perhaps, offset the stain of my own losses.

He laughs. 'Oh, quite the contrary, it's precisely what this country needs.'

'I didn't call to discuss politics, Roger. Your side won. It's over. I just want to know how you got away with it.'

'Not sure I'm following you there, Art. I'm rich, I get away with a lot — getting away with it is the main thrill. Is there something in particular?'

'In particular? Yes there is something in particular: three murders, perhaps more, people smuggling, modern slavery, assault, political interference, bribing cops, falsifying records. All of it points to you, but nothing...'

'I've committed no crime, there is not one shred of evidence that I have done any of those things, Lazaar. If others commit crimes and want to use the results of those crimes to gain advantage, that's their concern. I buy when the market is selling and sell when it's buying. That's what winning is, Lazaar — an art you have probably not practised much. There's a Malay saying, maybe you've heard it, *jangan makan dunia* — there's no need to eat the world. Winning means getting fifty-one per cent when the other side gets forty-nine.'

'But you have suffered losses. Dower, a multi-million dollar plane, Yusuf, Sam Codlin, looks like your mate Glendinning might be leaving. Gordioni's arrest can't have done your restaurant's reputation much good, not to mention a body found in a back room that looks like food poisoning...'

'Incidental failures are part of all success; some are tragic. Our insurers have actuaries that calculate the worth of valued employees, good people move on to better positions all the time, it's the way the world works.'

'How is snatching victory from the leaky boats of refugees a win, Roger?'

'You don't get it, do you, Lazaar? If people are silly enough to get on a boat and think they will find a new life here in Australia, they've got fucking rocks in their heads. We can't afford to listen to every fucking bleeding heart or take in every victim. At least now we've got a government prepared to send them back. We say who comes here Lazaar. Us. The Australian people.'

My drunken mind struggles to find purchase on loosely swarming thoughts. I'm too tired to be angry, too beaten to be of any use. Maybe I should call it a day. *Go Rest High on That Mountain* springs to mind, but one more question remains.

'What about the girl, Roger? That must have been quite a loss for you to go to such lengths?'

'The girl?' He pauses, as though thinking, and then says, 'If she is a loss, what has been won? In this game, just to win is not enough: your enemies must be seen to lose. That's a cold hard truth. The losers determine the winners. You lost. That's the other truth.'

I sit in the silence of a severed connection as Vince Gill's tenor — once described as one kissed by angels — overtakes my melancholy. I top up my glass while I think on the matter of truth and freedom. Does truth drift like water, shapeless, bounded by its container, always seeking the lowest point, forever pursuing the greater body lest it evaporate? I stare at my glass and it dawns on me that water, like the whisky in my glass, is unfree. Like all of humanity. But what is freedom? I sing the only words left to me: 'A bit of a bloody worry.'

ACKNOWLEDGEMENTS

No book is ever written alone. Not really. It might begin alone, but then others get caught in its web, and that web can take on surprising dimensions. This one began as part of a creative writing PhD inquiry, but it has taken many turns since then.

I am indebted to my very good friends David Moody and Jim Rossiter for their repeated and meticulous readings of the manuscript as it unfolded in its various permutations, and the many lengthy discussions we held. Peter Taylor, Sasha Wasley, Norman Jorgensen, David Whish-Wilson, Andrew Melrose, Paul Williams, Miki and Taylor all generously gave their time and considerate thoughts on early versions.

A big thanks to my editor Pam Hewitt whose rigorous attention to detail sharpened the work in ways I could never have imagined, to John Rando for casting an eye over the legal issues, and to the memory of Dr Ian Cook who gave me some insights into the workings of political parties. Of course, I have played fast and loose with some of this advice to suit to the fictive moment of this book and its poetic licence. Any perceived deviations from reality are entirely of my own making.

Finally, to my partner Judith Vun Price who stood steadfastly by me, challenged much of what I had to say and how I was saying it, and then turned it into the beautiful book it is with her extraordinary talent and visionary design craft, I thank you for making me feel like the luckiest author alive.

KP

*Kevin Price is a West Australian author who lives
on a rural property in the hills north of Perth.*

CPSIA information can be obtained
at www.ICGtesting.com
Printed in the USA
LVHW092300020522
717733LV00016B/720

9 780994 211552